SUPERNATURAL™

COYOTE'S KISS

SUPERNATURAL™
COYOTE'S KISS

CHRISTA FAUST

SUPERNATURAL created by Eric Kripke

TITAN BOOKS

Supernatural: Coyote's Kiss
Print edition ISBN: 9780857681003
E-book edition ISBN: 9780857685438

Published by
Titan Books
A division of
Titan Publishing Group Ltd
144 Southwark St
London
SE1 0UP

First edition July 2011
10 9 8 7 6 5 4 3 2 1

Visit our website: www.titanbooks.com

Did you enjoy this book? We love to hear from our readers. Please email
us at readerfeedback@titanemail.com or write to us at Reader Feedback
at the above address.

To receive advance information, news, competitions, and exclusive Titan
offers online, please register as a member by clicking the "sign up" button
on our website: www.titanbooks.com

A CIP catalogue record for this title is available from the British Library.

Printed and bound in the United States.

HISTORIAN'S NOTE

This novel takes place during season six, between
"Caged Heat" and "Appointment in Samara."

ONE

Letty was almost positive that the beautiful woman hadn't been part of their group when they left the Sonoran town of Altar, heading for the U.S. border. But as exhausted, dehydrated, and sleep deprived as she was, it was difficult to be sure.

Crammed into the first of several filthy, claustrophobic vans, nineteen-year-old Letty had felt self-conscious and anxious. She was one of only three females in a group composed primarily of rough, posturing men. A skinny, awkward girl that boys barely noticed back home in Tláhuac. But they noticed her now, and some of the men made crude comments about her, encouraging each other to pinch her meager breasts.

It had got worse after Marta, the only person who had been nice to her, had been bitten by a snake and had to be left behind. Marta tried to make Letty take her water, since she knew she was dying and didn't want it to be wasted, but

Letty couldn't bring herself to leave the older woman with nothing. Now, in the unrelenting heat with the heartless sun burning her scalp and blurring her vision, Letty wished she'd taken the water after all. Maybe if she had, she wouldn't be imagining things. Like the beautiful woman.

They'd made it over the border just before dawn and were hunkered down, waiting for nightfall. At which time another vehicle was supposed to pick them up and take them the rest of the way to the safe house in Phoenix. Their Coyote, a nickname given to border-crossing guides by the migrants they smuggled into the States, had left them. The spot where he told them to wait was nothing but a cluster of thorny brush and jagged rock. Barely enough shade to shelter a single person, let alone a large group. The Coyote himself had been picked up by another smuggler on an all-terrain vehicle (ATV), leaving behind a single two-liter bottle of warm, gritty water and dire warnings to stay hidden and listen for helicopters.

As morning became midday, the killing heat started picking them off one by one, like a lazy sniper. One of the young men who'd grabbed Letty's breasts was now unconscious, slumped like a drunkard and barely breathing. He'd stopped sweating. A young woman whose name Letty had never learned was already dead. The flies had found her. The water was long gone.

But the beautiful woman didn't seem phased by the heat at all. She sat in the sand with her legs crossed and the hood of her black sweatshirt up, shading her eyes. Her supple lips were not cracked and parched. Her smooth, pale skin was clean and untouched by sunburn. She didn't have a backpack. She didn't speak. She just watched the sun travel across the sky. No one seemed to notice her but Letty.

The unconscious man was dead by the time the promised vehicle arrived, a weary old cube truck with bald tires that did not look up to the task of navigating the rough, unpaved road. Two other men were barely alive and had to be dragged into the truck by their friends. Letty was so thirsty and so exhausted that she could barely stand, but she managed. She wasn't about to give up now. The beautiful woman was close behind her as she staggered to the rear bumper of the truck and climbed inside. It smelled like urine and human misery. The Coyote pulled down the roll door and padlocked it with a heavy chain. The engine rumbled and coughed, filling the airless space with the stench of exhaust.

Letty sat on her backpack and concentrated on not throwing up. She couldn't spare the water. That's when she realized the beautiful woman was now sitting right beside her. The woman had pushed back her hood and her wild curly hair brushed Letty's cheek, smelling like woodsmoke and copal.

"*My name is Letty,*" she whispered in Spanish to the beautiful woman, just to distract herself from the churning nausea.

It was too dark inside the truck to see the woman's expression or if she was even listening at all. If she was, she didn't reply.

"*I'm going to Los Angeles to work in my cousin's poultry shop,*" Letty continued, nervous and talking too fast. "*Plucking chickens. My brother thinks this is funny, because he calls me Chicken*

Neck. Ever since we were kids. Because I'm skinny, you know, like a chicken's neck. He won't think it's so funny when he sees how much money I'll be sending our grandmother. And soon, I'll have enough money to bring her and my daughter to live with me. My daughter's name is Marisol. She's three."

Even though it was too dark to see, Letty was suddenly certain that the woman was looking right at her, listening intently.

"*Shut up*," one of the men hissed, digging an elbow into Letty's ribs. "*You sound just like a chicken.*"

Letty shut up. Time passed. She could feel herself dozing, half dreaming of swimming naked through cool water.

Then Letty heard something that yanked her back into reality. Another engine. The crunch of tires. Another vehicle was approaching. There were a few short pulses of a siren and an incomprehensible foreign voice barked through a megaphone. A flash of desperate panic burned through the cramped and airless space and swiftly dissipated, leaving behind an apathetic kind of resignation. They were locked in. Nowhere to run. It was over. They were caught.

Letty was not proud of what she'd done to pay off the Coyote, and she knew in her heart that she could never put herself through that kind of hell again. This was her one and only chance to make it to the United States, to make a better life for her daughter. To make sure that Marisol would never have to do the kinds of things her mother had been forced to do. Now it was all falling apart. Her one chance, slipping through her fingers.

The truck slowed, then stopped. Without realizing she was doing it, Letty reached out and grasped the beautiful woman's arm. At least that's what she thought she had done. But what her fingers found didn't feel anything like a woman's skin. It felt first like the dirty, brittle hair clinging to a week-old roadkill dog and then more like the cold, chitinous plates of a scorpion's tail. Then flesh again, human flesh burning with a fatal fever and squirming with movement like busy maggots wriggling just beneath the skin.

There was a strange sound. An unnatural growl so deep it was more felt than heard, rumbling beneath a wet crunching like fresh bones being cracked for marrow. Letty yanked her hand away, letting out a small, airless scream. Her head was spinning with vertigo, as if the beautiful woman were a deep hole and Letty were falling into her. Falling, or drowning. The smell of copal smoke sharpened in the airless space and that's when the thing that used to be a beautiful woman leapt at Letty, not a hole anymore but real, all teeth and terrible, howling rage.

TWO

Supervisory Border Patrol Agent Marco Salazar watched the smuggler's truck approaching through night vision binoculars. Behind the wheel was a luckless Coyote named Fernando "Ojon" Ruiz Hierra. Ojon got his nickname because of his large bulging eyes, but it had become a joke around the station that Ojon couldn't see a 747 flying an inch from his nose. He was a loser, plain and simple, notorious for letting his charges die from dehydration before they even hit the border. But he was cheap, and there was no shortage of desperate migrants willing to take that risk in hopes of making it through to the land of opportunity. He'd been popped twice by Customs and Border Protection (CBP) and skated by both times by claiming to be just another migrant in the group. All their evidence against him was circumstantial and none of the people he smuggled would testify that he was a hired guide because of his connections with a local drug cartel. The second time, they'd tried to hold him on re-entering the U.S. as a prior deportee, but strings had been pulled and they'd had no choice but to send him back to Mexico again, along with all the others. Salazar figured it was only a matter of time before his connections decided Ojon was more trouble than he was worth and put him out of their mutual misery.

But it was looking like that time might come sooner rather than later. Now that they'd caught Ojon behind the wheel of a truck full of migrants, the charges against him would finally stick and he'd end up getting shanked in prison instead of gunned down in the street. Of course, taking him out of the picture wouldn't stop the endless flow of migrants, but maybe there'd be fewer senseless deaths in Salazar's sector.

Salazar's earpiece crackled, and then CJ's voice cut through the static. Not saying anything special, just confirming the visual on the approaching truck and asking for permission to move in. But the sound of her voice made him flush hot, suddenly sweating under his body armor despite the cool desert night.

Border Patrol Agent Cara Jean Hogeland had only been on his team for three months. She was twenty-seven, thirteen years younger than Salazar. Hardly a beauty, she had a long, horsy face and frizzy red hair that stuck out every which way, but she was six feet tall with legs that could kill a man and eyes that let you know she had your number. Salazar had been married for nine years and had never been unfaithful. CJ had made short work of that.

It had been a terrible idea from the start. Terrible because it would break Rena's heart if she ever found out and terrible because he was CJ's superior officer. The threat of a sexual misconduct charge was serious business in a division that was still more than eighty percent male, but even knowing he could lose both his job and his family over this kind of indiscretion, he just couldn't keep away from CJ. In cheap motels, in the back of his SUV, and one memorable occasion in the men's room at the gun range. He thought about her nearly every waking minute of every day. He thought about her when he really ought to be thinking about not getting shot. He was thinking about her right now as he watched her and her partner, veteran agent Davis Keene, move their vehicle into position for the intercept.

He gave Keene and CJ the go ahead, then shouldered his rifle to cover them, watching their SUV through the infrared scope. Both times they had arrested Ojon, he had made the same crazy headlong sprint into the brush. Both times he tripped and fell on his face within 100 yards and was easily apprehended. Yet, Salazar was willing to bet he was going to do the exact same thing tonight. Like somehow, this time would be different. No chance of that.

Salazar checked his watch. He figured they'd have Ojon in custody and the thirsty migrants processed and ready to be deported well before 3 a.m. Which would give Salazar three full hours with CJ before he had to go home to his sleeping wife and children.

Keene pulled their SUV into the road, cutting the truck off while CJ hit the spotlight. The truck braked in a swirling cloud of dust and Keene's voice boomed over the loudspeaker, telling Ojon to keep his hands where they could see them and not make any sudden moves. Of course, Ojon threw the driver's side door wide open and took off into the scrub.

Salazar didn't bother to shoot him. It was more entertaining to watch him run and fall. Keene took off at a comfortable pace after the fleeing Ojon. Salazar watched CJ's white-hot, shimmering shape in his infrared scope as she threw her head back and laughed. He thought about the way she'd throw her head back just like that when she was on top of him. He wiped his sweaty hand on the leg of his uniform pants and then put his finger back on the trigger.

CJ made her way around to the back of the truck, checked the padlocked chain wound around the door latch, then took a sudden step back, hand on the butt of her side arm.

Salazar's heartbeat surged, senses suddenly sharp and all thoughts of CJ's anatomy washed away in a gush of adrenaline. Something was very wrong. He could feel it in his gut.

"Talk to me, CJ," he said, instantly wishing he'd called her by her last name like every other officer on his team, but too concerned about her safety to worry about sounding overly familiar on an open frequency. "What the hell's going on down there?"

"Sounds like…" CJ replied. "Like he's got some kind of… zoo animal in there…" Salazar could hear a burst of terrified screams in the background. The truck was rocking on its axles. CJ drew her gun and took another step back. "Oh my God it's…"

"Hold your position, Hogeland," Salazar said, already half-running, half-sliding down the steep embankment toward the truck. "Keene, forget Ojon. We got a major situation here."

"I just got him zipped," Keene replied.

"Leave him!" Salazar said. "We'll pick him up later."

That was when the back of the truck burst open, roll-up door wrenched from its hinges and left dangling by the padlocked chain. Something leapt out and took CJ down, some kind of huge, lanky dog maybe, but whatever it was, it was inexplicably difficult to look at. Like its edges weren't solid, but jittering and shifting with a seizure-like intensity. It gave off waves of rage like heat off a desert road at high noon.

Salazar tried to draw a bead on it, but focusing on its roiling shape was almost impossible and made the backs of his eyeballs ache. All he could see was CJ, laying there in the sand, head thrown back like it had been when she was laughing, when she was making love to him. Only now that sleek, muscular neck had been torn wide open, a fine crimson mist filling the air around what used to be her face as her body still tried to breathe through a ruptured windpipe. And then suddenly, that fierce, feral rage was focused on him.

He got off two shots before it was on him, tearing the rifle from his grip.

Ojon knelt in the sand, hands zip-tied behind his back. He couldn't believe this was happening now, tonight. He had this blonde stripper in Phoenix who he was pretty sure would give it up the next time he saw her. He could tell she really liked him, not like all those other guys in the club. She obviously respected him, because of his reputation and connections to Las Maras. And even though she said she didn't do that kind of thing, he knew she'd feel different when she saw the fat roll he collected from this latest crossing. Not to mention the nice clean eighth of coke he was planning to give her as a tip. *La pinché Migra.* They'd probably take that too.

Truth was, he was getting tired of these Coyote runs. It was way too hard, guiding all these stupid goats through the harsh desert. Sure, the pay was good and it got him laid by desperate women that were dying to get to the States, but he felt like it was high time he moved up in the organization. Something cushy, like sitting in a big office somewhere, telling people what to do over the phone while getting a *chupada* from his sexy secretary. He figured he'd talk to his cousin Beto about that as soon as he was processed and released.

When he heard shots, Ojon scrambled awkwardly to his feet and spun toward the truck. He couldn't see what was happening from his angle, so he crept closer, peering through the brush and trying to get a glimpse of the action. When he did, he wished he hadn't.

At first, he thought he was looking at a naked woman with wild black hair, facing away from him as one of the CBP officers drew down on her. If there had been a woman like that in the group, Ojon was sure he would have noticed.

In fact, he definitely would have offered her his special discount. The officer was an older man, late forties with salt-and-pepper hair and a thick mustache. Ojon remembered him from one of his previous arrests, remembered that he was a real hardass. But he wasn't acting like a hardass now. He was staring at the naked woman with wide eyes and a look first of horrified recognition and then stunned disbelief. The disbelief became terror as the thing that looked like a naked woman melted into something different. Something terrible.

Ojon turned and ran.

THREE

Dean Winchester eased the Impala up to eighty miles per hour. It was a knockout of a day. Sunny and perfect, like a vintage ad for America the Beautiful. Sky so blue it hurt. The red rock canyons of Sedona, Arizona had given way to windswept dunes as they headed west, toward the California border. He had a belly full of good greasy burgers from a Mom and Pop roadside stand a few miles back. Iron Maiden's "Running Free" pumped through the speakers. His brother Sam rode shotgun, long legs bent at what had to be an uncomfortable angle and balancing his laptop on his knees, a scattering of clippings and photos spilling across his seat. The road seemed to stretch out forever. If Dean squinted, he could almost pretend things were the way they used to be. The way they were supposed to be.

Then the song ended and a new one came on. When Dean heard the opening riff of ACDC's "Hell Ain't a Bad

Place to Be" he reached out and switched the music off.

Sam didn't seem to notice or care that the music had stopped. He was utterly absorbed in whatever he was reading.

"Got something?" Dean asked.

"Maybe," Sam replied.

Minutes and miles rolled by in silence, broken only by the shuffle of pages and the click of keystrokes. Dean could feel the cumulative weight of everything he'd been trying to forget crouching between them like a solid living thing. The elephant in the room. So much left unsaid. So much that had already been said and could never be taken back.

"So," Dean finally said. "You gonna share with the rest of the class?"

"Border Patrol intercepted a truck full of illegals just south of Choulic," Sam responded. "A routine stop. Only something went wrong and the officers involved never reported back at the station. When they sent a back-up unit out to the last known location, they found fifteen mutilated corpses, including the three officers. COD is listed as 'wild animal attack.'"

"*Fifteen* corpses, at least three of which were heavily armed and probably wearing body armor? That's some animal."

"Our kinda animal," Sam said, clicking through to another page. "Truck door was busted open from the inside. Says here there's been some speculation that the smugglers involved may have been trying to import some type of large exotic mammal, like a tiger or a bear."

"Great." Dean rolled his eyes. "Not another damn werewolf."

Sam shook his head. "It gets weirder."

"Doesn't it always?"

Sam showed one of the photos to Dean, who glanced sideways to look at it.

"Can a werewolf do something like this?" Sam said.

The photo showed an official Customs and Border Protection SUV. Well, half an SUV. A little less than half, to be precise. The front half was perfectly normal, undamaged. The back half had been removed with surgical precision, metal and plastic melted shiny smooth along the cut edges. As if someone had drawn a slightly curved line in the sand and everything on one side of the line had simply vanished, while the rest remained untouched. On the ground nearby was the uniformed body of a CBP officer. His Kevlar vest was torn to rags. So was he. And he didn't have a head.

"Werewolves are stronger than any normal predator, but their claws can't go through Kevlar like that." Sam tapped the photo. "And what the hell happened to the SUV? It looks almost like some kind of large protective circle had been drawn and then everything inside the circle disappeared. Transported, maybe. But where?"

Dean glanced over at his kid brother. Sam was staring intently at the laptop screen once more. He'd caught the scent of something new and was intrigued. It was the closest thing to a human emotion that Dean had seen in his brother's face since Sam had been brought back from Hell.

Maybe this was just what they needed. Something to take their minds off the big picture.

Dean could feel the old, familiar excitement building inside him. The thrill of the hunt. He looked away toward the raw, jagged mountains. Was he kidding himself to think that they could forget the past and the weight of a potentially bleak and hopeless future and lose themselves in an interesting job? Maybe so, but that wasn't gonna stop him from trying. He needed a distraction too badly.

"Where the hell is Choulic anyway?" Dean asked, turning back to Sam.

The corner of Sam's mouth twitched, just a little. Dean chose to interpret that as a smile.

FOUR

Choulic, Arizona turned out to be pretty much nowhere. A few trailers, and a ranch with three stoic horses watching the Impala from behind a crooked, endlessly repaired fence. A gas station straight out of the forties that sold beer and Jarritos soda from a Styrofoam cooler, along with weird "Indian Curios." A billboard advertising a rattlesnake round-up that was supposedly "fun for the whole family." That particular episode of wholesale reptile genocide had already happened more than four months ago.

If the town of Choulic itself was nowhere, the actual location where the truck and the bodies had been found was even further away from anywhere. The road, such as it was, was barely more than two hardened ruts in the stony ground. The amount of abrasive grit and yellow desert dust that was rapidly coating the Impala's slick black skin was starting to give Dean heart palpitations. He silently promised her a carwash the second they got what they needed from this particular patch of nowhere.

Sam was out the passenger door even before Dean had come to a complete stop. Dean sat for a moment with his hand on the key in the ignition, just watching. Sam had the EMF meter out and was walking a careful grid across the area where the event had occurred. Dean killed the engine and got out himself. He already felt that there was something disturbing about the place.

The heat was all over him the second he left the air-conditioned comfort of the Impala. There was hot and then there was this. Within seconds, his T-shirt was soaked through with sweat. The sun was swiftly barbecuing the top of his head and forcing his eyes down to a tight squint even behind his dark sunglasses. Suddenly, the idea of wearing a cowboy hat made perfect sense. He tried to imagine what it would be like to cross this inhospitable desert on foot.

"How do people live out here?" Dean asked, stepping up next to Sam and pulling his damp shirt away from his sticky chest. "I've been here five minutes and I already feel like a 7-Eleven hotdog in a microwave."

"Yeah," Sam replied, smirking without looking up from the readout. "But it's a dry heat."

"Hell's a dry heat, too," Dean said. "It still sucks. Let me know if you pull anything. I'm gonna go get a cold beer and pour it down my pants." He looked around uneasily.

"I got nothing," Sam replied, shrugging. "The area's clean. Whatever happened here, I don't think it's tied to this location and it didn't leave behind any detectable fluctuations."

If there had been any ordinary physical evidence, blood or tire tracks or anything like that, the stealthy, endlessly shifting sand had erased it. Nothing physical and nothing electromagnetic. No sulfur. No visible hexes. Nothing at all except for a strange feeling in the pit of Dean's stomach. A sense of profound *wrongness* about what had happened there.

"Heads up," Sam said.

Dean turned to face his brother. Sam gestured to the left with his chin.

"Looks like we got company," he said.

There was a rocky ridge about twenty-five feet away from the road that Dean realized gave a perfect sniper's view of the location where the attack had occurred. At the crest of the ridge was a figure in black astride a matte-black custom Suzuki Hayabusa motorcycle. The figure's eyes were hidden behind the dark visor of a full-face helmet, but there was no doubt that the brothers were being watched.

For a handful of heartbeats, nothing happened. The three of them just regarded each other in silence. Then the Hayabusa's engine turned over with a throaty roar, the bike spun 180 degrees in a spray of gravel and dust, and the mysterious figure was gone.

As the sound of the bike's engine faded into the distance, Dean turned to Sam with a slight frown.

"Nice bike, the Hayabusa," he said. "But pretty noisy."

"Yeah," Sam said. "So?"

"So," Dean said. "Did you hear a motorcycle engine at any point since we got here?"

The desert around them was quiet and peaceful. The only sounds were the raspy, repetitive call of a small bird, the bone-dry rattle of wind through thorny brush, and the whisper of sand around their boots.

"Or how about on the drive out here?" Dean continued. "Hell, I don't think we passed a single vehicle on the road since that crappy pick-up about ten miles back."

Sam's eyes went wide. He got it.

"Whoever that was," Dean said. "They were already here. Waiting for us."

The brothers didn't discuss the appearance of the mysterious rider on the drive from Choulic to Bullhead City, but Dean found himself mulling over the incident, wondering. Could it have been an off-duty CBP officer who had taken a special interest in the case? If so, how did they know Sam and Dean would be there? Or did they? Was Dean reading too much into it? Could it be a simple coincidence that they both chose the same time on the same day to check out the location? But Dean didn't think so. Coincidence was a concept that normal people used to explain away things they didn't understand. Things Dean understood all too well.

Maybe it had been the perp, returning to the scene of the crime?

"Okay," Dean said, pulling the Impala up to a modest but immaculately landscaped Spanish-style home on a residential street. "Tell me more about Officer Headless."

"Davis James Keene," Sam replied. "Age forty-seven. Hardcore evangelical Christian. Born and raised right here in

Bullhead. Highway patrol officer for ten years before joining CBP. Wife Loretta doesn't work outside the home. Four kids. All boys, all grown."

"But the question is, what makes him different than the other two murdered Border Patrol agents?" Dean asked, killing the engine and pulling the keys from the ignition. "I mean all the corpses were in bad shape, but Keene's body seems to have suffered way more damage than the other victims. Like whatever did this was particularly pissed at him."

Too hot and sweaty—at least in Dean's case—to face putting on their FBI suits, they had decided to go plain-clothed for this interview, figuring the grieving widow would have other things on her mind than to question their attire. Dean opened the glove compartment and pulled out a pair of fake FBI badges and handed one to Sam. Sam took the badge and shrugged.

"I guess that's what we're here to find out," he said.

The woman who answered the door was surprisingly beautiful. From Sam's description, Dean had been expecting some kind of sweet, chubby church-lady type. Loretta Keene looked more like a retired fashion model. Mile-high legs under a short sundress. Elegant cheekbones and big blue eyes that were just starting to crinkle at their corners. Thick blonde hair pulled back in a casual ponytail. Her feet were bare, toenails perfectly polished. She looked tired, like she'd been crying.

Dean showed her his badge.

"Mrs. Keene?"

The woman nodded, let out a resigned sigh. She stepped aside to let Dean and Sam enter without asking them who they were or what they wanted.

The interior of the house was just as immaculate as the exterior. Tasteful, but not too expensive. Simple brown-leather furniture and lots of well-groomed houseplants. Photos of four good-looking, athletic boys at various ages. A fresh lemony smell of recently applied furniture polish. The large windows were crystal clean. Not a speck of dust or a single item out of place.

But the thing that Dean found the most unusual about the room was what *wasn't* there. Not one single religious object. No bibles. No crosses. No framed religious sayings. Nothing to indicate that they were in the home of an evangelical Christian.

"I'm Special Agent Crockett," Dean told the woman. "This is Special Agent Tubbs." Sam shot Dean a warning look, but Dean ignored him, face still deadpan serious. "We're investigating the unusual circumstances surrounding your husband's death."

Loretta Keene picked up a small spray bottle and started misting the leaves of a large potted ficus, her back to Dean.

"It's like he knew this was coming," she said, almost too softly for them to hear.

"What makes you say that," Sam asked, frowning slightly and taking a step closer to the widow.

She looked down at the spray bottle and shrugged.

"From the day Davis and I met, it was… We had this… this crazy kind of passion. That's the only word I can think of to describe it. Passion. He was the love of my life. We couldn't keep our hands off each other." She blushed and turned back to the plant, spraying it again, even though it was already soaked. "All my girlfriends said that would change once our first baby was born, but it didn't. Not then, anyway. Not until years later."

Dean looked at Sam but didn't say anything. They just waited for her to continue.

"This was fifteen years ago. Ritchie, our youngest, was seven. I remember because it was the day after his seventh birthday party. Everything was normal, the way it always was. Davis had just started working for the CBP. Nights, which was tough for me, because we really only saw each other for a short time each evening before he left. But we would always... Anyway, he left for work that night and..."

She finally turned to look at Dean. Her eyes were shimmering with unshed tears.

"I feel like that was the last time I saw my husband." She put the spray bottle down on the windowsill beside the damp ficus. "I'd like a drink. Would you boys like a drink?"

"We're not allowed to drink on the job, ma'am," Sam replied before Dean could say yes.

"I'd like a drink," she said again, to no one in particular, then drifted slowly out of the room.

"Crockett and Tubbs?" Sam said, leaning close to Dean and speaking fast and low. "Come on. Isn't that a little too obvious? You oughta stick with your usual obscure rock and roll names."

"Just trying to spice up our relationship," Dean replied. "But listen, never mind that." He tipped his chin toward the doorway though which Mrs. Keene had drifted. "Booze in the house. No visible religious stuff. All this sex talk. You sure about this born-again thing?"

Sam looked down at the file folder in his hand. Rifled through some papers.

"According to this, the Keenes have been active members of the Living Word Baptist Church for fifteen years."

"Fifteen years," Dean echoed.

Mrs. Keene returned with a heroic three-finger knock of straight Bourbon in a thick, square glass. She tossed back more than half the amber liquid and then drifted over to the glossy leather couch. She didn't sit, just stood there.

"You were saying," Dean prompted.

"Was I?" Mrs. Keene looked puzzled and slightly anxious, like she'd just woken up in an unfamiliar bed. She sat down after all.

"You were saying," Sam reminded her. "That you felt like the last time you saw your husband was fifteen years ago."

"Right," she said. "The day after Ritchie's seventh birthday party." She downed the rest of her bourbon. "Davis went to work that night just like he always did, but when he came home, he was like a different person. Shut down inside. He never touched me again."

She shook her head, shifting the empty glass from one hand to the other. Dean felt a terrible empathy for her, all alone in that clean, perfect house, as empty as her glass.

"I know something happened that night," she continued.

"But he would never talk about it. He made us all get baptized the next day. I went along with it because it was easier than trying to argue him out of it, but I never really believed. I haven't been back to church since his funeral. Closed casket, of course, since they never found his head." She was suddenly angry, bitter as frostbite. "I mean, what's the point? So I can listen to a bunch of sanctimonious hypocrites tell me that what happened to Davis was God's will?" She made a harsh, half-suffocated sound that was probably meant to be a laugh. "God's will? I don't want any part of a God that would let something like that happen to one of his followers."

Lady, Dean thought, *you don't know the half of it.*

FIVE

Border patrol officer Manuel Léon didn't know what to make of his new partner. Charlie Himes was a decent guy, but very guarded. Didn't joke around. Didn't say a single word that wasn't directly related to the job or responding to a specific request. He was the only black guy on the Tijuana River ATV team and he was also the oldest by a good ten years. Léon was the youngest. They were a Mutt and Jeff team, Himes tall and wiry and Léon short and stocky. Their CO called them Rocky and Bullwinkle. But despite their differences, they'd been working pretty well together for these past four days. Himes been showing Léon the ropes along the river, and although Léon might have preferred to partner with someone he could kid around with a little every now and then, Himes was a crack shot, had a black belt in Brazilian Jiujitsu, and held the highest arrest record in the unit. He was in better shape than most guys half his age. Léon could do worse.

Their designated section of the Tijuana River was barely what you'd call a river. It was more like sludgy trickle of toxic chemicals and raw sewage that ran along a wide cement channel littered with dead dogs, burning tires, and discarded needles. The stench was overwhelming, but that never stopped people from wading through the filth to try and make it to the American side. Himes claimed that you got used to the smell after a while. Léon wasn't sure if he believed that. There weren't enough showers in the world to wash the memory of that smell out of Léon's head.

It was just after midnight when they spotted a trio of junkies squatting and huddled together on the American edge of the river. Male in an illegible death metal T-shirt and dirty jeans. Long, tangled hair and lurid red Kaposi's sarcoma legions on his arms and face. Two females. One overweight and painfully young. Childish, pink-and-black T-shirt featuring a bad knock-off of Hello Kitty. Way too much bloated belly exposed between the hem of the shirt and the saggy waistband of her torn pink leggings. Faded pink hair, with a good six inches of black roots. Maybe sixteen, tops. Dead, hopeless eyes. If she was sharing needles, and who knew what else, with her male companion, she was probably already HIV-positive. Léon hoped she was just fat, and not pregnant. The second female wore a hooded sweatshirt, hood up and curly black hair spilling out from around its edges. Jeans and dusty hiking boots. What skin was visible was corpse pale in the harsh sodium lights. The first two were totally absorbed doing something furtive with their hands, probably prepping their heroin, but the second female sat stone still and seemed to be watching the border patrol agents. Léon couldn't see her eyes under the hood, but she gave him the creeps.

"Paid diversion," Himes said as they pulled their ATVs up on the lip of the channel.

"Paid?"

"Smugglers pay junkies to shoot up along the river," Himes told him. "Divert our attention away from their operations."

Himes lifted the visor of his helmet and raised a pair of compact binoculars to his eyes to get a closer look at the action. He watched the junkies for a silent minute, then handed the binocs over to Léon. Léon pushed up his own visor and scoped the trio for himself, adjusting the focus and zooming in on the male junkie's hands.

Sure enough, he was dumping something from a tiny plastic envelope into a metal bottle cap. The chubby girl was pressed up against him, holding a disposable lighter and a syringe. She had sparkly glitter polish on her bitten nails, and a cheap ring shaped like a star.

"Should we try to apprehend them?" Léon asked.

"We can try," Himes said. "But they'll probably run back over to the Mexican side."

"So, what?" Léon said. "We just watch them?"

Léon was zoomed in so tight that when something suddenly happened, it just looked like a fast shuffle and blur. He lowered the binocs, squinting at the three junkies. Now there were only two of them. They were both laying face down in the oily sewage, rivulets of crimson feeding out into the sluggish current. The chubby girl didn't seem to have a head.

"What the..."

He turned to Himes and saw that the second female was standing right beside them, between the two ATVs. She was inexplicably nude. Impossible, but not any less possible than her running all the way up to the top of the steep concrete bank in the half a second it took Léon to lower his binocs. Her chin and chest were slick with gore. Her eyes did not reflect any light, just swallowed it all and gave nothing back. She was holding something, something that Léon's baffled brain translated as a dirty red mop. But when he saw that the mop had streaks of pink, he realized what he was really looking at. It was a human spine with the head still attached, clotted pink hair brushing back and forth against the naked woman's bare toes.

Léon looked at his partner. Crack-shot, bad ass Himes. Highest arrest record on the team. He didn't draw his weapon. Didn't take action. He was just staring at the woman with a drowsy kind of dread, like a suicide on a ledge, looking down. Like he knew what was coming. Like he deserved it.

When the girl dropped the spine and leapt on Himes like a hungry animal, Léon scrambled sideways off his ATV, thought processes utterly short-circuited by what he was seeing. It would have made sense to punch the gas and speed away, but he wasn't thinking. Couldn't think. All he could do was stumble backward, hands up and head shaking in endless, wordless denial. Because the woman was changing, form and substance flickering like a fire, bleeding off into the air around her as she tore into Himes with raptor claws and a thousand jagged teeth dripping glistening venom like rattlesnake fangs.

Léon tripped and fell on his ass as what used to be a woman threw back what used to be a head and screamed. That sound, that agonized, furious scream, was the single most terrible sound Léon had ever heard. Then something happened that was so strange, stranger even than all the other madness of the previous impossible moments, that Léon could feel his mind snap like a broken bone. In a way, it was almost a relief, not to have to try and make sense of anything anymore. Because there was no way to make sense of what he was seeing.

The sky around the woman's head was unfolding. The earth was torn wide open like Himes' corpse and things started to fall upward, twisting like trash caught in a high wind. There was a blinding flash and a burst of excruciating pain like a plane crash inside Léon's head and then the woman was gone. So were the two ATVs and Himes' body. So was the lower half of Léon's body. Everything from the navel down was gone, neatly severed and bloodless for a surreal moment. Then, the blood came in a dizzy sickening rush, flowing down into the oily river and mingling with the blood of the dead junkies. Léon thought he heard the buzz of ATVs, backup on the way, but it didn't matter. It was too late.

SIX

Dean stood at the single window of a motel room. He'd been looking out at the freshly washed Impala sitting in the mostly empty parking lot, but now let the scratchy plaid curtain drop. The room was identical to every room he'd ever stayed in, nearly invisible in its generic blandness. The only thing that stood out and reminded him that he was in Arizona rather than Nebraska or Montana or Vermont was a creepy painting of an anthropomorphic saguaro cactus wearing a cowboy hat and a mildly demented expression on its prickly green face. When they first checked in, he'd been tempted to take it down and stash it in the closet, but discovered that it was bolted to the wall. Like anyone in their right mind would want to steal that atrocity.

Sam had his laptop set up on the rickety table on the other side of the narrow room, surrounded by open files and crumpled papers.

"So what have you got on little Ritchie Keene?"

"He's in a band." Sam said. "They're terrible."

"How about something useful? Like his DOB?"

"April 16th," Sam read off the screen. "1988."

"When Mrs. Keene was talking about whatever she thinks might have happened to her husband on the job," Dean said, "she referred to it as the day after the youngest son's seventh birthday party. Not the day after his *actual* birthday."

"Still," Sam said. "At least that narrows it down, gives us a window of about a week or so. I'd say we should look for something that occurred between April 10th and 20th, 1995."

"Looks like I'd better pay a visit to our friends at Customs and Border Protection," Dean said. "Where was Keene stationed?"

"There's no way either one of us is getting into a CBP station," Sam said.

"Why not?" Dean asked.

"Look," Sam replied. "I want to bag this creature too, but we need to play it smart. Weigh the risks. A CBP station isn't some podunk sheriff's office where you can fool everyone with slick talk and a fake badge. In case you haven't been keeping up on current events over the past eight years, the CBP and the Department of Homeland Security have combined forces to crack down on any possible terrorist threat to our great nation. And they take their jobs very, *very* seriously. I think it's safe to say they're basically Dean-proof."

"I'm deeply hurt by your lack of faith in my ability to sweet-talk," Dean replied, opening the closet door and pulling out a garment bag containing two unremarkable navy-blue suits. He unzipped it, removing the smaller of the two jackets. "I'm like the Chuck Norris of sweet-talking."

"I'm serious, Dean," Sam said. "Federal prison serious."

Dean pulled off his T-shirt and slipped into the white button-down that had been hung underneath the jacket.

"What? You're saying you couldn't go on without me?" Dean buttoned the shirt and draped a dull striped tie around his neck. "You love your dear big brother so much that it would break your heart if I went to prison?"

Sam looked away.

"I'm just trying to be practical," he said.

"Practical," Dean repeated, tightening the knot on the tie. "Uh huh. Just give me the damn address."

SEVEN

The Nogales Station of the CBP was probably one of the most unfriendly looking buildings Dean had ever seen. He'd seen prisons that looked more welcoming.

The officer at the archive check-in desk was female. According to her laminated photo ID, her name was Ariana Cruz. She looked way too young for the job. Wide, heart-shaped face and big brown eyes. Pretty, even with minimal make-up and her dark hair pulled back into a no-nonsense bun. The sweet, kid sister type. No wedding ring.

"You must be Ariana," he said, flashing the most charming smile in his arsenal. "Ray Sandoval told me that you were the one to talk to about pulling some old records."

"I'm sorry, you are…?" She blushed, dropping her gaze.

"I'm Special Agent Allman," Dean told her. "I'm sure Sandoval must have mentioned that I was coming."

He badged her with the FBI ID, holding it low, just to the left of his belt buckle. Trying to make her feel embarrassed about looking too closely at that area of his body and keep her focus upstairs, on his face.

"Well... I..." She picked up a clipboard, scanning over a list of some sort.

He took a step closer, one hand on her desk. He didn't want to overplay it and act all pervy. Just give her the impression that he liked what he saw but was trying to be professional about it.

"It took me three weeks to get all the paperwork together to cover the transfer of document custody," he told her. "I'd hate to have to go through that all over again."

"I'll need your badge number," she said.

Dean pulled out a very official-looking business card with the FBI logo and Bobby Singer's phone number. Held it out to her.

"If there's a problem you can contact my superior back in DC," he told her.

"I need to enter your badge number into the system for security cross-check," she said. "It's standard procedure."

"Listen, Ariana," he said, leaning in and lowering his voice, making it softer, more intimate. "I know you hate all that paperwork just as much as I do..."

She cut him off before he could continue.

"You've always had it easy with women, haven't you?" she said. A funny little smile curled in the corner of her mouth. "I can see why. And, you know what, I'd love to lie to you and tell you that I can get you past security if you take me back into the supply closet and show me a good time. Just for my own selfish reasons."

Dean couldn't help but laugh. Some innocent kid sister.

"But let's face facts," she continued. "Even if you rocked my world, which I have no doubt that you would, I still don't have the power to let you in without performing a security cross-check and issuing a bar-coded visitor ID. If you want to bypass security, you'll have to show my superior officer a good time."

A new voice, masculine, deep and slightly accented, spoke up behind Dean.

"That would be me."

Dean turned to face the owner of the voice. Latino, late fifties with thick, perfectly groomed white hair and incongruous pale-blue eyes set in a deeply lined face the color and texture of old saddle leather. He wore the same uniform as Cruz but with higher-ranking insignia. His photo ID read "Raphael De La Paz."

"Sorry, sir," Cruz replied, blushing even deeper and awkwardly shuffling papers on her desk. "This is Special Agent Allman, here about some old case files. I just need to get his badge number…"

De La Paz looked at Dean.

Dean couldn't remember the last time he'd felt so profoundly scrutinized. By a normal human being, anyway. It was like that unflinching gaze was riffling through the drawers of his mind. Dean was sure the game was up.

There was a fingerprint scanner beside the clipboard on Cruz's desk. If they printed him, it would only take a few clicks on a computer to call up Dean's less-than-sterling history with law enforcement. Sam had been right. This was a spectacularly bad idea.

"Come into my office, Agent..." De La Paz gave Dean another searching look. "What did you say your name was again?"

"Allman," Dean said, sweating in earnest now. He knew perfectly well that the older man hadn't forgotton the fake name he'd given Cruz.

"Right," De La Paz said. "Cruz, take a break. Smoke. Coffee. Facebook. Whatever."

"Yes, sir," she said.

De La Paz turned and headed down the drab, fluorescent-lit corridor. Dean saw no choice but to follow. As they walked, Dean noticed the older man limping slightly on his right leg. De La Paz opened a metal door labeled with his name and gestured for Dean to enter.

Dean stepped inside the cramped, windowless office. It was pin-neat and minimalist. Standard, government-issue metal desk, nearly bare except for a phone, a small, out-dated computer monitor, and a single framed photo facing away from Dean. Two identical chairs, one behind the desk and one in front. One wall was lined with large, alphabetized filing cabinets, making the small room feel even smaller.

De La Paz stepped in behind Dean and closed the door. There was barely enough room for the two of them to stand side by side in front of the desk. Dean wondered for a moment if maybe Cruz had been serious about him showing her boss a good time, but De La Paz just squeezed past him and sat down behind the desk. He motioned for Dean to take the other chair.

"I've worked Border Patrol for twenty years," De La Paz said. "Seventeen of those years in the field, before a Zeta bullet put me behind this desk. People tell you all kinds of stories. Some are true. Most aren't. You learn to know the difference just by looking at 'em. At their eyes. I never even listen to what people say anymore. I just look at their eyes."

Dean shifted in the uncomfortable chair, feeling like he was twelve years old again and back in the principal's office.

"I know you're not an FBI agent."

The uncomfortable chair squeaked under Dean's weight as he shifted again, a subtle torture device that amped his discomfort up to eleven. He ran every angle, every possible response over and over in his head and still came up empty. He looked down at his sweating hands. Some Chuck Norris.

"But I also know you're not a criminal or a terrorist," De La Paz continued. "You probably like to think of yourself as some kind of rebel, but you have the soul of a lawman. I see that in your eyes."

Dean squinted at the older man, wondering where he was going with this.

"You're carrying a hell of a lot of scar tissue for someone as young as you are." De La Paz sat stone still, never taking his eyes off Dean as he spoke. "But we all get calloused on account of the things we've seen on the job. Things we've done. Things the people we protect could never understand. Those things have made you cynical, but deep in your heart you still believe in justice, don't you?"

Did he? Dean had no idea how to answer a question like that.

"You know I oughta turn you in," De La Paz said.

"What's stopping you?" Dean asked. If De La Paz really was going to blow the whistle, Dean wished he'd just get it over with already.

"Maybe the fact that you remind me of someone." De La Paz pulled a bottle of top-shelf tequila from a desk drawer, along with two shot glasses. "A complicated, driven man with eyes like just yours. Met him back when I was your age. Still young enough to think I knew everything about everything." He looked down at the bottle, shaking his head with a slight smile. "That man sure proved me wrong." He opened the bottle, poured two modest shots. "His name was Winchester. John Winchester."

De La Paz held one of the shot glasses out to Dean.

"Pleased to meet you, Dean," De La Paz said, raising his shot glass and clinking it against Dean's.

Dean tried to no-sell his surprise, but he was pretty sure his jaw was in his lap.

"You knew who I was this whole time?" Dean asked.

"I had a pretty good idea." He smiled. "I suppose you might have been Sam, but you've got firstborn written all over you." He tossed back the tequila and set the glass down on his desk. "Now why don't you tell me what this is really about."

Dean looked at the older man for a moment, then at the tequila. He wondered what supernatural horror had brought his dad and this guy together, but figured this wasn't the time to ask. He just had to hope that they had both been on the same side. He sucked in a deep breath, downed the shot, and took a risk. A risk he was probably out of his mind for taking. He told De La Paz what this was really about.

Dean laid out everything they knew. Everything they'd found out up to that point. Including their suspicion that the thing responsible for the attacks wasn't human.

De La Paz listened without interrupting, poker-faced and giving Dean no idea if he was buying it or if he was planning to call the men in white coats to come take Dean away.

When Dean was finished, De La Paz nodded. He didn't immediately arrest him or call the men in white coats, he just sat there for a minute in thoughtful silence.

"So you're saying that you think someone, or some*thing*, had it out for Keene because of an event that occurred on the job fifteen years ago?"

"Pretty much."

More silence. Had Dean made a mistake, trusting De La Paz? Just because the older man knew their father didn't necessarily mean he knew everything. Maybe they just had a couple of beers and talked about baseball. But there was something about De La Paz that Dean couldn't quite put his finger on. Something that made Dean instinctively trust him.

The phone on De La Paz's desk rang, startling Dean a little.

"Excuse me," the older man said, lifting the receiver. "De La Paz."

He spoke for a minute in Spanish, his tone intimate and soothing, like he was telling someone not to worry. He covered the mouthpiece and whispered to Dean.

"My wife. Every time she sees something on the news, she thinks I'm in danger, even though I've been working archives for three years now."

De La Paz listened to whatever was being said to him, and suddenly, his eyes went wide. He made a quick excuse to his wife and hung up.

"What...?" Dean began, but De La Paz held up his hand for quiet and then started tapping away on the computer.

Dean waited, feeling that hot excitement building inside him again. He had the feeling that he was moving in on their prey.

"There's been another 'animal attack' against our field officers," De La Paz said. "Three, possibly four victims this time. One of them may have been Charlie Himes, currently MIA."

Dean waited for the older man to elaborate.

"Himes was partners with Davis Keene, back when they were rookies, but he put in for transfer to San Diego..."

De La Paz stood and pulled open a file drawer, riffling through files till he found the one he wanted. He laid it on the desk, flipped through it until he found a particular piece of paper, then turned it around so it was facing Dean.

It was an application for transfer. De La Paz tapped the date with a thick, nicotine-stained finger. It said "April 18th, 1995."

"...fifteen years ago," De La Paz said.

EIGHT

De La Paz led Dean down another hallway to a door labeled "DOCUMENTS." De La Paz swiped his ID through a bar-code reader next to the doorknob and pushed the thick metal door open.

"Welcome to the graveyard," he said.

The room they entered was a cavernous, dusty warehouse space packed with row upon row of floor-to-ceiling metal shelving. The shelves were lined with thousands of identical cardboard file boxes.

"We're working on getting all this old paperwork uploaded into the system," De La Paz said. "But it's a monumental task for which we are desperately understaffed. All the personnel files are in my office but any incident reports involving Himes and Keene from April of '95 would be stored here."

Dean walked with De La Paz down the dimly lit rows, past 1997 and 1996, until they found a section marked 1995. The file boxes were in rough chronological order, but not exact, so it took them a few minutes to locate the later half of April.

"Okay, fifteen, sixteen," De La Paz was saying under his breath. "Right, here's the nightshift report that covers April 17th and 18th." He pulled a file, opened it. "Officers Keene and Himes were teamed up with José Porcayo and Gilberto Brewer that night. At 8:37 p.m. on the 17th, there was a pretty substantial narcotics intercept. Three arrests, 500 pounds of cocaine seized. Then nothing all night until 2:58 a.m. on the 18th, when a small group of migrants was apprehended trying to cross the border, including an abandoned female infant, aged nine months, whose mother was never found." De La Paz shrugged. "Doesn't sound like anything out of the ordinary."

Dean scribbled down the names of the two other officers in a small notebook, but he could feel a mounting frustration making him antsy, impatient. He'd always hated this kind of research. Sam was the librarian in the family. Dean much would rather be duking it out with demons than shuffling through old paperwork.

"But wait," De La Paz said, just as Dean was about to thank him for his time and give up on this angle of inquiry. "This is strange."

"I love strange," Dean said, interest renewed. "Lay it on me."

"One of the migrants picked up that night was a sixteen-year-old kid named Anibal Obregon Hernandez. In his statement, he asked to file a complaint against the arresting officers. At first he claimed they raped and murdered a woman in the group. Several hours later, he changed his story and claimed the four officers, quote, 'put a magic spell on her that turned her into a coyote.' Unquote."

"Bingo!" Dean said.

"You don't really believe that's what actually happened, do you?" De La Paz said, thick white eyebrow arched at Dean.

"Maybe not exactly," Dean said. "Maybe that's just a scared sixteen-year-old trying to make sense out of something he didn't understand."

De La Paz shuffled to another page and swore softly in Spanish.

"What?" Dean asked.

"Hernandez recanted his testimony the next morning," De La Paz said. "The complaint was never filed. They found him hanging in the holding cell less than thirty minutes before he was scheduled to be deported. He'd made a noose out of his own T-shirt."

"Damn," Dean said. "Do you think the officers involved may have gotten to him somehow, forced him to change his story?"

"Look, I don't know much about magic spells or anything like that," De La Paz said. "But these officers were good men. Regular guys you'd play cards with on your day off or invite to a family barbeque. I didn't know Brewer that well, but Himes's little girl went to first grade with my daughter. These guys aren't some kind of evil wizards or satanists or anything like that. They're just... guys. I'm having a really hard time believing they would do something like what that Mexican kid described. Magic or no magic."

"Well, clearly something happened that night that scared the hell out of everyone who saw it," Dean said. "Where are Brewer and Porcayo now?"

"Brewer retired early on disability," De La Paz said, slipping the file back into the box. "Diagnosed with Post-Traumatic Stress Disorder. Porcayo left CBP to work in the private sector." He turned back to Dean. "You don't think that they're in danger too, from whatever *animal* is doing this?"

Dean nodded, slipped the little notebook back in the breast pocket of his jacket.

"That's exactly what I think," he said.

Dean shook De La Paz's thick mitt as he was leaving. The older man's grip was strong and warm. The way things were, Dean found it difficult to trust anyone, even his own family, and it was astoundingly rare for him to meet a normal person as honest and open-minded as De La Paz.

"You didn't have to help me," Dean said. "Thanks." He looked into the older man's pale eyes. "And if you want the truth, I don't know if I believe in justice anymore. I want to, but…"

"I understand," De La Paz said. "Good luck out there, kid. You're gonna need it."

Once outside the CBP station's air-conditioned cocoon, Dean trudged across the vast parking lot with his head down, feeling like an ant crossing a frying pan. He was sure the thin soles of his dress shoes were going to catch fire before he made it to the Impala. When he got there, the Impala's door handle was almost too hot to touch.

He was pulling off his sweaty, wrinkled jacket and tossing it into the back seat when he spotted the rider in black right on the other side of the razor-wire fence.

The rider was much closer now, less than ten feet away, standing beside the parked Hayabusa. While the face was still hidden beneath a black helmet, it was clear that the body beneath the distressed, well-worn leather pants and black wife-beater tank top was curvy, unquestionably feminine. Every inch of visible, caramel-colored skin was covered in tattoos, all intricate, Aztec designs. Serpents and jaguars and skeletons. Women in elaborate feathered headdresses wielding leaf-shaped obsidian knives. Arcane symbols. Most were rendered in only black ink but the large, anatomically realistic heart on the left side of her chest was in lurid color, all lush red and purple, surrounded by golden flames.

Like a gunslinger in a classic Western, she wore a low-slung, elaborately tooled black-and-silver gun-belt with a holster on each hip. The nose of each holster was bound to one of her thick, muscular thighs with a leather strap. But rather than old-school six-shooters, Dean could make out the modern, ergonomic grips of what looked to be a pair of Heckler & Koch tactical pistols. She was also wearing heavy, masculine boots and tight, wrist-length black leather gloves. She was not wearing a bra.

There was no way he could climb over the double razor-wire fence in time to catch her before she could get that bike fired up and away. And as much as he loved the Impala, she was no match, speed wise, for what was widely considered to be the world's fastest motorcycle. The Hayabusa would be pushing 190 miles per hour before he could get the Impala up to fifty-five.

Dean approached the barrier.

"Who are you?" he asked, gripping the chain link of the fence between them.

She didn't reply. Just regarded him for a moment through the smoked glass of her visor, then got back on her bike and was gone.

NINE

On the way back to the motel, Dean took care of a few errands. Gassed up the Impala. Bottled water and beer. Ammo run. Unsurprisingly, it was pretty hard to find rock salt in the desert. Not a lot of icy driveways. One smartass clerk told Dean that if he wanted salt that badly, he should just grab a pickax and drive out to the Death Valley salt flats. Dean ended up with an obscenely expensive ten-pound bag of fancy gourmet salt crystals that were infused with truffle essence or some nonsense. He almost felt bad for the local restaurant he'd conned the supplier into charging for the salt, but he was sure the next demon he shot with the stuff would appreciate the "complex, earthy aroma and crisp mineral profile."

He was deeply grateful that the endlessly glaring sun was finally sinking down behind the mountains by the time he got back to the motel. There was so much to process. So much he needed to tell Sam. Plans to be made. He figured the best course of action would be to have Sam dig up addresses for the other two men involved in the unexplained incident of April 18th, 1995 and then find them and warn them. Maybe stake them out, wait for their vengeful "animal" to show up and then gank the thing before it had a chance to hurt anyone else. But how could they pick which man to visit first? What if they picked wrong?

These were the thoughts running though his head as he fished the gaudy plastic key-tag from his pocket and unlocked the motel room door. He pushed it open, stepping gratefully out of the heat and into the room's dim, cave-like sanctuary.

"You're not gonna believe…" he began but stopped dead in mid sentence.

It wasn't Sam sitting at the table, hunched over the laptop. It was the rider in black.

Her helmet was off, revealing dark, almond-shaped eyes, a fierce, pre-Columbian profile and wide, smirking lips. Her crow-black hair hung in a pair of thick, waist-length braids bound with leather strips.

Dean lunged forward to grab her and she leapt up, kicking the chair at him, jumping onto the rickety table and then diving for the open window. He batted the chair aside and swore under his breath as he threw his body in her path, blocking her escape.

She squared off, facing him, eyes wide and gloved fists raised. Standing toe to toe like this, he realized that, despite the aura of tightly coiled menace she radiated, she was actually surprisingly petite. Five foot three inches, tops.

He had a good sixty pounds on her and was almost a full foot taller.

"Look," Dean said, palms out. "I don't want to hurt you."

Before he could blink, she'd scaled him like a cliff-face, taking a step off his knee and another off his hip and then throwing a sharp, spinning kick to his face. He was quick enough to dodge the full force of the kick, but still caught a glancing blow on the jaw. He staggered backward.

She made a run for the door, but he grabbed one of her flying braids and yanked her back toward him, wrapping his arms around her from behind. She dropped straight down and out of his grasp, slippery as mercury, and then ducked backward between his legs. He spun to face her, narrowly avoiding an uppercut to the junk. He was finally angry enough to take a serious swing at her, but he may as well have sent her a Christmas card last year to let her know the punch was coming. She slipped in under his swing and gave him three short, tight body shots in the time it took him to throw just one.

Fighting her was like trying to fight a hummingbird. She was so small and so fast, but she didn't really have enough power behind her punches to knock him out. Just piss him off. On the other hand, she still had those guns on her hips and she could decide to use them at any moment. Dean had a feeling she was a pretty quick draw.

He had no choice but to bull-rush her, using his size and strength advantage to power her into a takedown. He could tell he'd knocked the wind out of her and worked swiftly to immobilize her arms and keep both her hands up high, away from those pistols. She hissed and squirmed beneath him like an angry snake, and he was suddenly intensely aware of her braless breasts pressing against his chest and her leather-clad hips grinding against him as she struggled to free herself. She noticed him noticing and arch amusement flashed in her eyes. Dark eyes, just like Lisa's. He felt a swift flush of heat, followed almost instantly by a cold chaser of guilt. That's when he heard the soft, deadly *snick* of a switchblade.

Dean froze. He could feel the narrow blade pressed up under his chin as she rolled him onto his back and straddled him. Her face was inches from his. He could feel her breath against his lips.

"Take it easy," Dean said, chin held high and eyes wide. "There's no need for all this. I just want to talk."

"So talk," she said.

"Well for starters, how about telling me who the hell you are and why you're following us?"

"I'm Xochi Cazadora," she replied. "And I could ask you the same question."

She had a fairly strong accent that wasn't entirely Mexican. Something a little harder around the consonants

"Where are you from?" Dean asked, intrigued.

"*Tenochtitlan.* El D.F." She pronounced it *Dey Efey.* "You call it Mexico City. My bloodline is Aztec."

"You're not gonna cut my heart out, are you?" Dean asked, looking down to see the knife still too close to his chin for comfort.

She smiled. "Try me."

"Wait a sec," Dean said. "Isn't Cazadora a Spanish name? I thought you guys hated the Spaniards, because of that whole smallpox thing."

"My people don't have surnames." She eased back on the blade just a touch. "Cazadora isn't a name, it's a job description. It means *huntress*."

TEN

The door to the motel room opened and Sam walked in with an armful of upscale Mexican takeout. He arched an eyebrow at the sight of his brother sprawled out on the carpet and straddled by a hot tattooed chick in leather pants.

"Am I interrupting…?"

"She's got a knife on me, dude," Dean said.

"Hey, man," Sam said, setting the food on the table. "Whatever lifts your skirt."

Xochi closed the blade and stood, offering Dean her hand to help him up. He didn't take it, just stood up on his own.

"This is Xochi Cazadora," Dean said to Sam. "She's a hunter."

"Sam Winchester," Sam said, pulling a giant, foil-wrapped package from one of the brightly colored paper bags. "You've obviously met my brother Dean." He offered the package to Dean. Dean shook his head so Sam offered it to Xochi instead. "Burrito?"

Xochi looked back at Dean, the same amusement still there in her eyes. She took the burrito.

"Thanks," she said, pocketing her gloves, unwrapping the foil and taking a large, voracious bite. She frowned down at the burrito's contents. "What is this?"

"It's a chicken fajita burrito," Sam said with a shrug, taking out one for himself. "Don't you like Mexican food?"

"Whatever this is," she said. "It's not Mexican food." She shrugged, took another bite. "But it's much better than raw rattlesnake. Got any hot sauce?"

"Um, hello?" Dean said. "I hate to interrupt your little dinner party, kids, but I've still got a few questions over here."

Xochi walked over to the bags on the table, rummaged around until she found a large container of hot sauce and dumped it all on the burrito. Now that her gloves were off, Dean could see that her hands were heavily scarred. Knuckles crushed flat. Nails unpainted, cut short. A fighter's hands.

"I'm not following you," Xochi said. "You are not following me. Don't you understand? We are both following the Borderwalker."

"Borderwalker?" Dean eyed her suspiciously, trying to get a read on her. Figure out if she was on the level. "You mean you know what this thing is?"

She nodded. "I do. But I've been on the road a long time and I'm hungry. Tell me what you know while I eat, and then I will tell you what I know."

"How do we know we can trust you?" Dean asked.

"You don't," she said.

"Forget it," Dean said. "We don't need your help."

She paused for a moment with the burrito halfway to her lips, shot Dean a curious look, then went ahead and took the bite.

"Suit yourself," she said, chewing. "I will still eat your burrito."

"What do we have to lose, Dean?" Sam asked. "I think we should hear her out."

Dean frowned. Sam's face was unreadable.

"Give us a minute," Dean said. "I need to talk to my brother. Alone."

Xochi shrugged and took her dinner outside.

"We don't know anything about this chick," Dean said as soon as the door was closed. "We don't even know for sure if she's human. I don't trust her."

"Trust has nothing to do with it," Sam said. "I want to hear what she knows about this thing."

"Okay, so we just listen to what she has to say," Dean said. "And then she leaves, right? I don't want her tagging along with us."

"Why not?" Sam asked. "Because you don't want to let a girl into the Monster Club? Or is it because of what happened to Jo Harvelle?"

"What the hell does that have to do with anything?" Dean asked, feeling like he had lost the argument before it had even started.

"Look, from what I saw, this girl's got skills," Sam said.

"She can obviously take care of herself and she knows what we're dealing with here. Why not take advantage of that? We can use her to help us hunt this thing and if she tries to screw us over along the way, well, then I'll handle her."

"Handle her?" Dean frowned. "What do you mean handle her? Give her a stern talking to? Put her over your knee?"

"Is this gonna be another one of your Jiminy Cricket lectures?"

"You mean kill her, don't you?" Dean couldn't believe he was actually having this conversation. "Sam, what if she *is* human?"

Sam shrugged. Dean shook his head, made a disgusted noise.

"Just trying to be practical, huh?" Dean asked.

Sam didn't answer.

Dean had to look away from Sam. From the Sam-shaped thing standing next to him with nothing but calm, cold logic in those empty eyes. What difference did it make anyway? Why not have a whole team of enigmatic strangers whose motivations he didn't completely trust? He had been kidding himself, thinking this job would be just like old times. That version of their lives was dead and buried in a thousand different graves.

"Fine," Dean said. "She's your responsibility. I want you on her day and night, watching her, but if you think something's not right, you come to me. Come to me, you hear me? And I can't believe I'm the one saying this, but I have to say it anyway. The day we start ganking innocent humans is the day we become what we're hunting. Hell, you're the one who taught me that. Remember?"

Dean could see that Sam was seriously thinking about what he was saying, but he had no way of knowing what was really going on inside that head.

"Go on," Dean said with a resigned sigh. "Call her back in."

Dean filled Sam and Xochi in on everything he'd learned from De La Paz. Sam, in turn, laid out the details of the more recent attack, including several grisly photos. The gory details didn't seem to have any affect on Xochi's appetite. She had finished the burrito and was powering her way through the remaining tortilla chips. She would dunk each chip into the salsa and then pour nearly an entire packet of salt onto every single bite. He'd never seen anyone eat so much salt in one meal. It was making him thirsty just watching her. Even though he still didn't completely trust her, it was safe to say that she definitely wasn't a demon.

"Interesting," Xochi said. "But this information gives me more questions than answers."

"Yeah, well speaking of questions," Dean said. "It's quid pro quo time. What's a Borderwalker?"

"Do you have any beer?" Xochi asked.

Dean gestured grudgingly toward the dented mini fridge beside the television.

"Help yourself," he said.

She sauntered across the room and bent over to pull a bottle of Negra Modelo out of the low fridge. Dean tried not to stare. Sam made no such effort.

"A Borderwalker is a creature that used to be human," she said, popping the cap off her bottle and taking a swig. "Transformed by an ancient supernatural affliction that originated with a trick played on a mortal woman by the god Huehuecoyotl. He was smitten by a legendary beauty, so he tricked her into swallowing a lump of white copal that would make her fall in love with him. But the trick backfired and her love was so strong that she did not want him go back to the realm of the gods. She clung to him as he was shifting form to leave the realm of humans and her soul was caught in the portal, trapped in the borderland between the worlds. She became a shadow dweller, neither alive nor dead, lost between dreaming and waking, between beast and human. Like vampirism or your European lycanthropy, this affliction can be passed on to others, but only to women and only in the moments before their death. It's known as the Coyote's Kiss."

Dean walked over to the fridge to grab a beer of his own. He motioned for her to continue.

"Borderwalkers are found only in the deepest desert," she said. "And are generally very shy, rarely making contact with living humans. But they are attracted by dying women and will often make an offer to either guide their soul to the realm of the dead or pass on the legacy of the Coyote's Kiss, allowing them to live on in dream form."

"That's a very nice bedtime story," Dean said. "But you're way off base. Whatever it is that attacked those Border Patrol officers certainly isn't shy. It's murdered at least twenty people that we know of."

"Butchered them," Sam said. "Tore them to pieces. This isn't some mopey romantic ghost we're dealing with. This thing is a bloodthirsty killer."

"Isn't that why we're both here?" Xochi asked.

"I don't follow," Dean said.

"Aren't you here because of the…" She paused, searching for the correct English word. "The wrongness? You are hunters, like me. Our job is to keep the balance, no?"

"Our job is to gank monsters," Dean said.

"Now I don't follow." She looked genuinely puzzled. "You don't dive into the river and slaughter a crocodile in her nest. She is a natural part of life and death in that river. She belongs there. You do not. But if that same crocodile comes into your swimming pool and eats your dog and your baby, she is no longer in her natural place. She has disrupted the balance and must be killed. That's my job. It has been the job of my family for more than 500 years.

"Something is horribly wrong with this Borderwalker. She has become corrupted, her powers both intensified and twisted. I feel sure that understanding what happened on that night fifteen years ago is the key to understanding this tortured creature."

"Okay, but hold on a second," Sam said. "I'm still stuck on this." He handed the photo of the halved SUV to Xochi. "What the hell happened here?"

Xochi took the photo, ran her finger over the image.

"Borderwalkers have the power to transport people and objects between worlds," Xochi said. "In this case, it looks like our Borderwalker is so out of control that she is pulling things out of our world without intention. I believe that is also what happened to Davis Keene's head."

"Lovely," Dean said.

"That kid Anibal," Sam said. "The one who said he saw the border patrol officers turn a woman into a coyote. What do you make of that?"

"He may have seen her mortally wounded by the officers and then witnessed the appearance of the Borderwalker who turned her," Xochi said. "That would explain her vendetta, but it doesn't explain what went wrong in the transition."

"Why wait for fifteen years?" Dean asked. "Why didn't she come after these guys sooner?"

"In the Borderland between the worlds, where the transformation takes place, time passes differently. What seems like a single second can be a decade, or the other way around. There is no exact formula to it. Some take years. Some are instantaneous. Every transformation is different."

"So how *do* we kill it?" Sam asked.

"A normal Borderwalker is a shape-shifter, able to take on aspects of various desert animals such as the coyote, the scorpion or the rattlesnake. But she is weakest in her human form. If we can find a way to connect emotionally with her human soul she will become vulnerable to attack with ordinary weapons."

"That's all you, Dean," Sam said.

"Of course," Xochi said. "That's a normal Borderwalker. A normal Borderwalker cannot tear through a bulletproof vest. A normal Borderwalker would have no reason to even attempt such a thing. This creature that we are dealing with is driven by a kind of all-consuming rage. Her vendetta has transformed her into something unnatural. Something terrible. There is no precedent. I think it would be wise to assume there are no rules."

"What about silver?" Dean asked. "Works against most other shifters."

"Yes," Xochi said. "It does, but not against Borderwalkers. It will not kill her if used as a weapon, but may thwart her attack if worn for protection. Obsidian, perhaps, would be more effective…" She trailed off, seeming lost in reflection for a moment.

"Is there some kind of herb we could use?" Sam suggested. "The Borderwalker equivalent to wolfsbane or garlic? You mentioned something about copal. That's a kind of tree resin, isn't it?"

"Borderwalkers have copal smoke for blood," Xochi said. "And copal is often burned to help lost souls find their way back home on the Day of the Dead. But I don't think it would give us any advantage against her. However, *Cempoalxochitl*… how do you say… marigold? These flowers are very powerful and may offer us some additional protection."

"Marigolds?" Dean raised an eyebrow. "You mean those little orange puffballs in old ladies' window boxes?"

"Marigolds are the most sacred plant of my people," Xochi said with a thundery frown. "I wear them in my hair whenever I go into battle."

"No disrespect to your people," Dean said. "But we're not going to San Francisco here. I ain't wearing any flowers in my hair."

"I'm with Dean on this," Sam said. "I wouldn't even let them put a lei on me if I went to Hawaii."

"No problem," she said, shrugging. "I'm sure your big fat *cojones* will be more than enough to protect you."

"So what's the plan then?" Sam asked.

"We need to talk to the two remaining men," Dean said. "Find out what really happened that night. Maybe warn them, if they'll listen. Then stake them out and wait for our Borderwalker to show up."

"So, what?" Sam said. "We should split up? Each take one guy?"

"No," Xochi said firmly. "We stay together. It's the only way."

"What makes you say that?" Sam asked.

"Listen," she said, throwing a loaded gaze in Dean's direction, then turning and putting her hand in the center of Sam's chest. "I need you."

Sam grinned. "Anytime, baby."

"Not for that," she said. She looked up into Sam's eyes, searching. "I need you because of your... dislocated soul. The motivations of your gods are hidden from me, but I know that you are here for a reason."

"Hold on a minute," Dean said. "What do you know about his soul?"

"Nothing," she said. "Only that it is missing from his body. And that without him, this hunt will ultimately fail. We need to work together to fight this thing. It's the only way."

"Okay, so you need him," Dean said. "But why do we need you?"

Xochi looked him over.

"*¿Hablas Español?*"

"*Mas cerveza por favor,*" Dean said with a sheepish half-smile. "That's pretty much it."

She turned to Sam. "You?"

"I remember some of my high school Spanish," Sam said. "I can get my point across when I need to."

"What if our Borderwalker chooses to move south? You are familiar with the towns on the other side of the border? Nogales? Agua Prieta? Cuidad Juarez?"

Dean looked at Sam. They both shook their heads.

"These are some of the most dangerous places in my country," she said. "I'm sure you've seen the news. The gruesome executions. Torture. Women and children gunned down in the street. There is open war between the drug cartels, but I'm sure they will be happy to stop shooting each other long enough to give directions to a couple of lost *gringos.*"

"Point taken," Dean said. "But what makes you think we won't catch it here on this side of the border?"

"Maybe we will," she said. "Or maybe we won't. You like to gamble, Dean? I do not."

"So we stay together," Dean said. "But how do we know who to visit first?"

"I will go into the desert," Xochi said. "Pray to Huehuecoyotl and ask him to help us find his wayward granddaughter. His answers are not always trustworthy, but his lies often reveal more than the truth."

"I'll work on tracking down current addresses for the two

men," Sam said. "And any other information I can dig up on the recent killings in San Diego."

Dean nodded, pushed his fingers through his hair. He wasn't exactly happy with this uneasy alliance, but it seemed almost like it could work.

"I must go now," Xochi said. "But I will return in the morning."

She walked over to Sam, stood high on her booted toes and pulled his shaggy head down so she could kiss his cheek.

"Thank you for the food," she said.

"*De nada*," Sam said with a wink.

She turned and locked eyes with Dean. She came to him slow and slid her arms around him, curvy little body pressed against his like it had been when she was struggling under him on the scratchy carpet.

"And thank you, Dean," she said, low and close to his ear. "For giving me a chance to prove my intentions."

Dean gripped her by the upper arms and stepped back, out of her embrace.

"Yeah, okay great." he said. "See you tomorrow."

She paused for a moment, looking up into his eyes.

"Tomorrow," she said.

She turned and left. Dean closed the door and locked it. Let out a breath he hadn't realized he was holding.

ELEVEN

"Dude," Sam said. "What's with you?"

"What?"

"That chick's a hammer. I'll bet she could crack walnuts with that ass."

"Yeah, so?"

"So she's obviously into you," Sam said. "You ought to hit that while it's hot."

Dean went for a much-needed drink, bypassing the beer and going straight to the whisky he'd stashed in the bedside drawer beside the King James Bible.

"Come on," he said, breaking the seal and swigging directly from the bottle. "We've got more important things to think about right now."

"You're the one who keeps on saying you don't believe I'm really me," Sam said, hands held out in exaggerated disbelief. "But who the hell are you? My big brother, the unrepentant womanizer, just let an ass like that walk out the door because he's got more important things to think about?"

"Look, if you think she's so hot, why don't you...:"

Sam cut him off before he could finish.

"Why are you still doing this to yourself?"

"Doing what, exactly?"

"Not like it matters to me one way or the other, but you and Lisa have been separated for how long now?"

"You were the one who wanted me to be with her so badly in the first place," Dean said. "Besides, I'm just..."

"Just what?" Sam said. "Just not getting any. That's what. Look, you gave the whole apple pie thing a shot, but it didn't work out. Moping around and acting like there aren't any other women in the world isn't gonna change that. You need to lighten up. Have a little harmless fun. Clear out your pipes, because they're obviously starting to back up and overflow into your brain."

"Yeah, well," Dean took another swig. "If you had a soul, maybe you'd understand."

"You really think she hasn't been with anyone else since you left?"

Dean turned to face his brother, eyes narrow.

"I really think you oughta mind your own damn business," Dean said. He set the bottle down hard on the table, contents sloshing, nearly spilling.

"I'm just saying," Sam said, shrugging. Unruffled as a reptile.

"Well don't," Dean said, hands curling into fists.

He was itching to let Sam have it, but there was no point. He was right, of course. Just trying to be practical. Besides, it wasn't as if the idea hadn't crossed Dean's mind before. More times than he wanted to admit. Even though it made him crazy to think of anyone else touching Lisa, she deserved to find someone who could keep her safe and make her happy. Someone stable and decent and honest. Someone who could be a good role model for Ben. Someone who would never expose them to the kind of ugliness that Dean had brought into their lives. In short, someone who wasn't him.

So why couldn't he let go? Lighten up? Have a little harmless fun?

He grabbed the bottle by the neck and walked out the motel door.

Dean sat behind the wheel of the Impala, staring through the bug-splattered windshield at the motel parking lot. That car had always been more of a home to him than any house or any town anywhere in the country. It was where he went whenever he felt rocky. Disconnected. But sitting there that night, he just couldn't shake the feeling of emotional freefall. Like he'd completely lost sight of what he was supposed to be doing with his life. Sam's question was still echoing inside his head. *Who the hell are you?* Dean couldn't make things work with Lisa, but he couldn't just go back to who he used to be either. All he could do was keep busy, keep moving, and keep all his emotions crushed down and buried deep, like he always did. Numb up and nut up. Lose himself in the hunt. But it was the quiet times like this that got to him. Those long, lonely hours when night became morning, when no matter how much he drank, he just couldn't seem to drown all the doubt and regret. The bottle propped between his legs was half empty. The pessimists' verdict. Half empty, like he was. He took another pull, swiftly working his way toward completely empty. He thought of De La Paz, asking him if he still believed in justice.

When he first came out to the car, he had this absurd hope that Xochi would still be there, silently waiting astride her Hayabusa. He'd gotten into his head that if he saw her, he'd give her what she wanted. In spades. Toss her in the back seat of the Impala and prove to her that he wasn't so hung up on the past he couldn't have a little harmless fun. Prove it to himself. But she wasn't there. So he sat in the car alone, drinking himself maudlin. Still hung up on the past.

He took out his cell phone. Lisa's number remained on the screen from the previous dozen times he'd looked at it but didn't dial it. He stared at it until the little screen went dark to conserve power, then put the phone back in his pocket.

TWELVE

Xochi had parked the Hayabusa beside a dying Joshua tree and hiked off into the desert. She had nothing with her but a thin bedroll, a canteen and a small pouch containing sacred tools and herbs. She had a flashlight, but didn't use it. She didn't need it. Her night vision was sharp as a cat's, but she wasn't following a visible path. She was following ley lines. Veins of psychic energy that flow like blood just beneath the skin of the world. Leading her to a powerful nexus point where her prayer to Huehuecoyotl would be most likely to be heard.

The sky above her was cloudless, a heavy three-quarter moon low on the horizon. She searched the scatter of stars for the *Tianquiztli* cluster out of childhood habit, feeling reassured and centered when she found it. She could hear the frantic, high-pitched yipping of coyotes in the distance.

The harsh, moonlit landscape gave no indication that humans had ever existed and seemed to actively resent her presence. The slithering sand filled in her footprints seconds after she made them.

It took several hours for her to reach the nexus. As she walked, she thought of the two big green-eyed *gringos*. So infuriatingly American in their approach, all cowboy muscle and cocky, self-centered entitlement, yet she could clearly see that their destinies were inextricably intertwined with her own.

The older brother was going to be a problem, but he was a problem that intrigued her. Sure, he was distractingly handsome, a ripe mango, and she couldn't deny a certain raw physical attraction. But there was so much more going on under the surface. He was complicated, a haunted warrior. She knew she couldn't just break into a man like that the way she'd broken into his cheap motel room. She needed to find a way to earn his trust, and cheap seduction was not the way to do it.

As for the younger, soulless brother, she knew from the first second she saw him that he was the key. But why couldn't she see the shape of the lock?

The area around the nexus was no different visually than the hundreds of miles of surrounding desert. A slight indentation in the sand, to the left of a pair of large squarish boulders like dice thrown by bored gods. To the right, a thick stand of spindly creosote, an impossibly long-lived desert dweller that was already ancient back when the great city of *Tenochtitlan* was still young.

She unrolled her striped woolen blanket near the center of the indentation and started gathering kindling for a small fire. Once she'd collected enough, she dug a shallow pit, ringed it with smooth stones and stacked the gathered branches in a loose basket shape with the smallest underneath and the thickest at the top. She tucked a handful of dried leaves under the kindling and lit them with a silver Zippo. She was an old-fashioned girl, but not above modern convenience.

Once she got the fire started, she began to lay out ritual tools on the blanket. Bundles of herbs. A chunk of turquoise. A wooden cup. A pale flint knife with a handle shaped like a coiled snake.

She started with a spiritual cleansing, bathing her body in sage smoke and releasing all worldly thoughts from her mind. She mixed several of the dried herbs in the wooden cup, crushing them with the turquoise and then adding water from her canteen. The resulting brew was bitter and earthy, but she drank it down without hesitation. It left flecks of grit on her lips and tongue.

After throwing a handful of copal into the fire, she took the blade of the knife and held it to her sternum. It felt cold against her skin. Pulling in a slow, centering breath, she drew the razor-sharp stone blade across the tattooed heart on her chest. She clenched her teeth, hissing against the sting. Her blood gathered on the blade and she held it over the fire, letting fat droplets fall sizzling into the flames. A symbolic sacrifice to Huehuecoyotl.

"*Let me be open,*" she said, speaking in her ancient native tongue.

Then she waited.

It started with the coyotes. First one, then three, leggy gray shadows lurking around the perimeter of her vision. Soon more than a dozen, silently watching. Waiting, like she was. She was not afraid.

When Huehuecoyotl came, his form was human, a diminutive old man, as gnarled and brown as dried venison. Naked except for a tattered blanket clutched around his hunched and bony shoulders. But his eyes were young, dancing with wicked humor.

"*Little Xiuhxochitl,*" he said, calling her by her full name.

"*Huehuetque,*" Xochi replied, respectfully addressing him using the term for a wise elder. "*You honor this humble huntress with your presence.*"

"*You are a woman now,*" he said, his face flickering from canine to human and back again in the orange glow of her dying fire. "*A shadow warrior, like your mother. The flower blooms.*"

He held out his knobby brown hand, cupping a lick of fire in his palm. He swirled a fingertip though the captive flame and it began to coil itself into petals. When he handed it to her, it had become a flower, a lush yellow dahlia. After a few heartbeats, the flower became a fat horned lizard, regarding her with a cocked head and suspicious little eyes. When she moved her hand to put the lizard down, it shot angry jets of blood from its eyes, leaping away and leaving her arm streaked with crimson.

Huehuecoyotl laughed, flashing toothless gums and slapping his skinny shank like that was the funniest thing he'd ever seen. Xochi was familiar with his childish pranks and kept her cool, trying to stay focused on the matter at hand.

"I need your advice, Huehuetque," Xochi said.

"What will you give me in return?" he asked. *"A kiss?"*

He was no longer a scrawny old man. In the swift flicker of a shadow, he'd become Dean Winchester. Still nude, his tattered blanket now thrown back off one muscular shoulder. Xochi looked away, focusing her gaze on the heart of the fire.

"A kiss is what started this trouble," Xochi said.

"Trouble is what makes eternity worth enduring," he replied.

"Not this kind of trouble." Xochi raised her head to meet his gaze. *"This isn't a joke. People are dying."*

"Child," he said. *"Your people are always dying. That's what makes you human."*

"But even you must sense the wrongness of these events. It's unnatural. Balance must be restored."

"Must it?"

He was no longer Dean. Now he was a giant black coyote, standing on its hind legs and towering over her with a disturbingly human posture. But he still had Dean's green eyes.

"This world lost all sense of balance hundreds of years ago," he said. *"It was lost when the greedy priests of Tenochtitlan started using their sacrificial rituals for political and personal gain. You and your family are backward artifacts of a lost age. Adhering to principles that mean nothing in this modern world of unchecked chaos and destruction. Your mother knew this. That is why she took her own life."*

"Your lies can't hurt me," Xochi said. *"My mother died in battle. The death of an honored warrior."*

"Your mother gave up. She couldn't face her own obsolescence."

He'd shifted again, this time taking the form of her mother. The intimidating, barely remembered beauty who'd never held Xochi. Never tucked her in at night and soothed her fears. Who'd always been too busy hunting to bother with mundane things like birthdays or skinned knees. Who was gone before Xochi was old enough to hold a knife.

"With respect, Huehuetque," Xochi said, struggling to keep her voice level. She couldn't let him get to her. *"I did not call you here tonight to talk about my family. I want to talk about your family. This Borderwalker is your own spiritual granddaughter. She has become corrupted, lost in hate and fear. Help me find her and take away her pain."*

"You must go home to find her." He was an old man again. *"Go home, huntress. This is not about my family."*

Xochi studied him, trying to squint through the smoke of lies and catch a glimpse of the truth.

"Does she bite with coyote's teeth?" he asked. *"Or is she driven by the wind of beating wings?"*

"I don't understand…?"

"She is just the song. Ask yourself, who is singing?"

Then he was gone.

THIRTEEN

Whoever was banging on the motel door needed to die. It felt like they were banging directly on the inside of Dean's skull.

"Up and at 'em, Sunshine," Sam said, whipping the covers off Dean's aching head. "Your girlfriend is here."

"Tell her I'm indisposed," Dean groaned.

"Tell her yourself," Sam said, throwing the motel door wide open and letting in a vicious blast of sunlight like napalm.

"Aw, man!" Dean said, pulling the covers back over his face.

"Good morning, Sam," Xochi said. "Dean. I brought some presents for you two boys."

"You should give them to me," Sam said. "Dean's been naughty."

"Close the damn door, will ya?" Dean said from under the thin motel bedspread.

Once the evil sun had been banished from the room, Dean peeled open his dry sticky eyes and peered out from under the covers. The first two knuckles on his right hand were scabbed and sore. Did he get into a fight the night before? He certainly felt like he'd gotten his ass kicked.

Dean had a vague recollection of killing the bottle of whisky, then making the brilliant decision to stagger over to the bar across the road from the motel. He remembered trying to pick up a woman who didn't speak English and failing miserably. He remembered kicking a juke box that only played "Amor Prohibido" by Selena over and over no matter what songs he picked. After that, nothing.

When he looked up, he saw Xochi standing by the door, still dressed in the same clothes as the night before. She had a large, padded olive-green rifle bag slung over her shoulder and that same look of arch amusement in her eyes.

Dean sat up gingerly, put his sock-clad feet on the carpet and his aching head in his hands, running his fingers through his hair. He noticed that he was still dressed in last night's clothes too.

"Give me one of those bottles of water," Dean said. "My mouth tastes like demon ass."

"You'd know," Sam replied, tossing Dean the bottle.

Dean cracked open the water and hit it hard, downing more than half in one swallow.

"Well, do you want your presents or don't you?" Xochi asked.

She handed the rifle bag to Sam.

"What the hell do you have in here?" Sam asked, weighing

the bag in his hand, surprised by its weight. "Gold bars?"

"A hundred pounds of aspirin?" Dean asked. "That'd just about do it."

"Open it," she said.

Sam unzipped the bag and removed what looked at first like a baseball bat. But it was wider and flattened out, the wood darker. It took a second for Dean's sluggish brain to process what it really was. There were several wickedly sharp, obsidian blades set into the edges of the bat in matched pairs, eight on each side, like a frozen chainsaw.

"This is *Maquahuitl*," Xochi stated.

"Mack what?" Dean asked.

"*Maquahuitl*," she said again. Dean didn't feel any closer to being able to repeat that word than he had been when she first said it. "You can strike with the flat sides or cut with the sharp. In our case, you will want to cut. Edged weapons will inflict more damage to our Borderwalker than bullets and obsidian will be more effective than silver or steel. It is no guarantee, but it is better than empty hands."

Sam swung the bat appreciatively.

"Nice," he said. "There's one here for you too, Dean."

"And I have another gift," Xochi said. "Outside."

"This one is aspirin, right?"

She shook her head.

"A witness," she said.

She opened the door and walked out into the parking lot. Sam set the strange weapon on the table with a weighty *clunk* and went after her. Dean got himself upright, shoved his feet into his unlaced boots and reluctantly followed them out into the bright morning. The mindlessly beautiful day seemed like a personal affront to his current condition.

There was another rider sitting on the back of Xochi's Hayabusa. Helmet on, hands behind his back. It wasn't until Dean got closer that he realized that the man's hands were handcuffed to a bolt set into the frame of the bike.

Xochi pulled the helmet off his head, revealing a chinless, unshaven face and large, bulging eyes. One of them was blackened, swollen shut. He was gagged with a red bandana.

"I want you to meet my friend Ojon," she said, pulling out a ring of keys and unlocking the cuffs. "Watch him. He's a runner."

Sam stepped up and took Ojon by the wiry arm, helping him down off the bike.

"Ojon was there the night of the first murders," she said. "He's seen our Borderwalker in action and he's anxious to tell us all about it."

Ojon was jittery, twitching like he was about to crawl out of his skin. His shirt was soaked with foul-smelling amphetamine sweat. His one good eye pinballed around the parking lot like he was trying to watch every angle at once. Like he was sure the Borderwalker was about to show up and eat his face.

Dean stepped up and took Ojon's other arm and he and Sam tossed their witness into the motel room like bouncers giving him the bum's rush in reverse. Xochi followed close behind, closing and locking the motel room door.

Ojon got up off his knees, untied the gag and pulled it out of his mouth. The second Xochi stepped away from the door he sprinted across the room and grabbed the door knob, frantically yanking and twisting. The lock was about an inch up from the knob and if he wasn't so fixated on the doorknob, he could have just unlocked it and run.

Dean traded disbelieving looks with Sam and Xochi.

"Okay, okay," Dean finally said, stepping up and putting his hand over Ojon's. "Take it easy there, genius. We're not gonna hurt you."

"Keep her away from me," he said, turning and flattening himself out against the door. His voice was high and reedy, his accent thick.

"I'll try," Dean said, leaning in close and dropping his voice. "But, between you and me... Well I'm sure you've seen *Q*."

He looked at Dean like he'd just stepped off a flying saucer. Sam swallowed a snorting half-laugh.

"Come on, Ojon," Dean said. "Relax. Have a seat. We just want to ask you a few questions."

Ojon gave Dean a wary look, then scuttled over and sat on the corner of Sam's unused bed, as far away from Xochi as he could be while still remaining in the same room.

"I'd offer you a drink," Dean said. "But I don't think there are any alcoholic beverages left in this county after last night."

"I don't know nothing," he said, hands battling in his lap like he was a kid making invisible action figures fight.

"Just tell us what you saw that night," Xochi said.

"Nothing," he said again.

Xochi spoke to him in Spanish, her tone both intimate and menacing.

"A woman," he said. "I saw a woman."

"What did she look like?" Sam asked.

"Pretty at first." He looked up at Sam, then away. "Then…" He shrugged. "Not so pretty."

"Look, we're not paying by the hour here," Dean said. "Get on with it."

"You pay?" Ojon looked suddenly hopeful.

Xochi hissed in Spanish and took a step closer to him, gloved hand raised.

"Okay, okay!" Ojon threw both hands up, shoulders hunched up to his ears. "I see a woman. She is pretty, with light skin and curly black hair. This CBP guy, he look to her and he know her. He *know* her. Then she change. She change to a monster. Like… like…"

He turned to Xochi and said something in Spanish.

"What?" Dean asked.

"Something about scorpions?" Sam said.

Xochi nodded. "He says the woman became a hole full of scorpion tails."

"Charming," Dean said. "Can't wait to meet her."

"Tell us what happened to the SUV," Sam said.

"I no look. I run," Ojon said. His gaze stayed locked on his hands.

"Is there anything else you can tell us about her?" Dean asked. "Anything at all?"

"She… she had a tattoo."

"A tattoo?"

"Yes, a tattoo. On her neck. *Una mariposa.*"

"A butterfly?" Sam said, looking to Xochi for confirmation.

She nodded.

"Right," Dean said. "Sam, make sure you write that down." He turned to Xochi. "Look, he's not telling us anything we don't already know. I don't think we're gonna get anything useful out of this speed freak."

"One more thing," Xochi said. "I want his blood. For divination."

That sent him flying over to the door again. This time he realized he could unlock it and was halfway out before Sam grabbed him around the waist and dragged him back in. He was flailing and kicking, shrieking like a howler monkey. Dean kicked the door closed and picked up the soggy gag, stuffing it back into Ojon's mouth.

Despite his flyweight physique, it took all of both Sam and Dean's combined muscle to hold Ojon down. His skin was moist and clammy and he stank, like bad teeth and burnt plastic. Xochi pulled out a stone knife with a handle shaped like a snake and pressed the blade to his dirty neck.

"You're not gonna kill him, are you?" Dean asked out of the corner of his mouth.

"As much as I might like to," Xochi said. "No. I only need a small amount of his blood."

"She's right," Sam said. "If he was that close to our creature when she opened the doorway between the worlds, some residual bad mojo is probably still clinging to him. A divination using his tainted blood could point to where she's headed."

"Tainted blood?" Dean said. "This guy's blood is so tainted we could sell it to truckers to help them stay awake."

Xochi's gloved hands were steady as surgeon's as she nicked Ojon's throat with the knife, collecting his blood on the flat edge of the blade. She then picked up the cap from Dean's empty water bottle and let the blood run into it from the tip of the blade.

"Let him go," Xochi said. "We have no more use for him."

Sam and Dean eased up on Ojon. He eyed them both like it was some kind of trick.

"You heard her, slick," Dean said. "You're free to go."

Ojon didn't bother to remove the gag. He just bolted for the door, threw it open and ran out into the parking lot, where he tripped over his own big feet and ate asphalt about three feet away from Xochi's bike.

Dean closed the door, shaking his head.

"Write the names of the two men," Xochi said to Sam.

Sam tore a page from his notebook and did as she requested, setting the sheet of paper on the carpet at her feet. She knelt with the cap in one hand and the knife in the other. She spoke some words that Dean was pretty sure weren't Spanish and the blood inside the cap began to swirl like a miniature maelstrom. When she up-ended the cap onto the center of the page, the blood ran toward one of the names as if the paper were slanted in that direction. Crimson tendrils flowed around the name, obliterating it.

BREWER

"There's your answer," Xochi said.

"Okay," Sam said. "Brewer's in Yuma. We'd better hit the road."

Xochi stood, sheathing the knife.

"Before we leave," Xochi said. "May I wash myself?"

"Uh yeah," Dean said. "No problem. Be my guest."

"You'd better wash yourself too," Sam said to Dean. "I'm not gonna sit in a car for four hours with a guy who smells like a dirty bar rag."

"Ladies first," Dean said, gesturing toward the closed bathroom door.

"Thank you," she said. She paused with her hand on the doorknob. "But Dean, I have one question. What is Q?"

"Look," Dean said, suppressing a snicker. "You can't be in the Monster Club if you haven't seen *Q, The Winged Serpent.*"

"It's a movie," Sam said. "And you're probably better off not having seen it."

"Winged serpent?" She frowned. "They made a movie about *Quetzalcoatl?*"

"They made a movie about a cheesy rubber puppet flying around New York City and eating people," Sam told her.

"Aw, come on," Dean said. "I love that movie."

"Dude," Sam said. "We watched that movie when I was, like, five years old, and even back then I wasn't buying that monster for a minute."

"You help me win this fight," Xochi said with a wink. "I'll introduce you to the real thing. Then can I be in the Monster Club?"

"If we win this," Sam said. "You're in. Lifetime membership."

Xochi smiled and disappeared into the bathroom.

FOURTEEN

The three of them stood outside a greasy spoon diner. It was long and narrow, a fifties aluminum building that had been given an ugly brown-and-orange makeover sometime in the mid seventies. There was a Denny's on the other side of the highway, and so the little diner was nearly empty. The faded and peeling sign above the door read "ROADRUNNER GRILL" and featured a slightly altered knock-off of the famous cartoon character who was always making a fool out of the coyote. Dean found that strangely appropriate.

It was only 9 a.m. but rapidly becoming unbearably hot. Xochi had traded her black wifebeater tank top for a white one, making her lack of a bra even more evident. Her long hair was loose and fragrant, still damp from the shower. She wore the same beat-up, Mad Max leather pants. And her gun-belt.

"You know, I'm as paranoid as the next hunter," Dean said, gesturing at the pistols. "But are you sure it's a good idea to wear those to breakfast? I really don't think anybody's gonna try to shoot you in a diner."

"I have a carry permit," Xochi said. "Your country is very gun-friendly."

"But you aren't even a U.S. citizen," Sam said. "Are you?"

"No," Xochi said. "In fact, this is my first time visiting the United States. But I have a U.S. driver's license. And a birth certificate that says I was born in Los Angeles. A lot of people owe me favors."

"Come on, kids," Sam said, pushing the diner door open and motioning for Xochi to enter.

The single waitress, a tiny, birdlike woman in her mid-fifties with a big, bright red, utterly unironic eighties poodle perm, motioned for them to seat themselves. She eyed Xochi's guns but was smart enough not to say anything. Sam and Dean took opposite sides of the orange Naugahyde booth closest to the door. Xochi chose to sit beside Sam. Dean had no idea why that bothered him so much, and tried to concentrate on the menu instead. A big greasy breakfast was just the ticket to get on top of his lingering hangover.

"So how was your powwow with the coyote guy last night?" Sam asked Xochi. "Anything useful?"

"Huehuecoyotl is a trickster," Xochi said, looking down at the menu. "It is hard to see through his lies. He told me I had to go back to Mexico City to find the Borderwalker, but the divination proves that she is going after Brewer in Yuma next." She closed the menu and slid it over to the edge of the table. "He did say one thing that I think may be significant. He seemed to be hinting that a larger force is behind the actions of the Borderwalker. If that is the case, we may have a much more difficult fight on our hands."

The waitress came over to fill their coffee cups and take their orders. Xochi asked for a bacon cheeseburger with extra bacon.

"And chili cheese fries," she looked to Sam. "We can share, okay?"

"Chili cheese fries, for breakfast?" Sam shook his head. "Dean, you may have finally met your perfect woman."

"Chili cheese fries sound fantastic," Dean said. "Just what the doctor ordered. And I'll have a bacon cheeseburger too."

"You can't fight the forces of darkness with a stomach full of salad," Xochi said.

"Amen, sister," Dean said, raising his coffee cup.

Sam rolled his eyes. "You can't fight anything if you're dead from a heart attack."

"You really think people like us live long enough to die from a heart attack?" Xochi asked.

There was a beat of awkward silence at the table.

"Okay, and what can I get you, honey," the waitress asked Sam, with a desperately forced smile.

Xochi followed the Impala on her bike. Dean watched her in the rearview, wondering what the hell he'd been thinking, agreeing to let her tag along. Wondering what it would be like with her.

"Turn here," Sam said. "Here!"

Dean swung the Impala into a squealing, last-minute swerve to hit the turnoff Sam had indicated. Xochi followed smoothly behind them.

Gilberto Brewer was a vet, a marine with a couple tours in the Middle East before he came home and joined the CBP, and so Sam had been able to pull all kinds of info about him through Veteran Services. Never married. No living family. History of drug addiction and homelessness over the past fifteen years, on and off a county-run methadone program. Mostly off. Currently living in a crap apartment on the outskirts of Yuma.

It took them a few trips around the block to find the place, and then only by inferring the address based on the numbers on the adjacent buildings. It was as if people who lived there didn't want to be found. Once Dean got a good look at the place, he decided he couldn't blame them.

It was a dump, cheaply built in the eighties and already falling apart. Scabby stucco. Barred windows. There were only six units, all in a row like a cheap motel. Letters instead of numbers. Brewer was in the last one. End of the line, apartment F. That was about right.

Xochi pulled into the parking lot behind them. She removed her helmet and started twining her hair up into a big figure eight on the top of her head, fastening it with long pins and marigolds just like she said she would. The resulting crown of flowers looked weirdly incongruous with the rest of her scrappy un-feminine outfit.

"Here," she said, pulling handfuls of thick silver chains out of her backpack. "Put these on. If you won't wear marigolds, at least these may give you some protection around your face and neck."

Dean slipped the tangled chains over his head.

"I feel like the second-place Mr. T," he said.

"Just tuck 'em under your shirt," Sam said, putting on his own chains and slipping them under his collar.

"Bring the weapons I gave you," Xochi said. "Be ready."

"I don't know," Sam said. "I think this guy's gonna freak out if we walk in there holding spiked baseball bats."

"Don't worry about that," she said.

"What about you?" Dean asked Xochi. "What are you planning to use to fight the Borderwalker? Harsh language?"

"Exactly," she said, turning away and heading for the door to Brewer's apartment.

"Well isn't she a take-charge kinda girl?" Dean muttered, annoyed by how easily they'd both fallen into following her lead.

"She can take charge of me any day," Sam replied, hefting the rifle bag and slinging it over one shoulder.

When the two of them got to the door, Xochi was already banging on it with her gloved fist.

"So," Dean said. "Is there a plan... or..."

The door opened a crack, revealing a chain lock and a slice of pale, unshaven face. A single suspicious bloodshot eye looked them over.

"What do you want?"

Xochi kicked the door open, breaking the chain off its track.

Dean and Sam exchanged glances, then shrugged and followed her into the apartment.

It was dim and cavelike inside, with a smell like old socks and moldy carpet. It was pretty much all one claustrophobic room with a minimal kitchen off one side and bathroom off the other. The walls were a dingy, unpleasant peach, like the skin of a discarded doll. The furniture was a sorry cluster of mismatched thrift store refugees. No television. No computer. No stereo. No books. No visible source of entertainment of any kind, unless you counted the dope paraphernalia on the scarred coffee table.

Brewer was Latino, mid-forties, and balding, with pale, jaundiced skin and the sad, deflated build of a former body-builder gone to seed. He was dressed in a thin T-shirt that hadn't been white in years and cheap, shiny track pants. There was an ugly purple abscess in the crook of his left arm.

In moments, Xochi had Brewer backed up against the wall, a fistful of his stained T-shirt in one hand and a pistol in the other. She jammed the business end of the gun up under Brewer's chin and whispered to him in Spanish.

Dean stepped up beside her and put his hand on her shoulder, flashing Brewer a friendly reassuring smile.

"You'll have to forgive my partner, Mr. Brewer," Dean said, badging him with an FBI ID. "She's very… enthusiastic."

Xochi backed off with the gun and let go of Brewer's shirt, but stayed up in his face, letting him know that she might change her mind at any moment. Playing unhinged bad-cop counterpoint to Dean's calm, trustworthy good cop like they'd been doing it their whole lives, Sam stood like a silent wall behind them, arms crossed and using his size to intimidate and block access to the door. Maybe not exactly the way Dean would have played it, but it looked like they had this.

"I'm Special Agent Scott. My partner's Young…" Chin tip to Sam. "And Quintanilla." To Xochi. "We need to talk to you."

Brewer's eyes flicked to the syringe on the table, then back to Dean.

"Not about that," Dean said. "About an incident that occurred on the night of April 18th 1995."

"I don't know what you're talking about," the man croaked. But Brewer's expression told a different story. It said that he knew *exactly* what they were talking about.

"Look, Brewer," Dean said. "We can do this the hard way, if you prefer."

"Mr. Brewer," Xochi interrupted. "Excuse me, Mr. Brewer."

Dean shot her a questioning glance but she ignored him.

"What?" Brewer wiped his dry lips with a nervous, shaking hand.

"Do you have someone else living here with you?" Xochi asked.

Brewer frowned, gave a terse shake of his head.

Xochi stepped back, gestured with her gun.

"Then who is that?"

Dean followed her gaze through the doorway to the grungy bathroom. There was someone sitting on the edge of the bathtub, facing away from them. Silent, unmoving. Someone with curly black hair.

FIFTEEN

For a moment, nothing happened. The four of them stood frozen, just watching and waiting. Xochi felt the familiar adrenaline rush coursing through her limbs as she let her breath out slow and relaxed her muscles, preparing her body for action. Then Dean leaned close and spoke low out of the corner of his mouth.

"That her?" Dean asked.

"I think so, yes," Xochi replied.

Sam reached into the unzipped rifle bag and pulled out one of the obsidian-studded *maquahuitl*, moving slow and never taking his eyes off the woman in the bathroom.

Then the woman's head whipped around and she screamed, face splitting open into a bloody, gaping hole ringed with canine teeth. Blowtorch rage blasted Xochi with a power that was nearly physical in its intensity, but she stepped forward rather than back, shoving Brewer behind her and raising her right hand.

The Borderwalker stood. Sam tossed the *maquahuitl* to Dean and then pulled the other from the rifle bag. The brothers flanked her, Dean on her right and Sam on her left. Brewer cowered behind them.

When Xochi spoke the first word of the spell that would bind the Borderwalker and drive her back, the creature abruptly fell forward onto her belly. When she hit the bathroom tile, her body seemed to shatter into a hundred black fragments. Xochi was horrified when she realized the fragments were alive. Hoards of black tarantulas were swarming around her boots, heading for Brewer.

The boys were swearing and stomping their feet. Brewer was crouched up against the wall, arms thrown defensively across his face. Xochi spun and held her ground, continued reciting the spell.

The army of hairy arachnid bodies puddled like tar and then in a stutter-flash, reformed into a kind of jittery, roadkill marionette, dripping with maggots. As quickly as her brain could register this new shape, the creature shifted again, now more coyote-like but still possessing aspects of a tarantula. Shiny black mandibles instead of teeth and far too many bony legs. The only thing that was still human was that wild black hair.

Xochi could feel the telekinetic power building in her extended hand. She thrust that hand forward and twisted. The Borderwalker reacted as if Xochi had grabbed a fistful of her curly hair, head cranked back and shrieking like an animal in a trap.

"Dean!" Xochi cried, sweeping her hand to her right and bringing the snarling Borderwalker with it as if attached by an invisible leash.

Dean was right there with the *maquahuitl*, swinging like Mickey Mantle. That weapon could cut off a horse's head in one stroke but when it hit the Borderwalker it was like striking water. Her substance simply flowed around the blades.

"Again!" Xochi said.

Dean let the Borderwalker have it a second and third time. Aromatic smoke started to leak from gashes in the creature's body and the liquid flow of her shape became sluggish, not so quick to reform. She lashed out at Dean, black vulture claws striking sparks against the silver chains around his neck. Dean faded back, then spun and brought the *maquahuitl* down sharply, neatly severing one of her skeletal hands. The hand fell to the carpet, became smoke and was gone. Sam moved in smoothly behind Xochi, placing himself between the Borderwalker and Brewer with his own *maquahuitl* raised and ready. They were winning.

Then the door burst open on its busted hinges and the last person Xochi expected to see walked into the room. Someone she hadn't seen in more than ten years. Her older sister Teo.

Teo looked good, pin-up perfect as always. She was poured into high-waisted black-and-gold matador pants and a matching halter top with a plunging neckline. Teo was the one who got the boobs in the family and had always loved to lord her overflowing cleavage over her B-cup sister. She was six inches taller than Xochi in her pointy gold cockroach-killer heels. Her hair was piled high in a crown of flawless rockabilly curls and yellow marigolds.

But none of these details mattered, because the only thing Xochi could see when she looked at her sister was the leaf-shaped obsidian knife tucked into the waistband of her pants. It was very simple, rough-hewn and primitive. The handle and the blade were all one piece of glossy black stone, the only distinction being that the handle was smooth and the blade sharp. This was *Itztlitlantl*, a knife that had been in Xochi's family for hundreds of years, a powerful and deadly weapon that could only be wielded by a woman of Xochi's bloodline. A knife, that by right should be wielded by Xochi.

In that moment of anger, conflicted emotion and distracted attention, Xochi's telekinetic hold on the Borderwalker faltered. Instead of going after Dean, the Borderwalker tore loose and threw herself at Brewer. Sam was there to block her, but she shifted form again, flickering like fire flowing around Sam and then suddenly right on top of Brewer, ripping into him with furious claws and teeth. Sam slammed his *maquahuitl* into the back of the Borderwalker's head while Dean gripped the thing by the wiry pelt on her hunched back and pulled her off Brewer.

"*Well, what are you waiting for, little sister?*" Teo asked, speaking in their ancient native tongue. "*Kill her.*" She drew *Itztlitlantl* and shifted it skillfully from her left to her right hand. "*Oh, that's right. You can't.*"

"What do you want, Teo?" Xochi asked in English. "Can't you see we're busy here? Unless you've come to help…?"

Teo flicked the fingers of her left hand like she was brushing away lint. The Borderwalker reacted as if hit by a truck, flying backwards and slamming into the far wall. Xochi was stunned by this casual display of power. Teo had always been strong, but nothing like this. Sam and Dean both turned toward the newcomer, weapons held high, eyes narrow and suspicious.

"What the hell's going on here, Xochi?" Dean asked.

There was no way to explain everything with the Borderwalker struggling back to her feet. No time. But even if there were time, Xochi had no idea where to begin.

Teo stepped up to the cowering Borderwalker and prodded the creature's scrawny, trembling shank with the pointed toe of her shoe. She held *Itztlitlantl* in her hand but didn't strike. Almost like she was teasing the thing. Teasing Xochi.

Xochi was so angry, she felt ready to spit razor blades. That bitch had a lot of nerve to show up here, flaunting *Itztlitlantl* in Xochi's face. Like she had every right to wield it. Like she had never betrayed the family. Like Atlix was still alive and safe.

"*You have no right,*" Xochi cried, reverting to their native tongue. "*No right.*"

It was a bad idea, but Xochi couldn't help herself. She lunged forward, grabbed Teo's wrist and twisted, trying to force her sister to drop *Itztlitlantli*. Teo gave Xochi a sharp elbow to the face, knocking her back, bleeding from a split lip. Dean was between them and on Teo before Xochi could shake the stars from her eyes. The two of them went down, grappling, to the carpet.

Instead of attacking again, the wounded Borderwalker let out a miserable, desolate howl, clawing at the wall behind her. That wall suddenly opened into a yawning gateway and the Borderwalker tumbled backwards, pulling a few crumpled beer cans and a stray sneaker with her as she fell.

And just like that, she was gone. The gate snapped shut and all that was left was a the heavy, resinous scent of copal smoke.

Teo kicked free of Dean's grip and leapt, cat-like to her feet.

"*See what you've done?*" Teo said. Then switching to English she added: "Do yourself a favor and stay out of my way. You and these… beefcakes."

She spun on her heel and walked out the door.

Sam looked over at Dean, eyebrow arched.

"Beefcakes?"

Xochi ran to Brewer. He was bleeding from a hundred slashes, life swiftly draining out onto the filthy carpet. She knew what she had to do.

"Xochi," Dean said, clenching his right hand like it pained him. "Who the hell was that?"

"There's no time," Xochi said. "I'm going to have to ask you to trust me."

Xochi gathered Brewer up in her arms, ignoring the blood that soaked into her white shirt. She put one hand behind his neck and the other on his forehead, palm centered between his eyes. Unfortunately for Brewer, there was no time for seduction or easing her way in gently. She spoke the ancient words that would allow them to link minds and then unceremoniously kicked open the door to his memories just like she'd kicked open the door to his apartment.

She clawed her way through scattered flashes. Images from a lonely, alienated childhood. An awkward sexual encounter with an older girl who chewed gum the whole time. The smell of cordite, of burning bodies and fresh blood on hot Iraqi sand. That first luscious rush of heroin, like the world's coziest blanket wrapped around a wounded soul. She could feel the structures swiftly crumbling inside his mind, but luckily the memory of that night fifteen years ago was just under the surface, as vital and malignant as the minute it was formed.

Men running through the moonlit Arizona desert. Brewer is one of them. They are chasing a woman through the tangled brush. A woman with curly black hair. She is carrying a dirty bundle in her arms. They lose her, spot her and lose her again. Now they've got her trapped in a cul-de-sac of steep, jagged rock. She turns to face them, hands up, defensive, begging them not to hurt her. The bundle is gone.

That was where the memory went strange. While every other one of Brewer's memories, no matter how violent or ugly, seemed centered and intimate, this memory seemed to hit a bizarre kind of snag and all his senses were suddenly disconnected. He still had his vision but even that was strangely distant and colorless, like watching a black-and-white television with bad reception. He couldn't hear the woman screaming and begging as he punched and kicked her again and again. He couldn't feel her struggling body against his as he shoved her jeans down around her knees.

It was as if he was watching something happening through the windshield of a car driven by someone else. Feeling his memories, Xochi was glad for that anomaly, glad she did not have to share the sense memory of what it feels like to rape a dying woman.

Brewer is finished with the woman, and is standing back, watching Keene and Himes work her over. Porcayo has his back to the action, head in his hands and shaking. Brewer wants to turn away but can't. He is sure that someone is watching him, another woman standing just out of range of his vision, but he can't turn his head. Then Keene and Himes stand up, backing away from the dying woman and all of sudden, Brewer can move again. He can feel the gritty wind on his face. He can hear the woman's wet, labored breathing. Everything is normal again, the way it should be, except for what they have just done. He looks at his fellow officers and they look at him. No one says a word. They just walk away. Like it never happened.

Xochi found herself evicted from Brewer's mind just as suddenly and violently as she'd entered. She felt dizzy and disoriented from the abrupt transition. Brewer was dead in her arms.

"Let's get the hell out of here," Sam said. "Before the cops show up."

Xochi let Brewer's body drop to the sticky carpet and stood. She staggered a little and Dean was right there at her elbow to steady her. She leaned into him for a moment, glad he and Sam were there. She had no idea what would have happened if she'd had to face Teo alone.

"Right," Dean said. "Bacon cheeseburgers are on me. But in return, I want some damn answers."

She knew it was unfair to ask the big *gringos* to trust her when she wouldn't confide in them herself. But her feelings about Teo were so complicated, so contradictory. She hadn't talked to anyone about her sister in years.

She thought of what Huehuecoyotl had said, that she needed to go home to find the Borderwalker, suddenly understanding with the pure clarity of hindsight. He didn't mean that the Borderwalker was in her home town. He meant that she needed to look at her own family to figure out what was really happening.

"Okay," she said to Dean. "No secrets. It's the only way we can beat this thing."

SIXTEEN

"Start with the chick with the big knife and the bigger attitude," Dean said before biting into his second bacon cheeseburger of the day.

The three of them sat together in a different diner that may as well have been the Roadrunner Grill, or pretty much any diner Dean had ever been in. Xochi had taken a beat-up leather jacket from Brewer to cover the blood on her tank top, the over-sized man's jacket incongruous on her feminine frame. Dean couldn't help but notice that she had decided to sit next to him this time.

"That woman is my sister Teo," Xochi said.

"Well, what was she doing at Brewer's apartment?" Sam asked. "She a hunter too?"

"She used to be." Xochi frowned. "Still is in a way. I don't know."

"Come on, Xochi," Dean said. "You got to let us in. We can't fight this thing if we don't know the whole story."

"I'm sorry," she said. "You're right." She poked at her fries, but didn't eat. "Teo is my mother's oldest daughter, and so naturally she was to become the head of our family when our mother died. She was more of a mother to me growing up than our mother ever was. We kids were moved around to various aunts and cousins, always on the move, traveling with hunters, but we always stuck together.

"What about your dad?" Dean asked.

Xochi frowned.

"Never met him," she said with a shrug.

There was a beat of awkward silence at the table. Xochi pushed the salt shaker back and forth between her hands for a minute then continued.

"Teo is the best hunter I've ever known," she said. "Taught me everything. Spells. Weapons. Hand-to-hand combat. But she likes hunting too much. Do you understand? She hunts for sport. Torturing her prey, like a cat playing with a mouse. It's not about good and evil, it's just a game to her. Our job is to maintain balance, not to revel in bloodsport."

Dean thought of Gordon Walker, the hunter with the vendetta and the hard-on for killing vamps. Of Dean's own hard-earned lessons on when to kill and when to let live. But even Gordon, as far off the deep end as he may have been and even after he was turned, still believed he was doing the right thing. Black and white, that was how he saw it. Even he didn't hunt purely for sport. For the thrill of watching something suffer and die. Just the idea of it made Dean's skin crawl, like a dry drunk listing to stories about someone else's bender. Because, after all the time he had spent torturing souls in Hell, he knew exactly what he was capable of. Because he knew how easy it would be for him to go down that same road. Because he knew how much fun it would be.

He took a big slug of ice water, wishing it was whisky.

"There was…" Xochi began, then paused and shoved her plate aside, expression hard and distant. "A death. Our little brother Atlix."

Dean felt like he ought to say something to comfort her from the obvious pain she was feeling, but he couldn't find the right words. He just looked down at the shallow cut on his hand, feeling awkward and useless.

"The male children in our family do not hunt," Xochi continued. "Atlix was nineteen, a student at UNAM. The first and only member of our family to attend college. Such a smart kid, loved computers. He wanted to be a video game designer. We always joked that he was going to make millions killing make-believe monsters while the rest of us lived in poverty fighting the real thing.

"That never happened. He was kidnapped and murdered. It was… retribution. The children of *Xolotl*, monstrous dog-headed creatures native to Southern Mexico, they came for him in the night. They wanted revenge for one of their own that had been tortured by Teo." She curled her scarred hands into fists. "I was away on a hunt at the time. I rushed home as fast as I could, but I was too late. I couldn't save him.

"Because of Teo's irresponsible actions and indiscriminate killing, the elders made the decision to initiate me as the head of our family instead of her. But before the ceremony could be performed, Teo broke into the family temple and stole the sacred knife *Itztlitlantl*. Even if our brother were still alive, this act of sacrilege can never be forgiven."

Dean saw that whatever emotion or vulnerability she had let slip while talking about her murdered brother had been swiftly buried, hidden under the quick-dry cement of righteous anger.

"Right, okay," Sam said. "So what's Teo doing here in Yuma?"

"Honestly, I don't know," Xochi said. "Maybe she is after our Borderwalker because she wants the challenge of hunting difficult and unique prey. Maybe she wants to beat me, to take my victory for herself and show that she is still the better hunter."

"And what the hell did you do to Brewer after she left?" Dean asked.

She told them. Dean suddenly didn't feel so hungry anymore.

"So you think this weird disconnect you felt in Brewer's memory was some kind of psychological block?" Sam asked.

"Maybe," Xochi replied. "Or maybe possession."

"Possession?" Dean put his burger down. "Like demons?"

"No," Xochi said. "Much more subtle than that. I'm beginning to think Huehuecoyotl wasn't lying. I think there may be a larger force at work here. Something big."

"So what's the next step?" Sam asked, efficiently devouring the remains of his protein salad.

"The Borderwalker was injured in our fight," Xochi said. "It may take her several days to recover her strength.

Meanwhile we should go to the last man, Porcayo. Follow him. Learn everything we can about him and see if we can find anymore clues that will let us know who is behind this."

"Where's he at again?" Dean asked.

"Fullerton, California," Sam replied.

"Okay," Dean said, holding up a hand for the check. "Sounds like a plan."

"One more thing," she said, turning back to Dean and smirking, shooting him a mock dirty look. "Back when you were pretending we were FBI agents, did you name me after *Selena*?"

"I was on the spot," he said. "It was the first thing that popped into my head."

"Hey," Sam said. "It's better than Crockett and Tubbs."

"*Pendejo!*" She punched Dean in the arm. "I hate that whiny bitch. Next time you let me think of names."

SEVENTEEN

Dean was feeling a little light-headed that night when they pulled into a kitschy motel with a neon sign that read "THE PRICKLY PAIR." Beneath it was a large painting of a busty pin-up cowgirl in a checked bikini hugging a huge, blatantly phallic cactus. Dean was looking forward to the day when they stayed in a motel that didn't feature any cacti in its décor.

Xochi pulled her bike in behind the Impala and parked it under the sign.

"Okay," Sam said, heading toward the tiny office. "Two rooms, right?"

Xochi pulled off her helmet and shook her head.

"I'm fine," she said. "I have a blanket."

"What?" Dean asked. "You're just gonna sleep outside? On the ground? Screw that. We're getting you a room."

"Unless you want to share a bed with my brother?" Sam put in with a grin.

"Sam," Dean said. "Knock it off."

"You can use my bed," Sam said.

"With or without you in it?" Xochi asked eyebrow arched.

"Your choice," Sam said. "But if you want me in it, it won't be for sleeping. I don't sleep."

"I prefer my own room," she said with another one of her patented smirks. "Thank you."

"Don't thank me," Sam said. "Thank…" He pulled out his wallet and thumbed out a stolen credit card, reading off the printed name. "Duane Swierczynski."

Sam went into the office. Dean leaned against the Impala, still feeling fatigued and slightly off balance. That fight had really taken a lot out of him, and he figured he was still suffering residual effects from the night before. The cut from Teo's stone knife on his right hand throbbed as he opened and closed his cold fingers, massaging his wrist with his other hand. It felt inexplicably strange, like touching someone else.

"Dean," Xochi said. "Are you okay?"

"Fine," he said, clenching his right hand into a tight fist. "Just tired, I guess."

Sam returned with two keys attached to large plastic cacti emblazoned with room numbers 202 and 203.

"Upstairs," Sam said. He handed one of the cactus keyrings to Xochi. "You take 03, we'll take 02."

Sam and Xochi went ahead, while Dean followed close behind. As he watched Xochi walk up the stairs in those tight leather pants with her gun-belt straps cinched just below the generous curve of her ass, he started to sweat, feeling so light-headed he thought he might not make it to the top. Xochi certainly did have a spectacular ass, but no ass in the world was that good. What the hell was the matter with him?

He made it to the top and paused, gripping the metal railing. The weak, dizzy feeling passed as quickly as it had come and he shook it off, heading down the breezeway to their rooms.

"Goodnight, boys," Xochi said, keying open her room. "Tomorrow, Fullerton."

"Right," Sam said, opening their door. He held it open. "Dean, you coming?"

"In a minute," Dean said, looking out over the dusty parking lot.

Sam shot Dean a look.

"I just need a minute, okay?" Dean said. "I'll be right in."

"Okay," Sam said. He closed the door.

Dean leaned against the railing. The rough, peeling paint flaked off under his touch. He looked at the closed door to Xochi's room. Thought about knocking, but didn't.

She really was an amazing hunter, one of the best he'd ever seen. So graceful, so intuitive, utterly unflappable under pressure. They worked together like a well-oiled machine. Like tango dancers. Like they'd been doing it for years. She was everything he could ever want in a hunting partner and then some, and it was getting harder and harder to ignore the chemistry between them. Which was really the last thing in the world he needed. It didn't help that every time he found himself thinking about what it would be like with

Xochi, he would think of Lisa, see her standing alone on her porch, shrinking down to nothing in the Impala's rearview mirror. Of the stony finality in her voice when she'd told him to stay away from her and Ben. He thought of what Sam had said. Surely, she'd moved on with her life, right? Why shouldn't she? Why shouldn't *he*?

When he realized that he was just doing mental gymnastics to excuse sleeping with Xochi, he felt like a heel. The year he'd had with Lisa and Ben was the only time in his life when he'd ever been genuinely happy. And here he was trying to rationalize that away so he could spend a guilt-free night banging a chick with a nice ass.

Clearly, a drink was the answer. Hair of the dog that bit him. That was becoming the answer to way too many questions in his life, but he was too worn down to care.

He reached for the doorknob for room 202 and the dizziness suckerpunched him hard enough to rock him on his feet. The knob seemed to recede away from his fingers like scenery outside the window of a speeding train. He might have said Sam's name, or maybe he just thought it.

EIGHTEEN

The next thing he knew he was on his back on a sagging motel-room bed, looking up at a large brown water stain shaped like the state of Texas. Sam stood over him on the left and Xochi on the right. She was holding his right wrist in both of her hands. She looked beautiful and deadly serious.

"Dean," she said. "Why didn't you tell me you'd been cut by *Itztlitlantl*?"

"What?" He frowned. "You mean your sister's knife?"

"It is not her knife," Xochi said. "By right it is *my* knife."

"Okay, whatever," Sam said. "I don't care about your family drama right now, just tell us what's wrong with Dean. Is he poisoned?"

"Worse," Xochi said. "That knife was crafted by the great grandmother of my great grandmother's great grandmother," she said. "Carved from the tooth of a slain *Tzitzimitl*, a Star Demon. These are extremely powerful creatures whose obsidian bite can slice through souls. For this reason, they are also know as Souleaters.

"*Itztlitlantl* is the perfect weapon against ghosts and other unquiet spirits. It would also kill our rogue Borderwalker without a problem. But if it cuts a living human... The knife didn't just cut your hand, Dean. It cut into your soul."

"You've got to be kidding," Dean said.

"I wish I was," she said. "Your soul is wounded and must be healed."

"Awesome," Sam said. "It couldn't have been me that got cut with this thing."

Xochi looked up at Sam with an unreadable expression. Dean could see wheels turning inside her head but couldn't imagine what she was thinking.

"So what are you gonna do," Dean asked. "Give me a stick to bite on while you pop a few stitches into my soul?"

"I can do nothing for you," she said. "I'm no *curandera*."

"Okay so..." Dean frowned. "What happens now?"

"Your soul will die."

"Die?" Dean looked from Xochi to Sam and back again. "Whoa, what do you mean *die*?"

"It's not so bad," Sam said. "Not having a soul. I'm doing fine without mine."

"You don't understand," Xochi said to Sam. "Your soul isn't in your body, but it is still vital. Still alive. If the soul dies, the body is left a mindlessly animated, rotting corpse."

"A zombie?" Dean tried to sit up but couldn't. "You mean I'm gonna go all *Night of the Living Dead* and try to eat your brains?"

"You won't try to eat our brains, no," she said. "But when the soul is dead, or if it has been devoured by one of the *Tzitzimimeh*, the animated body is attracted to other living souls. It will obsessively chew and claw into living flesh in a desperate attempt to get at the soul within, like a moth banging mindlessly against a light bulb."

"Great," Dean said. "How long do I have?"

"It's a small cut," Xochi replied. "Twelve, maybe twenty-four hours." Her expression was grave. Dean felt sick to his stomach. He looked up at his brother.

"Sammy, you're not gonna let that happen to me are you?" Dean gripped his brother's arm. "If it comes to that, you'll take care of it, right?"

"Of course," Sam said. "I'll take care of it."

"You weren't supposed to answer that so quickly," Dean said.

"Sorry," Sam responded.

"So that's it?" Dean said. "We just sit here and wait for me to Romero out so Dexter here can pop a cap in my rotten brain and put me out of my misery?"

"There is someone," Xochi said. "Someone who can help you. But I don't know if she will."

Xochi pulled out her phone. Dialed. Turned away from Dean, speaking low even though he couldn't understand her anyway. The language she was speaking was neither English nor Spanish.

Dean couldn't understand her words, but he could gage her tone. It started pleading, then became angry. Then she broke off suddenly. She looked down at the phone.

"Well?" Dean asked.

She turned back to Dean, the answer in her expression.

"Great," Dean said. "Plan B?"

"Let me try again," Xochi said.

She went to the door and pulled it open, stepping out onto the breezeway. The door closed on another rush of incomprehensible words.

"What are we gonna do, Sam?" Dean asked.

"I don't know," Sam said. "We could ask Cass."

"I'm sure he's getting a little sick of us tugging on his trenchcoat sleeve every time one of us gets beat up in the playground."

"You got a better idea?"

Dean sighed and closed his eyes. The vertigo worsened, metallic nausea churning at the back of his throat.

"Hey, listen, Cass," Dean said, flexing the fingers of his injured hand. Cold streaks of numbness raced through his forearm. "I know you're real busy right now, what with the chaos in Heaven and all that…"

"No," Castiel said, standing suddenly by the bathroom door, looking rumpled, unshaven and put-upon, just like always.

"No what?" Sam asked.

"No I can't help you," the angel replied. "I'm sorry."

"You came all the way down here just to say you can't help?" Dean pressed the fingers of his good hand against his temple. "Why bother? Why not just ignore me like usual."

"I never ignore you, Dean," Castiel said. "I never ignore either one of you. Sometimes I'm able to come and sometimes I'm not."

"So why can't you help him?" Sam demanded.

"You are…" He seemed to be searching for the right words. "Out of my jurisdiction."

"I'm sorry, what?" Sam took a step forward. "Out of your jurisdiction? Since when do angels have jurisdiction?"

"You're dealing with a whole different system of government here," Castiel said. "Different gods. I'm not allowed to interfere."

"Come on, just because we're fighting Mexican monsters?" Dean said, struggling to sit up. The effort made his head swim. "There's got to be, what, a billion Catholics in Mexico, right?"

"And there are a billion demons in Mexico too. In fact they have one of the highest demon to human ratios in the world, second only to Uganda. And if you were fighting one of those demons I would be happy to help you, but you aren't. What you are up against is from a totally separate, independent spiritual realm. Upper management has a longstanding *laissez-faire* policy with other gods. By the terms of our recent agreement, they stay out of our business and we stay out of theirs."

"But *we're* your business," Dean said. "Me and Sam. Aren't we?"

"When you were up against Lucifer, did any Aztec deities show up to help you stop the apocalypse? Even though every one of their priests and chosen people would have also been destroyed if you had failed?"

"So, that's it then?" Dean asked. "I'm walking worm food and there's nothing anyone can do about it?"

"Your new friend is very capable," Castiel said. "Like Sam said, she's a hammer. You're in her hands now."

Xochi came through the door at that moment. Castiel was already gone.

"Good news and bad news," she said.

"Bad news first," Sam said.

"We must leave right away," Xochi said. "We have to cross the border, to Tijuana. My grandmother will not come to the United States."

"That's not so bad," Dean said. "Trip to TJ. We can have a few beers. Check out some strip clubs. Maybe get our photos taken sitting on one of those zebra-striped donkeys."

"Good news?" Sam asked.

"My grandmother is a powerful *curandera*," she said. "She will help Dean."

NINETEEN

Xochi went on ahead, with a promise to meet the brothers on the other side of the border. Said she had some things to take care of. Dean was in no condition to argue.

Sam helped Dean down to the Impala. Dean also wasn't in any condition to argue when Sam wanted to drive.

As the Impala ate up the long desert miles, Dean leaned his dizzy head against the window. They passed a wordless graphic sign warning of illegal immigrants. A trio of silhouettes, a running man, woman and child.

"Tell me something," Sam said

"What?" he asked.

"Are you still worried about Xochi trying to screw us over?" Sam asked.

"I don't know," Dean said. "I mean, I'm pretty sure she's human. She seems to be on the level, but… I just don't know."

He wasn't about to tell Sam what he'd really been thinking about Xochi. He'd never hear the end of it.

"I think…" Sam began, then faltered. "…I think this hunt is important. I can't say why, I just know it. It's not just about Xochi and this Borderwalker. It's bigger that that."

He drove in silence for a few minutes before speaking again.

"It's been a long time since anything seemed really important. I feel like I have to see this through, no matter what."

"Don't worry, Sammy," Dean said. "I'm not gonna check out on you just yet."

He hoped that was true.

Xochi had suggested they park the Impala in San Ysidro, on the American side of the border. Dean hated to leave his beloved ride, but not as much as he hated the idea of her getting stripped or stolen on the Tijuana street.

He had to lean heavily on Sam as the two of them staggered down the long cement walkway leading to the pedestrian border crossing.

The border guard who checked their IDs was beefy Latino guy with a thick neck and way too many big white teeth in his deceptively lazy smile. He gave Dean a casual once over.

"Is he okay?" the guard asked Sam.

"Him?" Sam hoisted Dean up a little straighter. "He's fine. Just been pre-partying a little hard."

Dean picked up on the ruse immediately and threw his uninjured fist into the air.

"DONKEY SHOW!" he bellowed with his best drunken slur. "WOO HOO!!!"

The guard shook his head, handed the IDs back to Sam.

"You two be careful out there," he said.

When they finally made it through customs they were funneled out into a maze of more zigzagging walkways, only these were lined with vendors. Kids Ben's age selling rock-hard gum and candy, faces stained with green and red rings from huffing paint. Old women selling plaster saints alongside weird, glossy knock-off statues of American corporate-owned characters. Piles of sombreros and maracas. Rugs featuring white tigers or Julio Iglesias or *La Virgen de Guadalupe*. Inflatable animals and piñatas shaped like masked wrestlers. In Dean's weakened condition, walking the gauntlet of street sellers felt like the Bataan Death March.

A cute teenage girl ran over and handed Dean a flyer advertising generic Viagra and Rogaine at bulk discount. Two steps later another girl handed Sam a flyer advertising a strip club.

"What are they trying to tell us here?" Dean asked looking down at his flyer and then at Sam's. "You know what, on second thought, don't answer that."

When they finally made it out onto the Tijuana street, Dean spotted Xochi right away. It was impossible not to.

She sat behind the wheel of a four-door '67 Impala. The number of doors and the fact that it rolled out of the Chevrolet factory the same year as his own were the only things the two vehicles had in common. This car had been chopped and channeled, sitting about a half an inch off the asphalt. It was painted a glossy, June-bug green impregnated with gold metal flakes. On the hood was an astoundingly gaudy painting of a muscle-bound Aztec warrior with a busty, mostly naked chick twined around one of his legs. As they approached, Dean saw the interior was done up in sparkly gold vinyl and lime-green fake fur. The hubcaps shined bright as diamonds.

When Xochi saw them she waved, punching the hydraulics and causing the car to hop and shimmy.

"Subtle," Sam said opening the rear passenger door, tossing his bag into the back seat and then helping Dean in after it. "No one's gonna notice us in this car." He got into the passenger seat, next to Xochi.

"I thought you said it was too dangerous around here to drive a nice car," Dean said. He was embarrassed by how good it felt to be sitting down.

"I said it was dangerous to drive your car," Xochi said. "Everyone knows who this car belongs to. No one will touch it."

"Whose car is it?" Sam asked.

"I told you," Xochi said, throwing the car into gear and peeling out. "A lot of people owe me favors."

Dean tried to pay attention to the scenery outside the car, but it all seemed to run together into a surreal, sodium-lit blur of illegible signs, beater cars and taco-cart smoke. Some kind of kick-ass old-school rock and roll was blasting out of the Aztec Impala's formidable, bass-heavy sound system but the lyrics were in Spanish.

Sam and Xochi were talking, laughing, but he couldn't hear what they were saying. His hand throbbed in time with his heart. His chest felt heavy, every breath leaden. When he closed his eyes, he felt like he was falling. He wondered if Xochi's grandmother was really going to be able to cure him and was struck with a sudden fear that he'd made a terrible mistake, agreeing to take on this job. A mistake that may never be undone.

He thought of the argument he'd had with Sam after leaving the grim prison where their grandfather had been torturing monsters. Sure, Dean put up a good front, but what if he really did die before Sam got his soul back? Dean knew he was the only thing keeping his brother tethered to his humanity. Without Dean, would Sam just give up? Resign himself to a life without emotion, without conscience? Dean couldn't let that happen. This wouldn't be the first time he'd been too damn stubborn to die. Probably wouldn't be the last.

Some time later, Dean had no idea how long, Xochi pulled the Aztec Impala into a narrow driveway leading up to what looked at first glance like an armored military compound. It turned out to be a motel. Surrounded by razor-wire fencing, guarded by guys in black-out SWAT gear wielding automatic rifles. They waved Xochi through with big smiles, giving Sam and Dean enthusiastic thumbs-ups.

"Where are we?" Dean croaked.

"It is a house of women," Xochi said. "We will be safe here."

"House of women?" Sam arched an eyebrow. "You mean a brothel?"

"Yes," she said.

"Awesome," Sam replied.

"Why all the security?" Dean asked. "Poachers?"

"The competition is very fierce," Xochi said. "Other houses have sent death threats to Tia Lupe."

"Hooker Wars?" Sam looked back at Dean with an expression of baffled amusement. "Now there's a reality show."

"We are so not in Kansas anymore," Dean replied.

A woman that had to be Tia Lupe came out to greet them. She was wearing a pink spandex dress that had been a bad idea ten years and fifty pounds ago. Too many rings on chubby, French-manicured fingers. Poofed-up bleached blonde hair and pencil-thin *chola* eyebrows.

"'Sup, *flaca*?" she said when Xochi rolled down the window. "Introduce me to your sexy friends."

"Sam in the front," she said. "Dean in the rear. Boys, this is Tia Lupe."

"Ma'am," Sam said.

She said something to Xochi in Spanish that was obviously dirty. Then she switched back to English.

"Your *abuelita* is in twenty-one. Just pull into the garage. You boys need any room service, all you gotta do is ring."

Xochi pulled out a roll of Mexican bills, pressed a few into Lupe's hand and did as she instructed.

Dean was amazed to see that each room had its own private garage. When he commented on it, Xochi laughed.

"That is so your wife will not see your car when she's out looking for you."

Sam helped Dean out of the back seat and through a connecting door into the room itself. The décor was super tacky, all red velvet and roses and gold sparkles, but he was happy to note there was not a single cactus in sight. The air-conditioning was cranked to eleven, meat-locker cold after the sultry Tijuana summer outside.

Xochi's grandmother was waiting for them in the room. Dean wasn't sure what he had been expecting, some kind of cliché Native-American wise woman or something like that, but he was not prepared for the woman Xochi introduced him to.

"This is my grandmother, Toci," she said. "She doesn't speak any English."

Toci was tiny like Dean had pictured she would be, but other than that, he couldn't have been further off in his image of her. She had a giant purplish-red beehive hairdo that was obviously a wig and added a good eight inches to her height. Heavy Cleopatra eye make-up behind owlish glasses and ten pounds of weird, kitschy jewelry hung off her skinny neck and wrists. She wore a black-velvet tunic with a sparkly gold jaguar head on the front, shiny gold-lamé leggings and gold, high-heeled cowboy boots.

She said something snide and dismissive to Xochi. It didn't sound like Spanish. Dean leaned against Sam in embarrassed silence as the two women went back and forth in some kind of heated exchange. Sam shook his head and led Dean over to the bed.

"Is she gonna help Dean or not?" Sam asked.

Dean lowered himself slowly and gratefully onto the bed. His head was spinning, muscles weak and shaking.

Toci said something to Xochi, tipping her head toward

Dean with her painted eyebrows raised expectantly.

"She wants me to tell you that it will hurt," Xochi said.

"I can take it," Dean replied.

Xochi translated his reply. Toci looked Dean up and down and then gave a curt nod. She said something to Xochi and Sam that needed no translation, accompanied as it was by a shooing gesture.

The two of them turned to leave. Xochi paused with her hand on the doorknob, looking back over her shoulder at Dean. She was obviously worried, but trying not to show it. Sam didn't look back at all.

Dean could handle pain, but he had no idea what to do when Toci started yanking at his clothes like a drunk bachelorette at a Chippendales show. When he tried to stop her from pulling his shirt off, she slapped his good hand and said something stern. Dean had never had any strong female authority figures growing up and had absolutely no idea how to cope with being bossed around and man-handled by a little old lady. He had no choice but to let Toci have the shirt. But then she started unbuckling his belt.

TWENTY

"Whoa," he said. "Look, lady, the cut's on my hand." He held his hand up as proof. "Hand! See? You don't need to…"

She shoved him backwards onto the bed and pulled his pants down to his ankles.

"Okay then," Dean said, looking up at his own mortified expression reflected in the mirrored tiles on the ceiling.

Toci unlaced his boots and took them off, then removed his jeans completely. Laying there on the bed dressed in nothing but crumpled white socks, he was really quite glad Sam and Xochi had left the room. Dean had never quite imagined his life might end like this. Naked in a Tijuana brothel with an eighty-year-old woman dressed like Janine from Spinal Tap sizing up his junk and looking distinctly unimpressed. He really wished the room wasn't so heavily air-conditioned.

He knew there was no point fighting Toci. Whatever she needed to do to heal him, even if it included some kind of mystical ancient Aztec prostate exam, he'd just have to take it and like it. It wasn't as if he had any other choice.

When she got down to business, Dean forgot all about feeling self-conscious. Xochi hadn't been lying when she'd warned him that it would hurt. It was all he could do to keep still and keep whatever moans of agony he couldn't stifle from cranking up into the girlier octaves.

What she was doing probably wasn't all that dissimilar to one of Castiel's angel cavity searches. But rather than sticking her hand into his chest, she was somehow teasing the wounded portion of his soul out through the cut on his palm. He hadn't been that far off when he asked Xochi if she was going to put stitches in his soul. Unfortunately, there was no such thing as spiritual anesthesia.

When she finally stopped, he let out a long, shaky breath and clenched his wounded hand. It still hurt, but it was a pain he could handle.

Toci threw a fuzzy red blanket over his shivering body, tucking him in with a surprisingly tender touch considering her previously gruff demeanor.

"Thanks," he said. "Um… *gracias*?"

She patted his chest and said something to him that he didn't understand, but it didn't seem to require a response. Then she called out for Xochi.

Xochi had clearly been waiting right on the other side of the door as she came in the second she was called. She had changed out of her blood-splattered tank top and into a cheap T-shirt that featured a pair of sexy female silhouettes and read "My friends got busy at Tia Lupe's and all I got was this lousy T-shirt." Her hair was bound back into the long twin braids she'd been sporting when they'd first met. No flowers. There was a brief exchange between her and Toci and then the older woman left the two of them alone.

"So what's the prognosis?" Dean asked. "Am I gonna make it?"

"Your soul is still very sick, but healing." She spotted the crumpled pile of Dean's clothing on the carpet and looked up at him with a very slight smile.

"It wasn't my idea, believe me," he said.

She didn't reply, just stood there with that same arch humor in her eyes.

"What? Isn't that part of this whole healing mojo thing?"

Xochi shook her head.

"You don't really need to be naked," she said. "I think she just wanted to check out your body."

"Are you serious?"

"No," she said, smile blooming. "I'm joking. Tight clothing restricts the flow of natural energy that you will need for the healing."

"I don't know if I believe you," he said. "I think all you Aztec chicks are up to no good. Trying to take advantage of a sick, defenseless *gringo*."

"If I wanted to take advantage," she said, "I'm perfectly capable of doing it while you are strong and healthy. Or have you forgotten already?"

Dean hadn't forgotten.

"Is your grandmother coming back?" he asked.

"She just went for some more supplies," Xochi said.

"She'll be back soon. She still has a lot more healing to do."

"Don't tell me that," Dean said. "I barely made it through the first round."

"I'm sorry," Xochi said.

He could see that she really meant it. Under the wisecracks, she was still worried.

"You know," Dean said, gesturing with his uninjured hand. "If we were in an action movie, this would be the scene where you tenderly dress my wounds. Then the wailing electric guitar ballad would kick in and we'd end up rolling around on the bed in a slow motion montage."

"If we were in *Q, The Winged Serpent*," Xochi replied, "this would be the scene where I sacrifice you to *Quetzalcoatl.*"

"I thought you said you'd never seen that movie."

She took her phone out of her pocket, tapped the screen a few times, then turned it to face Dean.

"I was curious," she said.

On the phone's screen, the Aztec priest was about to cut some poor bastard's heart out on top of the Chrysler Building.

"Sam is right," she said. "This movie is terrible. Look, he's holding that knife all wrong."

Dean laughed, the laugh trailing off into a weak cough. His chest felt heavy, his right arm still leaden and strange.

"So," Dean said. "Does this mean you won't tend my wounds?"

"I'm a great hunter," she said, crossing her arms and leaning back against the wall. "But I'm a terrible nurse."

Dean realized he didn't want to be alone.

"Just sit with me, then," he said, patting the bed beside him. "Talk to me."

"What do you want me to talk about?"

She stayed standing, arms still crossed. Wary.

"It doesn't matter," he said. "Please?"

She came over to the bed and sat perched on the edge.

"What's your favorite movie?"

"*Los Campeones Justicieros*," she said. "Mil Máscaras was my hero growing up."

"Mil always did have the pimpin' wardrobe. You gotta love a guy that's man enough to fight monsters in leopard spandex."

"That might be a good style for you," she said. "I can introduce you the best tailor in Mexico City. She makes ring gear for all the top *luchadores*."

"I don't know," he said. "When I'm facing off against an unholy soul-sucking abomination from beyond the grave, I want something a little more substantial than spandex to protect my future children."

"What is your favorite movie?" she asked.

"Hard to pick just one," he said.

"Not *Q*?"

"No," he said. "And if you ask me again tomorrow, I'll probably have a totally different answer, but tonight, I'd have to go with *The Monster Squad*. I want Shane Black to write all my dialog. Favorite band?"

"*Caifanes*."

"Never heard of them," Dean said.

"I also like the British band Led Zeppelin."

"Yeah?" Dean smiled. "What's your favorite Zep song?"

"'Ramble On,'" she said. "I feel like that song has so much meaning for me, for my life. You know?"

He looked up at her.

"Don't you have someone? Boyfriend?"

She shook her head.

"Girlfriend?"

"No," she said. "No one. I mean, I tried but…" She shrugged again. "I was a terrible wife too."

"What happened?"

"You know," she said. "Things don't always work out."

Dean didn't say anything. He could sense she wanted to say more. He waited.

"I tried to walk away… to be a normal person." She looked down at her scarred hands. "But this life. Hunting. It's the only thing I'm really good at."

He wanted to tell her that he got it, that he understood so well it hurt, but again he couldn't find the words. She crossed her arms again, turning her body away from him. Distant, sealing herself up.

"Maybe you just need to find someone more like you," he said.

She looked back at him.

"What do you mean?"

"I mean someone who really understands you," he said. "What you've been through. Someone who's been there. You know, someone you can trust to have your back in a fight."

"Someone like you, maybe?" She smiled, just a little. "Dean, you want to be my boyfriend?"

"Of course not," he said. "I just meant…"

"That is a beautiful dream," she said. "Warrior lovers, fighting side by side, going down together in a blaze of glory. But you and I, we are so much alike, aren't we? And as beautiful as that dream may be, I know that you don't really want that any more than I do."

"Then what do you want?"

"The same thing you want. The thing we've both wanted so desperately ever since we were children. The thing we both need and fear we may never be allowed to have."

"Yeah, what's that?" Dean asked, even though he was pretty sure he already knew the answer.

"A home," she said, like it was the most obvious thing in the world. Like he was crazy for asking.

She was getting way too close to messy, painful truths that Dean thought he'd buried good and deep. Feelings about Lisa and Ben, about his dead mother and Sam and all those long sleepless nights on the road. He needed to crack a joke, to reinforce the armor. To regain control of the conversation and steer it back to safer waters.

"Okay, so forget the whole blaze of glory thing," Dean said. "How about gratuitous, casual sex?"

He was only half kidding.

She laughed, but he could hear the relief underneath her laugh. She was as glad to change the subject as he was.

"That would be very nice," she said turning away from him again. "But I don't think you understand how badly you are hurt. You need to conserve your energy to heal your soul."

He put his uninjured hand on the small of her back, following the channel of her spine with his fingertips.

"You could lend me some of yours," he said.

She arched her back almost imperceptibly against his touch, making a wordless, throaty purring sound so soft Dean thought maybe he was imagining it.

Toci chose that moment to return, lugging a large woven plastic bag.

Xochi stood, exchanging a few words with her grandmother. The old woman took out a beat-up plastic two-liter soda bottle with no label and handed it to Xochi. It was full of something that wasn't soda. Something pale, milky and viscous. Xochi took the bottle and looked back at Dean. Her gaze was guarded, but he was almost sure he saw something there. Some kind of connection maybe. She turned and left the room before he could be sure.

Toci came to his bedside and pulled a second bottle of that strange beverage from the bag. She unscrewed the plastic cap and held it to his lips, telling him something he didn't understand. He had no choice but to drink it. Drink it or wear it.

Whatever it was, it was alcoholic. It tasted sort of like rotten pears soaked in moonshine and had an unpleasant, slimy texture. When she pulled the bottle away from his lips, there was a snotty clear stringer like Alien spit connecting the mouth of the bottle to his lower lip. His stomach did a slow lurching roll, but the warm familiar burn of the alcohol spread through him, relaxing the knots in his spine and dulling the pain in his hand.

Toci poured some of the gooey liquid into a plastic bowl and added a bunch of dried plants and powders. Dean couldn't help noticing a large amount of orange marigold petals. If this worked, he promised to take back anything bad he'd ever said about the humble little flower.

Round two was even worse, if that was possible. It seemed to go on for hours and when it was done, Dean was close to passing out. He hoped the moisture on his face was sweat and not tears.

The herbs had been steeping in the strange milky liquor while Toci worked, imbuing it with a bitter peppery scent. Dean thought she was going to make him drink it, but instead she gave him another, unadulterated swig straight from the plastic bottle and then used the stuff in the bowl to soak his hand.

She lit several candles in glass tubes, inscribed with various lurid designs: burning women and tattooed hands and curious symbols. Then, she pulled his hand out of the bowl and wrapped it in gauze. She spoke some melodic words over him and then turned and left him alone in the tacky room.

Dean drifted. Dreamed of Lisa. Of home.

TWENTY-ONE

Xochi found Sam sitting on the curb outside the garage connected to their room. A group of prostitutes were hanging around by the door to the office, eyeing Sam like he was a raw steak in a dog kennel. He was lost in thought, however; ignoring them completely.

Xochi sat down on the curb beside him. She unscrewed the cap off the bottle her grandmother had given her, took a long swallow and then handed it to Sam. He nodded and drank. Made a funny face, like a baby who'd been given a chili pepper for the first time.

"What the hell is that stuff?" Sam asked, wiping his lips on the back of a big fist.

"*Pulque*," Xochi said. "Help me finish the bottle and I'll show you how to spit the last sip in the shape of a scorpion."

"Poolkay?" He took another swig. "It's kinda weird, but I kinda like it."

"It's made from fermented *maguey*, very thick and sticky,"

she said. "When you get to the bottom of the bottle, you spit that last sticky mouthful onto the floor and if the *pulque* is good, your spit will look like a scorpion."

"I'll drink to that," Sam said, taking one more swig and then passing the bottle back to Xochi.

She drank deep, and tried to organize her chaotic thoughts.

"Sam," she said. "I know I can say this to you and you will not react badly, but I need to make sure you and I understand each other."

"Okay," Sam said. "Shoot."

"What happened to your brother is my fault," Xochi said. "He was cut because he was trying to protect me. For that I am sorry." She paused. Passed the bottle. "He is not out of danger. There is still a chance that he may not make it."

"I know," Sam said. He drank. No reaction.

"He's a good hunter," she said. "I like fighting next to him. If he dies tonight, I will own that responsibilty for the rest of my life."

She could still feel Dean's touch on the base of her spine. She held her hand out for the bottle. Sam handed it back to her. She took a swig.

"What I must ask is this," she said. "Sam, are you still with me in this fight, no matter what happens to your brother? Because I want Dean to make it… to fight with us… but I *need* you. Do you understand? If he dies, you and I can still do this. But without you…"

"No problem," he said without hesitation. "I'm in. No matter what."

"Thank you," she said.

The two of them drank in silence for a few minutes. They watched the prostitutes share cigarettes and hustle clients. One of the younger ones got lucky. Xochi watched her steer her tipsy American prey into one of the rooms, shamelessly clipping his wallet before she'd even unlocked the door.

"What does it feel like," Xochi asked. "Not having a soul?"

"It doesn't feel like anything," Sam replied. "I mean, I can tell something's missing. Like I know I'm supposed to be upset by the idea that my brother might die, but I'm not. Because I know you and I can handle this hunt without him." He looked at her, then away. "The thing is, when I know there's something I'm supposed to be feeling, something important, I just can't seem to leave it alone in my head. Even if I'm not sure what it is, I keep on thinking about it. Thinking in circles. It's like…" He swirled the milky contents of the bottle, staring into nothing for a moment before taking another swallow. "It's like having a pulled tooth. You can't stop touching the space where it used to be with your tongue. It was much worse when I first came back. But now… I think I'm getting used to that hole. Sometimes I think I'm better off this way."

He handed the *pulque* back to Xochi and she looked into his eyes, green eyes like Dean's, but flat and lifeless. She suddenly felt like a monster.

What Sam was going through was horrible, a unique and profound kind of torment that she could only imagine, and never once had she even bothered to think of what it was like for him. All this time, she'd looked at the big *gringo* as nothing more than a useful tool. A piece of the puzzle presented by her visions. A weapon that she knew would be critical to her victory. She still had her soul, or whatever tattered shreds might be left after everything she'd been through, and yet here she was thinking just like Sam. Thinking only about winning this fight no matter what the cost. But every day this boy spent without his soul, he was becoming less and less human. He shouldn't be wasting time hunting with her, he should be fighting to get his soul back. Before he gets too comfortable with that hole.

"No," she said, handing him the bottle. "You're not better off like this. Now, for this hunt, maybe, but not in the long run."

"You don't know the whole story," Sam said. "I have my reasons." He drank. Wiped his lips. "Look, I don't want to talk about it anymore. All you need to know is that I'm gonna see this thing through with you. You can count on me."

Xochi nodded. She wasn't going to argue with that.

"You know," Sam said, passing the bottle back. "There's something I've been meaning to ask you about. Something that's been bothering me for a while now."

Xochi drank and waited for him to elaborate.

"This knife your sister has," he said. "The one that cut Dean. You say it could kill our Borderwalker?"

"Yes," she said.

"So why didn't she use it?"

"What do you mean?"

"I mean she had her shot, why didn't she take it?"

Xochi frowned.

"Dean stopped her," she said. "Then the Borderwalker crossed over before she could…"

"No." Sam shook he head. "Dean only went after her when she threw that elbow at you, but she had plenty of time before that. I think she didn't want to kill the thing."

"Why not?" she asked.

"You tell me."

Xochi took another thick, sticky swallow from the bottle, but any kind of comfortable intoxication that may have been building up was swiftly burned away by thorny, unanswered questions.

Was Teo just toying with the Borderwalker, or was there something more sinister behind her actions? Why was she there in the first place? How did she fit into all this?

They drank together in silence for a few more minutes. The bottle was nearly empty.

"Tell you what," Sam said suddenly. "Why don't we forget about all this and get a room." He leaned close to her, put an enormous paw on her thigh. "I'll let you do you anything you want to me. Anything. Upside of having no soul." He drank. Smiled. "No inhibitions."

"You know, your brother also asked me to make love with him tonight."

"Yeah, well," Sam said, dipping his chin and raising his eyebrows. "I'm bigger."

She laughed. Took the bottle.

"No thank you, Sam," she said.

"Okay," he said, taking his hand off her leg and showing

her his palms. "You're into him. I get it. Anyway, to be fair, he needs it way more than I do."

"I'm not 'into him'" she said. "I just… We have more important things to worry about right now."

"Man," he said, rolling his eyes. "You two are like peas in a frickin' pod."

Sam stood and took his wallet from his hip pocket, extracting a few American bills and then handing the wallet to Xochi.

"Hold this for me, will you?" he said. "I'm gonna order up some room service."

He walked over to the group of prostitutes by the office. Xochi watched with amusement as he struggled to communicate with them using his high school Spanish. He was right, he could get his point across when he needed to. He walked away with two of the best-looking girls, one on each arm.

Xochi sucked the last of the *pulque* from the bottle and spit the gooey dregs on the cement between her boots. The resulting blob didn't look much like a scorpion. More like a spiny butterfly.

She thought about checking in on Dean, but knew she didn't need to. Toci was with him and he would either make it or he wouldn't. Having Xochi standing around staring at his bare chest wasn't going to speed up the healing process.

She thought about Teo. About what Sam had said. About what Huehuecoyotl had said. She wondered once again what they were really up against.

TWENTY-TWO

When Dean woke up, the first thing he saw was the back of Xochi's neck. No tattoos on that particular area, just smooth brown skin and a few little wisps of black hair that had escaped her braids. He'd only had a couple mouthfuls of that weird liquor, but if he'd somehow managed to score with Xochi after all and didn't remember a thing, he was going to be seriously pissed.

Taking more detailed stock of the situation, Dean saw that she was fully dressed, sleeping on top of the covers with her back to him. Highly unlikely that she would have bothered to get dressed again after the horizontal mambo out before falling asleep.

He reached out to wake her, brushing her tattooed arm with his fingers.

She reacted with the speed of a striking rattlesnake, grabbing his wrist and rolling toward him, switchblade open in her other hand.

"Good morning," Dean said. "Coffee?"

She let him go, closing the knife and looking sheepish.

"Sorry," she said. "I guess I'm a little jumpy. How are you feeling?"

He paused for a moment to take internal inventory. Opened and closed his bandaged hand. He felt good. Better, in fact, than he had in months.

"Okay, I think," he said.

"Good," Sam said. Dean hadn't even noticed his brother, sitting silently in a plush red chair on the far side of the room. "We gotta get out of Dodge and beat the Borderwalker to Fullerton."

"I'm glad you are still with us, Dean," Xochi said, rolling away from him and sitting up, stretching her arms above her head. "Toci said your soul is very strong. Almost as strong as a woman's."

Dean laughed.

"I guess I'll take that as a compliment."

Xochi stood, rolling her neck to work the kinks out while stepping into her boots. Sam stood too, slinging his bag over his shoulder. Laptop already packed up and ready to hit the road.

Dean lay there for a moment with the fuzzy blanket clutched against his bare chest, eyeing the inside-out scatter of his clothes on the carpet.

"Um... I'd better..." He flapped his hand in the directions of his clothes. "You know."

"What?" Xochi asked. "You're shy? You only allow old ladies to see you naked?"

She snickered and cut him off before he could come up with anything resembling a snappy retort.

"We'll be waiting in the car," she said.

Xochi dropped them back off at the pedestrian border crossing, promising to meet them in Fullerton. When Dean pressed her to set an exact meeting place, she refused. She said that she would find them.

Getting back into the U.S. was a much bigger deal than getting out. Drug-sniffing dogs were walking along the line. Guys with rubber gloves and humorless scowls searched through Sam's laptop bag for nearly half an hour. For once, Dean actually hadn't done anything questionable but he still felt anxious and convinced they'd find some reason to detain him. He could only imagine how much harder it would have been if he or his brother looked even vaguely Latino.

When they finally made it back to American soil, Dean was so happy to see his own car he almost kissed the hood.

"Think she can tell we've been rolling in another Impala?" Sam joked as Dean got behind the wheel.

"Don't listen to him, baby," Dean said, patting the dash. "I swear, she meant nothing to me. I didn't even drive, honest."

The journey to Fullerton was pretty uneventful. They passed more of the running immigrant family signs and some sort of weird power plant that looked like a giant pair of silicone breasts. Traffic was light, almost non-existent. Even with a stop for chow and coffee, they still made it to Porcayo's place in record time.

Fullerton was suburban and unremarkable. Porcayo lived in an unremarkable house on an unremarkable street. It was a Witness Protection kind of neighborhood. The kind of place you forgot the second you left.

"Okay," Dean said, pulling up to the curb a couple of houses down from the target. "What have we got?"

"José Ibarita Porcayo," Sam read off the screen of his laptop. "Forty-nine years old. Works at HandyMart, a franchise hardware store, during the day. Security for an office building at night. Married to a grade school teacher, Irma Diaz Porcayo, for twenty-one years, until her death six months ago. Cancer. Just one kid. A daughter, Claudia, fifteen. Looks like she was adopted."

"Did you say *fifteen*?" Dean raised his eyebrows and leaned across the seat to look at the laptop's screen.

"Fifteen years and nine months to be exact," Sam said. "You thinking what I'm thinking?"

"Abandoned female infant," Dean said. "Age nine months. Mother never found."

"You think he actually adopted the daughter of the woman he and his buddies raped and murdered?"

"That's how it looks, doesn't it?" Dean sat back, stunned.

"I'll see what I can dig up in the way of adoption records," Sam said, keys clicking. "You keep an eye on the house."

Dean couldn't even imagine what it must be like for Porcayo, living every day with that girl. Raising her as his own. Did he see her mother every time he looked at her?

Then, as if invoked by Dean's speculation, a teenage girl came walking down the street. She was short and a

little chubby, a gothy Hot Topic baby bat. Crayon red
streak in her hair. Too much eyeliner, applied with a
heavy, inexpert hand. Steel ring through her pouty lower
lip. Unflattering black skinny jeans and a red-and-black
striped T-shirt with a cute, cartoony skull on the front.
Emily the Strange backpack. She walked with her arms
tightly crossed, shoulders curled inward with the tense,
wary body language of someone trying to avoid the
attention of bullies. Dean was pretty sure this was Claudia,
and his suspicions were confirmed when she turned into
the target house, opening the front door with a key on a
chain crowded with dangling bats and beads and big-eyed
Japanese anime figures.

"It's only 11:30," Sam said peering at his watch. "Shouldn't
she be in school?"

"Cutting class maybe?" Dean suggested.

"We should probably to talk to her," Sam said.

"Well we obviously can't just kick the door down and
shove a gun in her face," Dean said.

He looked down the street, wondering where Xochi was
and how long it would be before she showed up. Weird,
how quickly he'd gotten used to having her around. It
didn't seem possible that just two days ago, he wasn't even
sure she was human.

"Do you think she knows?" Sam asked.

"About her mother's murder?" Dean shook his head. "No
way. And I'm not gonna be the one to tell her." He cut Sam
off before he could speak. "Neither are you. Trust me on
this. We don't go there unless we absolutely have to."

"One other thing," Sam said. "Remember that the Borderwalker just showed up inside Brewer's apartment. It's not like we're gonna see her walking down the street before she attacks. By the time we realized anything was going down inside that house, it would be too late."

"So what," Dean asked. "We break in and set up a duckblind in the bedroom closet?"

"I think we should head over to HandyMart," Sam replied. "Have ourselves a chat with Dad."

TWENTY-THREE

The HandyMart was a cavernous, sprawling warehouse with piles of plywood and PVC piping stacked to the mile-high ceiling. Fenced outdoor garden center off to one side, full of leggy juvenile citrus trees and brambly pink-and-red bougainvillea. Aisle after aisle of bathroom fixtures and closet organizers and every shape and size of screw ever invented. It smelled like hot sawdust and fresh paint.

It took them nearly twenty minutes of searching the aisles to find Porcayo. They eventually spotted him in the light fixture section, one hand on a shelf and his face turned away from them. He had thick, wavy black hair and dark brown skin. Maybe five-foot eight with a stocky, muscular build. He wore neatly pressed khaki pants and a green HandyMart polo shirt, plus a cheery yellow apron with his name on it and a smiley face button that said "Happy to Serve You!"

"Excuse me," Dean said.

Porcayo turned to them, startled. Dean saw that the man had been crying. His square-jawed, handsome face was contorted and ugly with grief, dark eyes bloodshot and raw. He pressed a shaking hand to his lips. Dean felt instantly uncomfortable and embarrassed for the older man.

"Welcome to HandyMart," Porcayo said, voice cracking slightly. "How can I help you?"

Dean was at a loss for a moment, confronted with the intense emotion in the man's tortured face, but Sam jumped right in, stoic and unruffled.

"Mr. Porcayo," Sam said, badge in hand. "I'm Special Agent Kolchak. My partner Agent Summers. Is there somewhere we can speak in private?"

"Is this about Claudia?" Porcayo asked. "She's a good girl, really. She's just been through so much. Losing her mother…"

Sam and Dean exchanged a look.

"Well," Dean said. "It is and it isn't. But we really should discuss this in private."

Porcayo pulled in a long, shaky breath. Wiped his lips again.

"Yeah, okay," he said.

He led the brothers into a grungy little breakroom near the public toilets. Dusty drop ceiling and scuffed linoleum. Cheap card-table with a few dented metal folding chairs. There was a pair of vending machines on the far side of the room, one filled with generic, off-brand soft drinks and the other an array of unappetizing, fossilized snacks. A staticy television bolted to the wall played some kind of animal show featuring badly lit home video clips of cats and dogs knocking over toddlers. Dean got the distinct feeling that the corporate masters of HandyMart would really rather their employees didn't take breaks.

"Why did you think we wanted to ask you about your daughter?" Sam asked.

"Well," Porcayo looked at the television screen for a moment, then down at the toes of his beat-up work boots. "The skipping school, the shoplifting and then that destruction of public property thing two weeks ago. My wife..." He swallowed hard. "When she got sick again... Claudia started acting out. Irma, my wife, she always used to say that I'm too soft on Claudia, that I don't discipline her enough. She was right, I know. But now, with Irma gone..." He spread his hands, palm up. "I just don't know what to do anymore."

Dean thought the guy was going to break down again. Dean couldn't help but feel for him, and he had to remind himself of what Porcayo and his buddies had done to Claudia's real mother. Apparently, Sam didn't need to be reminded.

"This isn't about shoplifting," Sam said. "This is about rape. Rape and murder."

Porcayo staggered as if Sam had slapped him. He gripped the back of one of the folding chairs to hold himself up and then lowered himself slowly into the seat.

"I saw the news," Porcayo said. "They're all dead. Keene, Himes and Brewer." He looked down at his calloused hands like they were stained with blood. "It's her, isn't it?

"Yes," Sam said.

"And now she's coming for me."

"I'm afraid so."

Porcayo put his head in his hands.

Dean was extremely glad to have Sam take the wheel on this one. He knew he shouldn't be so sympathetic but he couldn't help it. After all, if Porcayo really had been possessed in some way and unable to control his actions, he could hardly be blamed for what had happened that night. Plus he'd tried so hard to make up for what he'd done, taking the kid in and raising her as his own. Having her there every day as a living, breathing reminder of his unspeakable crime. Without him, who knows what would have happened to that baby.

"Look, Mr. Porcayo," Sam said. "We can help you, but…"

Porcayo took an orange plastic box cutter from a pocket in his apron and thumbed the blade open.

"Whoa," Dean said, grabbing Porcayo's wrist before he could slash open the inside of his forearm. "Okay, take it easy now."

"Let me go!" Porcayo hissed, struggling against Dean and kicking over the chair.

"Just take it easy, José," Dean said. "Can I call you José?" Dean repeated Porcayo's first name in a soft voice, trying to calm him down. "Please, José, just listen. We're here to help you. You and Claudia, okay?"

A petite Latina with disproportionately big hair and big gold loop earrings pushed the door open with her shoulder, texting on her cell phone. She was dressed the same as Porcayo, khakis, polo shirt and a yellow HandyMart apron, but somehow managed to make her outfit look provocative and ultra-feminine. She paused in front of the door for a moment, thumbs flying on the tiny keyboard and eyes riveted on the screen. When she looked up and spotted Dean and Porcayo, frozen with the boxcutter held high above their heads, she did a broad, comical double take, bumping backwards into the door.

Sam badged her.

"Official business," Sam said. "I'm gonna have to ask you to step outside, ma'am."

For a second she just stared at Sam, over-glossed lips hanging slackly open.

"Um," she finally said. "Yeah, okay. I'll just… come back later."

She backed out the door, never taking her wide, disbelieving eyes off Dean and Porcayo.

When she was gone, Porcayo let go of the box cutter, letting it clatter noisily to the linoleum. Sam picked up the fallen chair and set it upright. Dean eased up on his grip, and guided Porcayo back to the chair. Porcayo sat, shoulders slumped, hopeless and defeated. He didn't cry. He just sat there, staring at nothing.

"Nobody calls me José," he said, his voice a dull monotone. "Except my mother."

"So what do they call you?" Dean asked.

"Joey," he said.

"Listen to me, Joey," Sam said. "If we're going to stop her, we need you to tell us everything about what really happened on the night of April 18th 1995."

"Look, man, I was there," Porcayo said. "And even I'm not sure what really happened."

Dean and Sam didn't press him, they just waited for him to continue.

"I'm not trying to cop out and say it wasn't my fault," Porcayo said. "But something happened to the four of us that night. Something I can't explain. I've been over it and over it in my head, every night for fifteen years. Trying to understand. I mean, I'm no angel. I got into some trouble when I was growing up. Fights, that kind of thing. But in all my life, I would never hurt a woman. Never."

He got up and walked over to the soda machine. Put in some coins and pulled out a can of cola. Popped it open and took a sip. He didn't sit back down.

"Before my father took off, he used to hit my mother." He looked down at the can in his hand as though the nutritional information was profoundly fascinating. "He hurt her so bad she couldn't have no more children. I was her only son, and she made me swear to her every day that I would never be like him. I have a lot of anger inside me, just like his anger. It's in my blood, and I know I could be like him if I'm not careful. That's why I would never let that anger out on a woman, no matter what. Before I met Irma, I was dating this chick who used to get all crazy, throwing stuff and slapping me. She stabbed me in the arm with a pen one time. I never did nothing back to her, I just walked away. My friends made fun of me for years because of that, but that's how important my promise was to me. I just don't understand how a promise that was so important could go right out the window for no good reason. That poor woman didn't do nothing to me. She was just trying to get away."

"At any point during the attack," Sam said, "did you feel like you were not in control of your body?"

"Yeah," Porcayo said. "That's exactly how I felt. I kept on trying to stop, even just to turn my head away, but I couldn't. It sounds crazy, I know, but…"

"We believe you, Joey," Dean said.

"What can you tell us about what happened after the assault?" Sam asked.

"We…" Porcayo wiped his lips again. "We just left her there. We all had control over our bodies at that point, but… We didn't do anything to save her. We were all so ashamed of what had happened that we just walked away. That still haunts me."

He finished the soda. Crushed the can.

"When we had rounded up all the other migrants in the group, I went back to her. I felt so horrible about what had happened that I went back to try and help her. She was gone. I don't mean dead, I mean gone, like she had never been there. That's when I heard a baby crying. That's when I found Claudia."

"My wife couldn't have kids. She had to have a hysterectomy because of cervical cancer when she was just twenty-three and she thought no man would ever want to marry her. But she was so smart and so pretty. She was my angel, the best thing that ever happened to me. Better than a guy like me deserved." He choked up and had to pause for a moment. "She was so happy when I brought home the paperwork to adopt Claudia. She never knew anything about what really happened. Neither one of them ever knew. I told them her mother died trying to cross the border."

He looked up at Dean.

"Is Claudia in danger?"

"Perhaps," Dean said. "We really have no way of knowing. I don't think so, but I also think it would be a good idea for her to stay with relatives or friends, until we catch this thing."

"You really think you can stop her?" Porcayo asked.

"We're gonna try," Sam said.

TWENTY-FOUR

Dean followed Porcayo's crummy little blue Toyota back to the unremarkable house, while Sam rode with Porcayo to make sure the older man didn't pull a runner. Dean parked the Impala while the Toyota pulled into the garage, slung Xochi's rifle bag over his shoulder, then got out of the car.

By the time Dean got up to the door, Sam already had it open. Porcayo stood beside him.

"Is Claudia here?" Dean asked, handing the rifle bag to Sam.

Porcayo shook his head.

"She's still at school."

"I hate to break it to you," Dean said. "But we saw her come home about an hour ago."

Porcayo frowned. Took a cell phone out of his pocket. Dialed. Waited.

"Where the hell are you?" he said into the phone. "You better call me as soon as you get this message..." He hesitated for a moment. "I'm not mad, *mija*. Just please call okay?"

He ended the call and stared down at the phone, tears welling in his eyes again. He swiped at the tears with his knuckles, gritting his teeth against their onslaught. He raised the phone, clenching it in his fist and looking like he was about to throw it for a moment, but didn't.

"If something happens to her," he said. "Because of me…"

"Why don't we go inside," Dean said.

"Yeah, sure," Porcayo said. "Of course."

The house was generic and unremarkable on the outside, but on the inside the décor was quirky and colorful. It was painfully clear to Dean that the romantic vintage movie posters and charming folk-art had been selected by the late wife. All the funny little wooden animals were dusty, sad and neglected. There was a pair of gaudy red women's reading glasses sitting on the coffee table, next to an empty coffee cup and a paperback romance novel. Dean was pretty sure it wasn't Porcayo's book. Or Claudia's. The room felt like a shrine.

"Can I get you something?" Porcayo asked. "Beer?"

"Yeah," Dean said. "That'd be great."

Porcayo led them into a large kitchen that was overrun with dirty dishes, take out containers and beer cans.

"I'm sorry it's so messy," Porcayo said. "I keep telling Claudia to clean up around here once in a while, but she don't listen."

He shrugged and opened the fridge. Pulled out a six-pack of Budweiser that was one of the only items left inside. Handed a can to Dean, one to Sam and took one for himself, then shoved some of the debris on the counter aside to make room for the remaining three cans.

"What about you?" Sam asked, gesturing at the mound of dishes. "Your arms broken? Don't know how to operate a faucet?"

He looked at Sam with an expression of baffled scorn, as though Sam had suggested he levitate the plates using psychic powers.

Dean cracked his can and sucked down a foamy mouthful.

"You know," he said. "I really don't think we ought to be here, in this house. We probably shouldn't be encouraging the Borderwalker to show up in a residential neighborhood full of innocent families. What if she goes off like she did with that truckful of immigrants? What if Claudia comes home?"

"You're right," Porcayo said. "I couldn't let that happen."

"Okay," Sam said. "So where should we go?"

"I work night security in an office building down in Santa Ana," Porcayo said. "After the cleaning crew goes home, the place is empty until eight the next morning."

"What time do you start?"

"Ten."

"Man," Dean said. "Don't you ever sleep?"

Porcayo shook his head ruefully.

"Not really. I try to take naps between the two jobs, but I get nightmares."

Sam looked at his watch.

"Ten o'clock?" he said. "That's way too late. We need to go somewhere right now."

"We could drive out to the desert," Dean suggested. "Aren't Borderwalkers more likely to show up in the desert?"

"That's not a bad idea," Sam said.

"Listen, guys," Porcayo said. "Are you sure I shouldn't go alone? I mean, she wants me, right? Why not just let her have me?"

"That's very noble," Dean said. "But we have no way of knowing if she'll stop after you and no way of tracking her next victim. This could be our last chance to take her out. Now maybe you feel like you deserve to die for what you did, but those poor people in that truck didn't deserve what happened to them. This creature is totally out of control and we need to stop it."

Porcayo hung his head and put his untouched beer down on the counter.

"I understand, but…" he began.

There was a small sound from the living room. A padded thump like something fell over and landed on the carpet.

"Do you have a cat?" Sam asked.

Porcayo shook his head.

Dean stepped in front of Porcayo and put his hand on the frame of the doorway leading back into the living room. The bright striped sofa had four huge, parallel gashes across the seat cushions, puffs of fuzzy white stuffing bulging out. The paperback romance novel had fallen to the floor.

TWENTY-FIVE

"Oh come on," Dean said. "Couldn't you just wait a few more minutes?"

A hand reached up from behind the couch, too many long hairy fingers like spider's legs clutching the sofa's back. Then another hand, this one looking oddly dissimilar to the first. There was a low, rumbling growl that sounded more like the Impala's engine than a living thing. Dean could feel the sound in his bones and the hair on his arms felt suddenly staticy, like there was a free-floating electrical charge in the air.

"Dean," Sam said, unzipping the rifle bag and handing one of the heavy Atzec weapons to him.

"Where the hell is Xochi?" Dean asked, taking the weapon.

"Not here, obviously," Sam said. "Got any other ideas?"

"I'm sorry," Porcayo said, stepping in front of Dean and through the door to the living room. He said something else in Spanish, his tone emotional and apologetic.

The Borderwalker leapt up onto the back of the sofa, perching like a vulture, bare taloned feet digging into the cushion. She seemed mostly human, but cadaverous and abnormal in the joints. Limbs asymmetrical and covered in patchy snake scales. Eyes matte-black and terrible. For the first time, Dean noticed the tattoo Ojon had mentioned: a lacy black butterfly on the left side of her scrawny neck. She didn't seem to have any other ink. Her long, bony jaw dropped to her chin, that now familiar shriek echoing through the room.

Dean remembered what Xochi had said about connecting emotionally with the Borderwalker's human soul. How she would be rendered vulnerable to normal weapons. He stepped up beside Porcayo.

"Listen to him," Dean said. "He saved your daughter's life."

She looked at Dean with her head tilted like a curious animal. She screamed again and her face shifted first into the face of a coyote, then melted down to a canine skull with only a few shreds of desiccated meat clinging around the empty eye sockets.

"I don't think she understands English," Porcayo said.

"Then tell her in Spanish," Dean said to Porcayo. "Tell her how much you love Claudia."

Porcayo took another step closer to the Borderwalker, hands held palm up, voice soft and calm as he spoke gently to her in Spanish. Meanwhile, Sam was slowly inching around the perimeter of the room, that Aztec Louisville Slugger held low and ready to swing.

The Borderwalker's face shifted again, back to human, but expressionless, features cold and static. Her curly hair was full of dirty feathers. Dean had no way of knowing if Porcayo was getting through to her or not. Dean's hands were sweating, making the wooden handle of the Aztec weapon slick in his grip.

Porcayo took another step, now less that six feet away from the Borderwalker. She could easily pounce on him and tear him to shreds, but he was a rock, utterly fearless. He was a completely different person from the broken man who'd tried to slash his wrists in the breakroom at the HandyMart. Like his whole life had been leading up to this moment. The Borderwalker leaned forward, face a skull again and twisting on a long, vulture's neck as she hooked her long claws into her own chest, tearing at her skin and opening up her ribcage like a book. Inside was a deep, impossible hole, a bottomless well, slick red walls crawling with fire ants. Looking into that hole made Dean feel like he was looking down from the top of a skyscraper. He felt inexplicably sure that he was about to fall into her and had to resist the powerful urge to grab onto something to keep himself from plummeting. That's when the front door opened.

"Dad?"

Claudia stood in the doorway, keys in one hand and a blue raspberry Slurpee in the other.

The Borderwalker's skeletal canine head whipped around at the sound of Claudia's voice. When the Borderwalker saw her daughter, all the monstrosity sluiced off of her like rainwater, leaving behind an ordinary human woman in dusty jeans and a black sweatshirt. She reached out an ordinary hand toward Claudia. Dean could see amazed recognition lighting up Claudia's eyes.

"Mama?" Claudia whispered.

Sam was right there beside the Borderwalker with the obsidian-studded weapon, raising it for a decapitating swing. Claudia saw what he was about to do.

"NO!" she screamed.

Claudia dropped the Slurpee and ran to her real mother, throwing her body in between the Borderwalker and Sam. Sam had to check his swing at the very last second to avoid hitting the sobbing teenager.

For a split second, no one seemed to know what to do. Dean had his own weapon raised but didn't know what he was going to do with it. He tried to think of something to say to make Claudia understand why they couldn't let her mother live, but he couldn't find any words. In that moment, he wasn't really sure he knew why himself.

Then Dean heard a gunshot. He swore and spun toward the sound, weapon at the ready. It took him a second to spot the bullet hole in the large picture window. When he turned back toward the Borderwalker, he saw Porcayo take a crooked, staggering step toward him. There was a perfect, bloodless hole just above Porcayo's right eye. He looked surprised and slightly confused, like he was trying to remember the name of a song playing on a distant radio. He took another step, stumbling like a drunk, and then fell to the carpet.

Before Dean could react, there was another volley of multiple-caliber gunshots, followed by something crashing through the window. Dean leapt reflexively back from the flying glass and saw to his amazement that the something was a woman. A leggy brunette with the lean, sinewy build of a long distance runner. She wore a thin, filmy dress that had been torn to shreds. Her feet were bare.

She immediately rolled into a crouch, eyes wide and hair studded with glittering shards of broken glass.

"Wow, are you okay?" Sam asked, taking a step closer to her.

She hissed at Sam, flashing a mouthful of blood-webbed canine teeth, and leapt at him. As she lunged, she shifted so that by the time she connected with Sam, she was no longer human, but rather an enormous snarling panther. The heavy Aztec weapon was unwieldy for close combat, and Sam furiously wrestled with the beast, trying to kick it back far enough to take a decent swing.

"What the…" Dean managed to say, but was interrupted by Xochi appearing in the broken frame of the window.

"Dean," she cried. "Silver!"

She had marigolds in her hair again and a pistol in each hand, firing with one while simultaneously tossing the other to Dean. Dean didn't need to be told twice.

Xochi's shot had hit the panther woman in the chest and she dropped, shifting as she fell. She was human again by the time she hit the carpet. Xochi stepped up and followed up with an efficient double tap to the fallen shifter's head, but there were three more women coming in fast behind her, all in various stages of transformation. Two of them had guns, firing at the brothers as they ran.

Dean pushed over a large bookshelf for cover and hit the carpet behind it. He picked off one of the shifters with Xochi's pistol while another rolled and dove behind the sofa. The Borderwalker reacted suddenly and violently to this strange invasion, tearing loose from Claudia's embrace and sprouting a thousand scorpion tails, face split open into a howling pit.

"Sam," Dean cried. "Claudia!"

Sam was already on it, pushing Claudia behind him and letting one of the panther women have it with the Aztec weapon. The screeching shifter fell into the coffee table, snapping it in half. Dean finished her with the last silver bullet in the clip.

"Out!" he called to Xochi, holding up the empty gun where she could see it.

She wordlessly pulled a second magazine from one of her pockets and tossed it to Dean. He released the empty and caught the full clip in mid-air, snapping it smoothly into place just in time to fire at the third panther woman. At that point, two more shifters had joined the fray, one going after Sam while the other hung back in the empty window frame, taking potshots at Dean and Xochi. Meanwhile, the Borderwalker was attacking Porcayo's corpse, screaming with unhinged, irrational fury.

Xochi dove across the room and behind the fallen bookshelf, pressing herself up against the wall beside Dean and swapping out her own spent magazine.

"It's good to see you, Dean," she said.

"You too," Dean said. "But who are your little friends?

They aren't Borderwalkers are they?"

"*Nagual*," Xochi said. "They are helping Teo, but I'm not sure why."

"So who else is on the guest list for this little shindig?" Dean asked. "Dracula maybe, or the Creature from the Black Lagoon? Or how about Hitler? Because I don't know about you, but I think this party could use a few more monsters."

"Well…" Xochi began.

That's when Teo walked in through the broken picture window.

TWENTY-SIX

What happened next happened so fast it made Dean's head spin.

Teo leapt on the Borderwalker's back, but instead of ganking her with the obsidian knife, she spoke a rapid gush of words that seemed to form into glowing blue strands, snaring the writhing Borderwalker like a spider's web.

The ceiling above them split wide open, gaping like a hungry gullet and Teo and the Borderwalker fell toward it, spiraling impossibly upward into the void. There was a sound like a thunderclap, like a sonic boom, and they were both gone. The two remaining shifters did a quick fade, transforming into doe deer and taking off through the broken window.

For a few heartbeats, there was just silence in the room as the three hunters waited to see what would happen next. Nothing did.

"What the hell just happened?" Sam asked, checking out a couple of nasty claw-marks on his forearm. He grabbed a crumpled red tablecloth and pressed it to the bleeding wounds.

"Teo has saddled the Borderwalker," Xochi said. "Rode her through the gate into the Borderland between worlds."

"Okay," Dean said, frowning and handing Xochi's pistol back to her. "Why?"

"I don't know," Xochi said, holstering both the pistols. "But I do know this. The Borderwalker's power to transport people and things goes both ways. She can also bring things from the worlds beyond through the Borderland and into our world. I think maybe Teo is planning to unleash something ancient and terrible. We have to find a way to stop her."

"This job's too hard," Dean said to Sam. "Let's be firemen instead."

Sam laughed, shaking his head.

"Where is Claudia?" Xochi asked.

They found her huddled underneath an end table, knees tucked up under her chin and eyes squeezed shut.

"Are you all right?" Xochi asked gently, offering Claudia her hand.

"Don't touch me," the girl responded.

"We need to get out of here," Xochi said. "Now."

Claudia started crying, face buried in her hands.

Xochi looked up at Dean. He could see that she was silently asking him to do something to comfort Claudia, but he wasn't any better at nursing the wounded than she was. Dean had never considered himself the boo-boo kissing type. Normally Dean would have relied on Sam for that kind of emotional aftercare, but in his current soulless state his brother was worse than useless in that department.

"Listen, kid," Dean began, kneeling down awkwardly beside her.

Claudia threw her arms around him, sobbing against his chest.

"Yeah, well…" He patted her back awkwardly, looking up at Xochi. Xochi gave him an encouraging thumbs-up. "Okay, come on, let's get you out of here."

He stood slowly and she stood with him, clinging to him like she was drowning. Xochi and Sam both headed for the broken window frame, Xochi waving for Dean to follow. Dean lifted Claudia in his arms and carried her through the debris, wreckage and bloody carnage that used to be her home.

When he got out to the Impala, his arms full of sobbing teenager, he just stood for a moment, unable to let go of her to get the keys from his pocket.

"I'll drive," Xochi said. "Where are your keys?"

"Yeah," Dean said. "Look, nothing personal, but I don't really like other people driving my car."

Dean could hear sirens in the distance.

"Unless you plan to drive with her in your lap," Xochi said with an arched eyebrow, "you'd better change that policy."

Dean looked over to Sam, who raised his swaddled arm and shrugged. He was clearly way too amused by this exchange to offer any help.

"Right front pocket," Dean said eventually. "But don't touch the stereo."

He lifted Claudia a little higher in his arms so that Xochi could reach into his pocket, trying not to think about how weird and uncomfortable this felt.

Xochi unlocked the Impala's doors and Dean tried to put Claudia down in the back seat, but she clung to him with panicked desperation and he had no choice but to get into the back seat with her. Sam got in the front passenger seat and Xochi slipped behind the wheel.

Xochi revved the Impala and put her in gear, pulling away from the curb. Dean had to resist the urge to watch the road and lecture Xochi on her driving. After a while, Claudia slowly started to wind down, easing up on the death grip she had on Dean. He looked down and saw that the front of his shirt was smeared with black blotches from her runny eyeliner.

"You okay?" he asked her.

She shook her head.

"Would you be?" she asked.

"Believe me, I've been there," he said.

She was looking up at him, black make-up running down her chubby cheeks and eyes narrow and suspicious.

"I lost both my parents to this kind of action," Dean told her.

"What?" Claudia looked away, tears welling back up again. "That's supposed to make me feel better?"

"I'm just saying," Dean told her. "You don't always get to choose what happens to you and your family, but you can choose how you react. Know what I mean? You can either let it chew you up or you can keep fighting no matter what. I chose to keep fighting. Now it's your turn to choose."

Dean could see that his words were getting through to her, but he could also see they were having another, unfortunate side effect. Now she was looking up at him with big puppy-dog eyes.

"Hey Xochi," Dean said, pulling his hand away from Claudia and stuffing it into his pocket. "Why don't you pull into that diner. I think we really need to talk some stuff over. Figure out our next move. There's no point just driving around aimlessly."

Really, he just wanted to get out of the back seat and Claudia's adoring gaze.

"No problem," Xochi said, hitting the turn signal.

She pulled into the first available slot in the parking lot, killed the ignition and tossed the keys to Dean.

"Thanks for trusting me to drive," she said. "It was a real pleasure. This is a beautiful car."

"Don't get used to it," Dean said, pocketing the keys.

This diner was called "ORBIT BURGER," a mid-century classic, all futuristic angles and atomic-age details. The sign was shaped like a rocket ship and the décor inside continued the space-faring theme.

The four of them took a table all the way in the back, as far away from other patrons as they could get. Claudia sat beside Dean in the booth and so Xochi sat opposite her.

Sam took off into the men's room with a first-aid kit while the other three stared at the menus and didn't speak. In the end, none of them actually felt like eating, so they just got coffee. Claudia asked for a chocolate milkshake but then barely touched it. When Sam returned with a neat, white bandage on his arm, he slid into the booth beside Xochi.

Xochi was intensely relieved to be reunited with Dean and Sam. She'd felt sure from the beginning that they needed to stick together and now more than ever, she knew that was true. It had been a hell of a fight trying to make her way back to them. Teo's pet *Nagual* were on her the whole way, hounding her and thwarting her at every turn. What had her sister got herself into?

"Where to begin?" Xochi asked. "This is such a mess."

"First things first," Dean said. "Claudia, where can we take you? Someplace safe, grandparents or friends maybe?"

"I'm not a child," she said. "I'm not going to Grandma's house, I'm going to find my real mother."

"Don't even think about it," Dean said. "You can't…"

"I can," Claudia said. "She's all I have left."

"There's no way…" Dean began.

"It's my choice," Claudia said. She turned to Dean. "I choose, right? You said so yourself."

"Claudia," Dean said. "You have no idea…"

"Don't I?" Claudia picked up her napkin, shredding the edge with a chipped black fingernail. "I know where she is right now. I've always known. And if you won't help me get to her, then I'll go alone."

"You know where she is now?" Sam asked. "Are you sure?"

"Ever since I was little, I've had these…" Claudia looked down at the shredded napkin. "They're like dreams, but they don't always come when I'm sleeping. We have a bond. I can't really explain it. It's like I can see her, my real mother, inside my mind. Her name is Elvia. I bet you didn't know that. Elvia Revueltas."

"No," Dean said. "We didn't know that."

"For the longest time," Claudia continued. "She was lost. Wandering alone, scared and hurting. Then I saw her in Choulic. In San Diego. In Yuma. She was so angry. So angry. I never told anyone about her. They would just say I'm crazy, but I'm not, am I?"

"So where is she now?" Sam asked.

Claudia looked at Sam with a hard frown.

"What, you want me to tell you where she is so you can kill her?"

"I'm sorry, but we have no choice," Xochi said. "What your mother has become, it's unnatural. She needs to be put down, like a sick dog. You have to help us find her."

"No," Claudia said. "Tell them Dean, there's always a choice. Isn't there? Isn't there?"

Dean didn't answer. He had no idea what to say.

"Screw you people," Claudia said, standing up. "I'm not helping you kill my mom!"

An old Mexican man a few booths down looked up over the edge of his Spanish newspaper at Dean and Claudia, frowning.

"Keep your voice down," Dean said.

"Okay, just hang on a second," Sam said. "Please, sit down. I think I have an idea."

Claudia paused warily, then sat cautiously on the edge of the booth, ready to bolt.

"Dean," Sam said. "Remember when you got turned into a vampire?"

Claudia's eyes went wide.

"Oh yeah," Dean said, hard stare locked on Sam with half-buried fury flashing in his eyes. "I remember."

"You're a vampire?" Claudia asked, like she hadn't heard anything else.

Xochi could see that Claudia was rapidly developing a massive crush on Dean. The rush of teenage hormones flooding the booth was thicker than the greasy smoke coming off the grill in the kitchen.

"Whoa, hold on," Dean said. "First of all, being a vampire isn't sexy, okay? Not even a little bit. I'm dead serious. It was one of the worst things that's ever happened to me, and I've been to Hell so you better believe I know what I'm talking about. Second, I'm not a vampire anymore, because…"

He looked up at Sam, suddenly understanding.

"You think there's a way we can cure the Borderwalker?"

Dean turned to Xochi. "Is that possible?" he asked. "To turn the Borderwalker back into a normal human?"

"I don't know," Xochi said. "But I know who would. Huehuecoyotl. If he can tell us how to transform her back into a human, then she will be unable to open a gate between the worlds. She will be useless to Teo."

"Okay," Sam said. "So we talk this coyote dude into giving us a way to cure the Borderwalker, but we'll still need to find her."

"I think she's in Mexico," Claudia said. "Somewhere close to the border, but not Tijuana. I don't know where that woman is taking her, but she's very scared and confused. Promise me you won't hurt her. Please?"

"I cannot promise that," Xochi said. "I won't lie to you, but I can promise to try this other plan first. If we fail, we may have no other choice. This hunt has become so much bigger than simply putting a suffering animal out of its misery. I think my sister is using the Borderwalker for something big. Something terrible."

There was silence for a moment at the table. Xochi could see the gravity of her words sinking in for Claudia but also for Dean. Claudia looked terrified and unsure. Dean just looked grim and determined.

"How about the panther chicks?" Dean asked. "Where do they fit into all this?"

"The *Nagual* are a race of shapeshifting witches," Xochi said. "Both male and female. They can take on various animal forms, but cannot imitate other humans. Not all are evil; it depends on which gods or goddesses they serve. Why they are helping Teo capture the Borderwalker remains to be seen."

"Okay," Sam said. "Next step?"

"We should go to Mexico, find my sister and the Borderwalker," Xochi said. "We can find a place to talk to Huehuecoyotl along the way. But first..." She turned to Claudia. "I need to ask you something important."

"Okay," Claudia said.

"What do you know about the night of your real mother's death?"

"Xochi, come on," Dean said. "Do we have to get into that right now?"

"I have my reasons," Xochi told him. "Please, Claudia, it's important."

"Nothing," Claudia said. "All I know is that she died trying to cross the border. We have this... I don't know what to call it, this weird kind of link, but I can't see anything about what happened to her that night. It's like she's blocking that part from me."

Xochi closed her eyes, pressing her fingers into her temples. She really wished there was some other way to do this. With everything else that Claudia was going through, she didn't need be confronted with her father's awful secret.

"I'm so sorry to ask you this," Xochi said. "But I need information about what happened to your mother, and there are only two people who witnessed her unnatural transformation. One of them is dead, by his own hand. The other is you."

"Me?" Claudia frowned. "But I was just a baby. I don't remember anything about that night."

"You don't consciously remember," Xochi said. "But the memories are there inside your head. I can help you access them if you agree to let me in. I think there is a larger force behind what is happening to your mother. If I can see exactly what went wrong that night, it will help us find who is responsible. Find them and stop them."

"All right," Claudia said quietly. "What do I have to do?"

TWENTY-SEVEN

"I don't know about this," Dean said over his shoulder.

He was back in the driver's seat, where he clearly belonged. Sam rode shotgun, as usual. Xochi was in the Impala's back seat with Claudia. She felt more than a little apprehensive about linking minds with the young girl, but she also knew that the world was full of hurt and heartbreak. No one could be protected from that ugly truth forever.

Xochi herself was hunting full time by the time she was Claudia's age, staring death in the face every single day. More than that, Xochi was beginning to understand that Claudia was going to be a critical piece of the puzzle. As important to the success of the hunt as Sam. Maybe even more important.

"I'm okay," Claudia said.

Xochi hoped she was right.

"Just remember," Dean said. "Your dad—he was a good person. He saved your life. What you see that night, it wasn't really him, okay?"

"Whatever," Claudia said. "I'm fine." She turned to Xochi. "I'm ready."

Xochi gently cupped the back of Claudia's head, pressing her palm to the girl's forehead.

"This may feel... strange," Xochi told her. "Don't fight it, just try to relax."

Then she began to recite the spell, easing her way slowly in.

The first thing Xochi encountered was a flood of memories, not of the Borderwalker, but of Irma, Claudia's adopted mother. A woman with kind hazel eyes and gentle hands. Thick brown hair swept up into a simple twist at the nape of her long neck. A heart-shaped locket on a gold chain. She had an almost ethereal beauty, delicate, girlish and a little too thin, but always smiling. She stood in the kitchen with Claudia's grandmother, cooking a huge pot of *menudo* on Sunday after church. In the backyard wearing a yellow dress, laughing and raising a hand to shade her eyes from the sun. In the living room, reading on the couch with her slim legs curled up underneath her, holding the book far away from her eyes because she refused to "throw money away" on new reading glasses when the ones she had were "perfectly fine." In Claudia's room, helping her make tea for dolls. Her father was there too, winking and pointing to his scratchy cheek, asking for a kiss. Lifting her up so high, seeming impossibly big and strong. Teaching her funny songs with bad words in them and her mother chasing him out of the kitchen with a wooden spoon. Him taking her mother's hand and kissing it.

There were also memories of her mother in the hospital. A skeleton in pink terrycloth, barely breathing and lost in morphine haze. Claudia standing there nauseous and wracked with guilt for wanting to run away. For not wanting to touch that cold, wasted hand. For wishing she'd just hurry up and die already.

Xochi worked her way backwards, moving like liquid flowing through the years. As the memories got older, they became more disjointed, non-linear. Flashes and blurred images that Xochi had to pick apart and decipher. When she came upon what seemed to be a memory of being tucked inside a zipped-up windbreaker, she decided to dig deeper. There were other feelings associated with this memory, warmth and safety and a smell of drugstore aftershave. She worked through the tangled strands of this memory and into what preceded it. That was where she found what she was looking for.

Claudia is alone. Alone and cold and frightened in the middle of the night. Sand under her cheek and scratchy branches and curious insects and she wants to cry but is petrified, frozen in terror. Men are running, huge boots thundering past the place where she is hidden. The men's eyes are all wrong, hot and glowing from within, like cinders. She can see Elvia, her mother. The men are hurting her, kicking her and tearing her clothes. Doing other things that Claudia doesn't understand.

Xochi breathed a sign of relief when she realized that the men in Claudia's memory are just looming monstrous shapes. She carefully kept her own thoughts about the unfolding scene to herself, trying to stay detached as she watched and waited.

The men seem to be finished with Elvia. They step away, one by one, but the last man reaches down and touches her. Touches Elvia on the neck and a terrible dark stain forms, like an inky bruise. The stain takes the shape of wings. A butterfly.

A cold, creeping dread surged through Xochi's veins. How could she have missed all the signs? How could she have been so blind when the answer was right there all along?

The men walk away, heads hung low and eyes no longer glowing, slump-shouldered shadows disappearing into the night. Then, a woman. A tall, silent woman with no clothes on. The woman crouches over Elvia, comforting her and whispering, shifting fluidly from human to coyote and back again. Elvia reaches out to take the woman's hand and the black butterfly on her neck begins to spread like a disease across her pale skin, ugly barbed tendrils that reach out to infect the coyote woman. There is a hole opening in the night sky, a huge pulsing wound between the stars. The coyote woman lets out a shriek of unbearable agony as the black tendrils begin to eat into her flesh like acid, exposing raw, smoking bone. A torrential gush of strange power is flowing like blood from the coyote woman and into Elvia's convulsing body as the two of them slowly levitate into the air, falling away from the bloody sand beneath them. Then the coyote woman bursts into a shower of wet black rags that disintegrate before they hit the sand and Elvia disappears into the wound in the sky, a long crooning howl echoing through the desert night.

Then the big man in the windbreaker, and Claudia zipped up safely inside.

Xochi fought to keep her breathing calm and steady as she gently withdrew, disengaging herself from Claudia's memory. She came slowly back to herself in the back seat of the Impala, taking her hand off Claudia's forehead. The girl's smeary soot-ringed eyes flickered, then opened.

"Trippy," she said. "Was that real?"

"I'm afraid so," Xochi said.

"Well?" Sam asked.

"It is so much worse than I thought," Xochi told him.

"So," Dean said. "Let's hear it."

"It is *Itzpapalotl*," Xochi told them. Just saying the name out loud made her skin crawl. "The Clawed Butterfly. Queen of the *Tzitzimimeh*."

Dean didn't know what he was hoping to hear from Xochi about her spelunking into Claudia's head, but that definitely wasn't it.

"Wait a minute," Dean said. "These zee-zee... whatdayacallits, aren't they those Star Demons you told us about? The soul-eaters?"

"Yes," Xochi said. "Those are the ones. And *Itzpapalotl* is the most powerful of them all. It was she who possessed those men and made them rape Elvia. It was she who put her unclean mark on the dying woman's neck so that her rage would be intensified and her transformation corrupted. I believe she is planning to use Elvia's unnatural power to transport her and her sisters through the Borderland and into our world. The *Nagual* helping Teo are obviously her servants."

"Wait a minute," Claudia said. "Who were those men who attacked my mother? Are those the men she's been hunting?"

"Oh boy," Dean said softly under his breath. "Here we go."

"That's right," Sam said, oblivious to the awkwardness.

"Well, then why did she come after my dad?"

Dean looked at Claudia in the rearview mirror. She wasn't stupid. He could see in her face that she already knew the answer to her own question.

No one said anything. They didn't have to.

"Remember what I told you," Dean said. "Your father saved your life. Hell, he saved all our lives today. He's a good man. What happened that night wasn't his fault."

Dean took one more look in the rearview. Claudia's expression was conflicted, but he knew that there was nothing he more he could do for her. She'd either find a way to come to terms with what her father had done, or she else wouldn't and there was nothing that Dean could say that change that. So he changed the subject instead.

"So, Xochi," he said. "Where does your crazy sister fit into all of this?"

Xochi took a breath. "My family has always worshiped the moon goddess *Coyolxauhqui*," she explained. "All female children are dedicated to her from birth, including Teo. But when she wasn't chosen to be the head of the family, she renounced *Coyolxauhqui* and all things relating to the spiritual realm. She said she cared only for the carnal pleasures of this life. I will never forgive her for what she did, but I still can't imagine her becoming involved with something as loathsome and deadly as the *Tzitzimimeh*. Teo is not evil, she is just misguided."

"I realize that she's family and all," Dean said. "But I got news for you. If she's an active part of a plan to ferry these Star Demons into our world, that's straight-up evil my book."

"I'm with Dean on this," Sam said. "Just a scratch from a dead one's tooth almost killed my brother. What's gonna happen when we have a whole pack of these things on the loose? And not only will we have the *Tzitzimimeh* to contend with, but we'll also have all their soulless, zombified victims running around. Am I right?"

"Right," Xochi said. "It would be the end of civilization as we know it."

"End of civilization as we know it?" Dean asked. "Sam, didn't we just stop an apocalypse last Tuesday? There's gotta be a quota for that kind of thing, right? You know, one per family?"

Dean glanced in the rearview mirror and caught a glimpse of Xochi's face. She wasn't laughing.

"Okay, before we start waxing apocalyptic," Dean said. "A more practical question. Where are we going, exactly?"

"We need to cross the border," Xochi said. "Not Tijuana. Nogales, I think would be best. I have a friend there who can help us."

"I'm tired," Claudia said in a very small voice.

Dean's head was so full of everything he'd just learned that he had almost forgotten she was there. They had to be crazy bringing a young girl like her into a dangerous hunt like this. But without her, he realized, they would never be able to find the Borderwalker in time to stop her from opening the gate for the Clawed Butterfly and her minions. They had to face that Claudia could get killed on this hunt or wait and get killed along with the rest of the human race once the Star Demons had been unleashed. But the fact that they didn't seem to have a choice didn't make the idea of something happening to Claudia on Dean's watch any more appealing.

"Get some sleep, kid," Dean said to Claudia. "It's gonna be a long drive."

TWENTY-EIGHT

Dean stopped for gas just outside Yuma. Sam got out to stretch his legs and Xochi headed off to the ladies' room. Claudia was still out like a light in the back seat. She'd been through so much; her young mind had obviously tapped out. Dean didn't have the heart to wake her.

"Want anything?" Dean asked Sam.

"No, thanks," Sam said.

Dean went into the minimart and walked over to the coffee machine, pulling a large cup from the dispenser below. Xochi came up next to him, taking a cup for herself.

"Milk?" she asked Dean, holding out a handful of single-serve half-and-half containers.

Dean shook his head, filling his cup to the rim with steaming black brew. He watched with amazement as Xochi dumped the contents of a half a dozen of the little containers into her own empty cup, followed by an equally ridiculous amount of sugar.

"Want some coffee to go with your milk and sugar?" he asked, holding out the carafe.

"Just a little," she replied, offering him her cup. "I suppose you think you're more tough than me because you don't put sugar in your coffee."

"No," Dean said. "I'm tougher than you because I know all the lyrics to 'Eye of the Tiger.'"

"Yeah?" Xochi said. "Well, I know all the lines from *Die Hard*. In English and in Spanish."

"I once ganked a demon with a match book and a handful of pocket change."

"Last week I killed six mummies with my *chonies*," she said. "And I was wearing them at the time."

"*Chonies?*"

"You know, panties."

"Damn," Dean said. "You win."

"Good." Xochi smiled. "Then you buy the coffee, tough guy."

Dean laughed and fished out his wallet.

When they got back out to the Impala, Sam was leaning against the back passenger door.

"Xochi," Sam said. "Why don't you ride up front with Dean for a while? I've got a bunch of info here on the *Tzitzimimeh*. I really ought to go over this stuff and see if I can find anything that'll help us."

Dean could see what Sam really was doing, pushing him at Xochi again, but he couldn't be bothered to argue. It's not like Sam was exactly a font of scintillating conversation these days anyway and it wouldn't suck to have someone to talk to for the rest of drive.

Sam settled into the back seat with his laptop and Xochi got in up front. When she reached for the stereo, Dean swatted her hand away.

"Hey, what did I tell you?" Dean asked. "My car, my tunes, okay? Don't like it, buy yourself some ear plugs."

"Why don't you sing 'Eye of the Tiger' for me?"

"Careful what you wish for," Dean said, pulling out of the gas station.

He turned on the radio. Led Zeppelin's "Rock and Roll."

"See, there you go," he said.

Xochi grinned.

"That's just what I would have picked," she said.

To his surprise, she started singing along. Her singing voice was actually pretty good, powerful and a little husky, like whisky and cream.

"Been a long time, been a long time…"

Dean joined in with her, unable to kill the big dumb smile on his face.

"Been a long lonely, lonely, lonely, lonely, time," they sang together.

"Come on, Dean," Sam said from the back seat. Dean could see him rolling his eyes in the rearview. "Do we really need to listen to the theme song for your sexual frustration?"

"Led Zeppelin?" Claudia said, turning her head against the window and covering her face with one arm. "Ugh! That's like total grandpa music."

"Grandpa music?" Dean said. "Look, you two chuckleheads can walk to Nogales."

"What?" Sam asked. "If we don't shut up, you're gonna turn this car right around?"

"That's right," Dean said. "And no ice cream for either one of you."

Dean looked over at Xochi. Her dark eyes were full of mirth, lips curled up in one corner. He shook his head and pulled back onto the highway.

In the back seat, Sam plugged a pair of earbud-style headphones into his laptop and handed them to Claudia. She put them in and smiled. Dean didn't even want to know what kind of musical atrocity was being perpetrated back there. "Rock and Roll" ended on the Impala's stereo and Cream's "Sunshine of Your Love" came on.

"Has it really been that long?" Xochi asked, sipping her coffee.

"What do you mean?" Dean asked.

"You know."

"No," Dean said, answering way too fast. "I mean, not really, no."

"Okay," Xochi said, shrugging.

He looked up in the rearview at Sam. Sam met his gaze for a second, eyebrow raised, before looking back down at the screen of the laptop without comment. His silence was somehow more damning than a snarky retort. Dean had no idea why the whole world had taken a sudden avid interest in his sex life, or lack thereof.

"Dean," Xochi asked. "What did you mean before, when you were talking about stopping an apocalypse?"

"Long story," Dean said. "But I tell you what. If we

succeed in stopping this one, I promise, I'll buy you a dozen drinks and make you sorry you ever asked."

When they finally arrived in Nogales, Arizona, Xochi directed them into a neighborhood that may as well have been on the other side of the border. Dean spotted where they were going before Xochi pointed it out.

Chevy Atzeca. A body shop. The entire wall in front of the place was painted with an enormous mural that depicted a hopping '64 Impala with angel wings, a crying woman in a fedora and the words *Bajito y Suavecito* in ghostly white script. The large metal gate was open, and there was a group of bald, heavily tattooed gangbanger types hanging around in the driveway, eyeballing Dean as he pulled up. One of the young men had a huge blue-gray pitbull on a heavy chain and a gun butt protruding from his waistband

"I don't like this," Sam said from the back seat.

"Relax," Xochi said. "These guys are on our side."

Dean didn't like it either. After all his dire warnings to Sam not to trust Xochi and keep an eye on her to make sure she didn't try to screw them over, he was starting to seriously wonder if that wasn't exactly what she had done.

The guy with the dog strolled over to Dean's window, lifting his goateed chin in an acknowledgment so subtle it was almost unperceptable. The dog sat at his master's side, looking up at Dean with his wide pink tongue out and a dumb, friendly expression that was seriously undermining the whole tough-guy routine.

"'Sup, Xochi," the guy said. He had a heavy accent and spoke like a ventriloquist, lips barely moving. "This Dean Winchester?"

"Yeah," Xochi said. "Dean, this is Lil' Sleepy."

"How you doing?" Dean said. He made himself smile, trying to stay relaxed and casual. The temptation to crack a Snow White joke was almost unbearable, but he somehow managed to keep his trap shut.

"Nice ride," Lil' Sleepy said. "Go on in."

Dean pulled in. The sullen bangers cleared out of their way and then shut the gate behind them.

Although the neighborhood was questionable at best and the outside of the building dilapidated, everything inside the body shop was top of the line, tricked to the nines. In addition to all the standard equipment: compressors, oxy/acetylene torches, and MIG welders, they also had a computer-programmable tubing bender, an automatic tungsten-carbide cold saw, and a brand-new five-station hydraulic ironworker. With equipment like that, they could pretty much build a whole car from scratch. No wonder they had a bunch of armed guys hanging around in the driveway. Just that saw alone was probably worth around a hundred grand.

"You sure about these guys?" Dean asked Xochi quietly.

"Of course I'm sure," Xochi said, looking mildly offended. "I trust Chato with my life. He's a good friend. Works on cars for all the border-town hunters I know. Engines too, not just bodywork."

"Chato?"

A stocky, sawed-off Mexican guy in a grease-stained coverall walked up to Dean's window. He was five-foot-four tops, but he had the single most astounding pompadour hairdo Dean had ever seen. It had to be at least six inches tall, slick and shiny as black glass. He was wiping his filthy hands on a rag, hands that were easily as big as Sam's, if not bigger, and looked weirdly disproportionate on the ends of his short, stubby arms. A name patch on the breast of his coverall read CHATO.

"Beautiful," he said, eyeballing the Impala like she was a naked playmate.

"Dean, Sam, Claudia," Xochi said. "This is Chato Aguilar."

"Pleasure to meet a fellow Chevrolet enthusiast," Dean said.

"327?" Chato asked, hand on the hood.

"Of course," Dean replied.

Chato squatted down and peered underneath the back end of the car with a penlight.

"Your skid plates are looking a little worn," Chato asked. "I could take care of that for you. Hook you up with some sick hoppers too. Just charge you for parts. Any friend of Xochi's…"

"Nah," Dean said. "You know what? I'm good. I'm more of a do-it-yourself kinda guy."

"What we need is a place to crash for a few hours," Xochi said. "And a safe place to leave Dean's car while we're down south."

"You got it," he said. "My shop *es tu casa.* Ashley!"

A bouncy, freckled and slightly buck-toothed blonde in tiny cut-off shorts sauntered in and gave Xochi a big hug, speaking rapid-fire Spanish even though she was clearly white as Wonder Bread. She was also hugely pregnant.

"My wife Ashley," Chato said to Dean.

"Ma'am," Dean said.

"Hi," she said with a toothy smile. "You guys hungry? We got the grill going out back."

"Sounds fantastic," Dean said.

"Thanks," Sam said.

Claudia didn't say anything. She still seemed kind of shut down, moving like an automaton.

"You hungry, kid?" Dean asked her.

She shook her head.

Ashley came over to Claudia, a concerned, motherly look on her face.

"You okay, honey?" she asked.

"I'm tired," Claudia said.

"Lemme get a bed made up for you," Ashley said, putting an arm around the girl. "The rest of you, go on out back. Grab a couple of beers and help yourself to some *carné asada.*"

Dean was tremendously relieved to have someone with real mom-skills take over the job of dealing with the traumatized teenager. He was more than ready to get back to doing something he was actually good at. Like drinking beer.

TWENTY-NINE

Dean woke to find himself sprawled out on a sofa with a bare female foot pressed against his cheek. The foot was attached to a slender, tattooed ankle, which in turn was attached to Xochi, fully dressed and currently passed out facing the opposite way on the sofa. She had fallen asleep with her gun-belt on. Dean wondered if he was getting close to some kind of personal record for the number of nights spent sleeping with a woman that he wasn't actually sleeping with.

The sofa was inside a small office. Sam sat at the cluttered desk, engine parts and order forms shoved aside to make room for his laptop. Posters of sexy women posed with sexy cars covered the wall behind him. There was a coffee machine sitting on a low table beneath the single window, nearly full and busily belching out fragrant steam. Dean extracted himself from under Xochi's legs, got himself relatively vertical and shuffled like a zombie toward the coffee.

"Oh look," Sam said when he noticed that Dean was up. "It walks among us."

Xochi made a low, pained groan and put one of the cushions from the sofa over her head.

Dean poured coffee into a cup emblazoned with the *Lowrider Magazine* logo and took a slug.

"Where's the john?" he asked.

"Through there," Sam said, indicating a doorway on the far side of the room. "But there's no door."

"Great," Dean said, looking over his shoulder at the semi-conscious Xochi. "Watch her."

Dean managed to rid himself of about ten gallons of recycled beer without waking Xochi. When he came back into the office, he saw that she had her eyes open, peering blearily out from under the cushion.

"You are a bad person, Dean Winchester," she said, slowing sitting up and pushing her tangled hair back from her face.

"I'm a bad person?" He walked over to the coffee machine and poured her a cup, loading it up with milk and sugar. "You're the one who started with the mezcal."

He handed her the cup and then topped up his own.

Xochi reached into her back pocket, pulled out a flat silver flask and added a generous knock to the coffee. She held the flask out to Dean.

"Hell yeah," Dean said, offering his cup.

"*Salud*," Xochi said, pouring a shot into his cup.

Sam made an exasperated noise, shaking his shaggy head.

"You know, I used to think it was kinda cute how similar you two are," he said. "Now, not so much. It's hard enough dealing with one Dean every day."

"I'm not like him," Xochi said, standing and pocketing the flask. "*He* is like *me*."

"Except," Dean said, smirking. "Well… you know." He frowned. "Hey, wait a minute. You're not really a dude, are you?"

Xochi laughed.

"Of course not," she said. "That's why I'm clearly the superior version."

"I won't argue with you there," Dean said. "I like your version better, too."

Xochi glanced through the open doorway into the bathroom.

"Is there no door on the toilet?"

"Yeah," Dean said, flapping his hand in the general direction of the other door. "You know what? I'll just… be out there. Sam? Sam!"

Sam looked up from his laptop screen.

"Oh yeah, right," he stood and followed Dean out into the garage.

If Dean thought it was hard to leave the Impala at the California border for one night, he was even less thrilled about leaving it with a near stranger for who knew how long.

"Are you sure about this?" Dean asked Xochi yet again as he watched Chato cover the Impala with a tarp. "I mean, I'm not gonna come back for my car and find she's got six-inch-tall windows and an Aztec warrior painted on the hood?"

"I'm sure," Xochi said. "She is in good hands."

Dean believed her, but he still called Bobby and gave him the address of the garage.

"Just in case," Dean said into the phone.

"In case what?" Bobby asked. "In case you go and get your dumb ass killed?"

"Well, yeah," Dean said. "Or something like that."

"What the hell are you two up to down there anyway?" Bobby asked.

"Something big," Dean said. "Don't wait up."

He ended the call.

Xochi was in the midst of hooking a trailer with two dirt bikes to a beat-up brown Land Rover.

"Where'd you get these?" Dean asked.

"The bikes are mine," Xochi said. "I won them in a poker game a few months back. The Rover..." She shrugged, tipped her chin toward Lil' Sleepy, who was noisily demonstrating his name, snoring in an old bucket seat propped up against a stack of tires. "It belongs to Lil' Sleepy. He sold it to me last night for a dollar and a bottle of mezcal. We'd better get going before he wakes up."

"Forget I asked," Dean said. "What are we gonna need dirt bikes for anyway?"

"We will need to go out into the deep desert to call Huehuecoyotl," she said. "These will be much faster than hiking, and with the Borderwalker on the move, every minute counts."

Claudia appeared from a back room, looking worn and rumpled but determined.

"How you doing?" Dean asked.

"Okay, I guess," she said. She looked Dean over. "Rough night?"

"What would you know about something like that?"

She rolled her eyes dramatically.

"I'm not stupid," she said. "I'm not a virgin either."

"You know what?" Dean said. "I do not need to know that."

Sam came out of the office, gear packed up and ready to go.

"Are we gonna have a problem crossing the border?" Sam asked.

"Claudia," Xochi asked. "You have your passport?"

Claudia nodded.

"We used to go visit my dad's relatives in TJ every weekend," she said. "I always have it."

"They are never very concerned with people going out," Xochi said. "Only coming in."

"Yeah," Dean asked. "But what about the stolen car?"

"Stolen car?" Claudia asked.

She looked impressed. Sam looked annoyed.

"It's not stolen," Xochi said. "I bought it and Ashley did up all our paperwork for us last night. Registration, vehicle permit and tourist card. Mexican insurance. That kind of thing. Anyway that's not our main problem. Our main problem is that we cannot bring any weapons."

"What?" Dean shook his head. "No way."

"Listen to me," Xochi said. "Coming in, they search for drugs and people. Going out, it's money and guns."

"I'm not going into this hunt naked," Dean said. "That's just crazy."

"I know a guy," she said. "He'll hook us up on the other side of the border, but for now, this is the way it has to be."

She unbuckled her gun-belt and walked over to the tarped Impala, holding out her hand to Dean for the keys. He reluctantly gave them to her. She pushed back the tarp and popped the trunk, lifting the false bottom and adding her pistols to the rest of the arsenal. Then she held out an empty hand to Dean, fingers curling inward in a "gimme" gesture.

"Oh no," Dean said.

"Oh yes," Xochi said. "Trust me on this. It would be different if we were crossing on foot, but we need the bikes and CBP is much more careful with vehicles because they are more likely to carry a large shipment of contraband. You can keep any bladed weapons, just nothing that the gun dogs can smell."

"Dammit," Dean said, slapping his beloved Colt 1911 into Xochi's outstretched palm.

"Sam?"

Sam nodded and handed over his own .45.

"Ammo too," Xochi said.

Sam and Dean emptied their pockets into the trunk of the Impala while Claudia looked on with amazement at the growing pile of weapons.

Once they were all stripped down and harmless as civilians, Xochi closed the trunk and tossed Dean the keys.

"I hate this," Dean said.

"Don't be scared," Xochi said, with a sarcastic smile. "I'll be here to protect you."

"Let's get on the road, already," Sam said.

THIRTY

Getting across the border was more boring that stressful. Traffic was backed up and creeping along. Guys with dogs and mirrors on sticks strolled up and down the lanes, peering in through windshields. People in the cars had that dull, thousand-yard stare you see in any morning rush hour anywhere in the world. There were traffic lights over each lane, either red or green. If you got a red light you had to go get a full inspection. Dean got a green light. No problem.

When they finally made it through to the other side, they passed underneath a big sign that read "*Bienvenido a Mexico.*" Xochi directed Dean onto the astoundingly named Periférico Luis Donaldo Colosio Murrieta, bypassing the more touristy shops and cheap pharmacies and heading down into the gritty heart of the other Nogales.

"Pull over here," Xochi said, indicating a large, bland franchise hotel that seemed set up to cater to foreign business travelers.

Dean did as she requested, though it was easier said than done. He had to battle several mobile vendors, a pair of kids engaged in a scrappy fist-fight and a swearing woman in a pick-up truck, in order to get the Rover to the curb.

"Sam, take Claudia and check into that hotel," Xochi said. "I don't want her anywhere near the business Dean and I will be doing, but I also don't want her to be alone. The truth is, you two are much more important to this hunt than we are. I can't risk anything happening to either one of you."

Sam frowned. "Am I gonna get arrested for trying to check into a hotel with a fifteen-year-old girl?"

Xochi shook her head ruefully.

"Not in Mexico," she said. "In fact, you probably won't be the only one."

"I hate it here," Claudia said, arms crossed and slouching in an elaborate expression of distaste. "It's worse that TJ. It's gross and dirty and my phone doesn't work." She reached out and put her hand on Dean's arm. "Why can't Dean stay with me?"

"No," Dean said, pulling away from her. "You know, I can't. See, I really gotta… go do this other thing right now. You'll be fine with Sam."

"We won't be long," Xochi said. "Go on." Xochi handed her backpack to Claudia. "Hold on to my things for me. We'll bring back some fresh clothes for all of us too, okay?"

Sam got out of the car and led the theatrically pouting teenager over to the hotel. Dean watched Sam push the door open and let Claudia go ahead of him. It really did look bad, this Gigantor American with no luggage leading a tiny Mexican teenager into a border-town hotel. What made it worse was that there were tons of people around, not bangers or obvious criminals, just ordinary citizens going about their daily business and no one even looked twice.

Once Sam and Claudia were safely inside the hotel, Xochi got out of the back seat and came around to the driver's side.

"Better let me drive," she said.

Dean was happy to let her take the wheel. Driving in this town was like a bad video game. He slid across to the passenger side and she got in behind the wheel.

"What are we doing again?" he asked.

"You want guns, don't you?" she asked, pulling the Rover out into traffic and heading south, away from the border. She took a few, seemingly random turns, laying on the horn to clear dogs and ice-cream vendors and women with huge carts of laundry out of their way. Dean tried to keep a fix on where they were in relation to the hotel, but soon got utterly turned around in the chaos.

Eventually, Xochi turned down a narrow side street and parked. There was a tiny hair salon that didn't look open across the street and some other sort of establishment whose business wasn't immediately obvious to Dean. The building they wanted was a sad, crumbling little structure that seemed too square and featureless to be a private house, but too small to be any kind of commercial building. It was painted bright blue, the thick paint cracked and peeling to reveal an earlier, pink-and-white birthday-cake color scheme. The doors and windows were heavily barred, the bars painted pink to match the previous color scheme and never redone. All the streets they'd been down so far were jumping with pedestrians, but this street was nearly deserted.

Xochi pulled out her cell and dialed. Spoke a few words, nodded and pocketed the phone.

"He's there," she said. "Let's go."

She got out of the Rover and Dean did the same. Dean watched as she called a kid who looked about Ben's age over to the car. She started doling out money, pointing to the car. The kid winked and lifted his T-shirt, revealing the handle of a gun protruding from the waistband of his jeans. Xochi thanked him and then motioned for Dean to go with her into the blue building. He followed close behind her, not happy to be going into something like this unarmed. Especially because everyone else seemed to be armed except for him. He had no choice but to trust Xochi on this.

They entered a dim, musty hallway lined with about twenty electric meters. It seemed impossible to Dean that a building so small could house so many different households. Xochi headed to the back and took a set of sagging stairs up to the second floor. Dean followed without comment.

The first door at the top of the stairs was open. Xochi went right in and motioned for Dean to join her. She shut the door after him and turned a key that had been left sticking out of the lock.

It was an empty room, empty except for a tall, wiry man in his late thirties with a stoned, beatific smile and a black duffle bag. Thinning hair slicked back into a rat-tail, a large, broken nose and a pinkie ring. He wore immaculate, sharply pressed jeans and a shiny red cowboy shirt unbuttoned at the throat to reveal way too much werewolf chest hair. His dinner-plate-sized belt-buckle had the letters "BM" spelled out in red rhinestones.

"Dean," Xochi said. "This is Baby Malo."

Dean couldn't imagine why anyone so hairy would be nicknamed "baby" anything but he was willing to roll with it. The guy seemed friendly enough.

He said something to Xochi in Spanish and then switched to English. "I couldn't get HKs. Glock okay?"

"Did you get the Benelli?" Xochi asked.

He said something else in Spanish and unzipped the bag, pulling out a gorgeous, brand-new 12-gage tactical M4 in desert camo. He handed it to Dean.

"Damn that's nice," Dean said, checking the chamber and finding it hot and ready to rock. "I take it this isn't loaded with salt, right?"

Xochi shook her head, taking a Glock 17 from the bag and looking it over.

"Standard rounds, yes, but I have a friend in Chihuahua who makes 12-gage slugs in solid silver. For the *Nagual.*"

Dean whistled.

"Yeah, that'll do it."

There was a sudden heavy pounding on the door. Dean spun reflexively toward the sound and Xochi did the same. Baby Malo didn't wait to see who it was, just took off through a door on the far end of the room, leaving the bag behind. A deep, masculine voice called out from the other side of the door. It needed no translation.

"*POLICIA!*"

Dean swore and lowered the shotgun. Of all the potential problems he might have imagined they'd encounter on this hunt, getting arrested for buying guns in Mexico certainly wasn't one of them.

"What do we do?" Dean asked Xochi.

"Come on," she said, grabbing the bag of guns and taking off after Baby Malo.

The next room was furnished, two small beds, a sofa and a card table with four chairs. There was so much furniture that it was hard to maneuver in the narrow space. Xochi jumped up onto the couch, walking across the cushions and heading for a barred metal door that seemed to lead to some kind of balcony. Dean could hear the door back in the other room splintering. The cops would be in any second. He followed Xochi out onto the balcony, and found her with one leg over the railing.

"Jump," she said, and was gone.

Dean looked over the edge and saw a weedy little yard surrounded by high brick walls. There was a weird plastic ride-on toy for kids sitting in the corner, a large yellow duck with wheels and a saddle like a horse. Xochi crouched in the middle of the yard with the Glock in one hand and the bag in the other.

"Hurry," she hissed.

It sounded like the cops were through the door and into the empty room next door. Dean didn't need any more incentive. He jumped.

He hit the packed dirt hard but managed to hold onto the shotgun. Xochi kicked open a door on the ground level and Dean followed her back into the building. He could hear heavy-booted footsteps upstairs and men's voices. That's when his phone started to vibrate in his pocket.

Xochi was trying several doors and finding them all key locked. Dean took out his phone and looked at the screen. It was Bobby Singer, calling on the line that he only used in case of dire emergency. Dean took the call.

"It's not a good time, Bobby," Dean said.

"Are you crazy?" Xochi said, looking back over her shoulder before starting to kick at one of the locked doors. "Put that away!"

"Dean," Bobby said, his familiar drawl dropping in and out. "What the hell's going on down there?"

"Look," Dean said. "I got a major law enforcement situation here…"

"Yeah," Bobby said. "Well, I just got a call from your brother's phone. Some Mexican guy telling me to wire twenty-five grand or they'll kill Sam."

THIRTY-ONE

Xochi kicked the door one last time and it finally gave. On the other side was a single cop.

He looked about eighteen. Bad skin and a sorry, adolescent excuse for a moustache. He was dressed in black fatigues and a black Kevlar vest with "*POLICIA*" in big yellow letters. He looked like a startled cat, AK47 pointed at his dusty boots.

Xochi dove back, away from the door. Dean dropped the phone and reflexively raised the shotgun, drawing a bead between the kid's eyes.

"Dean?" Bobby's tiny voice echoed from the phone on the floor near Dean's boot. "Dean, you there?"

The kid looked absolutely terrified, nearly cross-eyed staring down the barrel of the big gun. This was their chance to get away, but Dean couldn't help remembering what he'd said to Sam about ganking innocent humans. He just couldn't pull the trigger.

Six other officers came barreling down the stairs, pouring in behind the kid and screaming at Dean in Spanish. An older guy with a real, grown-up moustache stepped into the room, ripping the shottie out of Dean's grip and throwing him against the wall.

Xochi let out what was probably a colorful string of Spanish profanity and dropped the Glock before another officer did the same to her, kicking her legs apart and patting her down with obvious enthusiasm. The nervous kid picked up Dean's phone, ending Bobby's call and slipping the phone into a zippered plastic bag. The guy with the thick moustache cuffed Dean and led him out of the building.

Out on the sidewalk, three more officers had wrestled Baby Malo to the ground. One of them had a knee pressed into the small of his back and was cuffing him, while another pressed a handgun to his head.

Dean was unceremoniously stuffed into the back of a dirty-white police cruiser. Officer Moustache didn't bother to cup the back of Dean's head to stop him from banging it into the door frame. As tense as he was about his own situation, Dean couldn't think about anything except Sam. Sam, and Claudia. Where was Claudia during all this? Did the people who had Sam also have Claudia? It had clearly been a serious mistake to bring her with them. Maybe a fatal mistake.

The cops put Baby Malo in the back of the cruiser with Dean.

"No, no, wait a second," Dean began.

They didn't wait a second. They just slammed the car door and rapped on the roof to tell the driver to take off.

As the cruiser pulled out into traffic, Dean twisted back to see Xochi being led out of the building between two big bruisers.

"Where are they taking Xochi?" Dean asked.

"Jail," Baby Malo said. "Just like us. Only it'll probably take her, like, twice as long to get there."

"What?" Dean tried to look back again, but they'd already turned a corner. "What do you mean by that?"

"I mean those guys will want to spend some time with her before they bring her in. That's how it is with women prisoners."

If Dean's hands weren't cuffed behind his back, he would have put his head in them. How had this happened?

Dean and Baby Malo stood together in a crowded holding cell inside the Nogales police station. There were probably twenty-five men in the ten-by-ten cage made of flimsy chain-link fencing. Several rattling electric fans did their best to circulate the stale air, but it was still unbearably hot and stank of stale sweat and urine. Outside the cage were three hostile, perspiring guards with automatic rifles—in case anyone got the idea that it might not be that hard to pull the chain-link loose from the connecting poles.

There was a single long metal bench along the left side of the cell, but it seemed to be "reserved" for the small group of tattooed bangers who guarded it like dogs and wouldn't let anyone else anywhere near it. As soon as they had entered, Dean noticed a strange kind of hierarchy in the cramped space. Those higher up on the food chain were allowed to stand closer to the door, where you could almost catch a whiff of fresh air coming from the distant windows. Those at the other end of the spectrum were forced to hang out beside the long cement trough in the floor that stood in for a urinal, slanting down to a stinking hole in the far corner of the floor. Baby Malo was somewhere in the middle and Dean, by association, was allowed to stand beside him. Dean didn't even want to think about what would have happened to him if he had been alone.

Dean wished there was room enough to pace. He was feeling anxious, frustrated and impotent. Even though he knew it would be a terrible idea, he was itching for someone to pick a fight with him, just to give him something to do with his hands, and somewhere else to take his head. There was no worse feeling in the world than knowing your friends and family were in danger and not being able to do a damn thing about it. He'd just have to count on Bobby to stay on it until Dean could find a way to get himself out of this mess.

"You know," Dean said to Baby Malo, just to say something, "I could have happily lived the rest of my life without ever experiencing this particular odor."

"This here is the high-roller suite," Baby Malo said. "Wait till they process you and move you into the real cells."

"This is seriously screwed, is what it is," Dean said.

"You're telling me?" Baby Malo said. "This is my third time for weapons."

"It's not just that," Dean said. "I think somebody kidnapped my brother."

"That's messed up," Baby Malo said, heavy eyebrows drawn together in a frown. "Your people better pay."

"That's why I've got to get the hell out of here," Dean said.

"What's your brother look like?" Baby Malo asked.

"Big." Dean indicated Sam's approximate height in the air, several inches above his own. "Six-four, 190. Brown hair, kinda longish. He was with a young Mexican-American girl with a bright-red streak in her hair."

"Six-four?" Baby Malo's frown deepened. "Doesn't exactly sound like an easy snatch."

"Look, I don't know anything here," Dean said, frustration closing his throat and making his voice tight. "All I know is what I heard."

"Okay, listen," Baby Malo said. "Lemme ask around a little. See if anyone has maybe heard something about it."

Baby Malo moved through the crowd, talking low out of the corner of his mouth. Dean stood alone, clenching and unclenching his fists. Sam and Xochi were both perfectly capable of taking care of themselves, but he couldn't stop obsessing over where they were or what was happening to them. And what about Claudia? It made him absolutely crazy to be locked up like this.

Baby Malo worked his way back to Dean, shaking his head.

"Nobody knows nothing," Baby Malo said. "No word of any big *Norteamericano* getting snatched by any of the usual gangs."

A gruff male voice called out Dean's name.

"Winchester?"

Two handsome, stone-faced Mexican guys who could have been twins were waiting on the other side of the door to the cage. Their get-up was remarkable similar to the uniforms of the police and armed guards. Black, military-style combat fatigues, bulletproof vests and black ball caps. The only obvious difference was that the now familiar word *POLICIA* on their caps was followed by the word "*FEDERAL.*"

"*Federales?*" Baby Malo whispered. "You in deep now, *guero.*"

"Take care of yourself," Dean said. "And thanks."

"You the one who better take care," Baby Malo replied.

Dean came forward as the guard unlocked the door. There were some comments from the bangers on the bench, but Dean had no idea what any of it meant. The *federales* cuffed Dean again and led him through the sweltering station, out into the street. He was sizing up his captors and the street around them, seriously considering just making a crazy break for it when he spotted Xochi in the back of a big black SUV. Her head was down, hands obviously cuffed behind her back. He was glad to see her, relieved she was okay, but seeing her made him worry even more about Sam and Claudia.

The twins stuck Dean in the back seat with Xochi and then got into the front. The front and back of the SUV were separated by a heavy wire-gauge screen. There were no handles on the inside of the two back doors.

Dean was appalled to see Xochi sporting a shiny new black eye. Her shirt was torn and soaked with blood.

"Damn," Dean said. "What did they do to you?"

"Don't worry," she said. "Most of this isn't my blood. Those cops picked the wrong little girl to play with."

Her voice sounded a little slushy, like she had a mouthful of marbles. He was kind of surprised when she leaned into him like she was about to kiss him on the cheek. But she didn't kiss him, she whispered in his ear.

"These men are not *federales*," she said, so softly he could barely hear her over the grumbling of the engine. "They are *Nagual*."

THIRTY-TWO

Dean was too stunned to speak. They'd barely been in Mexico for six hours and things were already going to hell at the speed of light. The traffic along the main drag was horrible, snarled up and inching along so slowly that they were being regularly passed by pedestrians. There was some sort of massive accident up ahead and tempers were flaring hot, people hanging out of their cars and shaking their fists. The stench of exhaust made Dean's eyes burn, even with all the windows rolled up.

"Where are they taking us?" Dean whispered.

"They are probably planning to take us out into the desert and kill us," she said. "But don't worry."

She did something so peculiar then, that for a minute Dean had no idea how to respond. She bent down and pressed her lips to the palm of one of his cuffed hands. He felt the heat of her breath and a brief flicker of her tongue against his skin that sent chills down his sweaty back. He really didn't need to add vaguely, pointlessly, horny to the stew of anger and fear and worry already churning in his aching belly. It took him several baffled seconds to realize what she had actually done: She'd spat something into his hand. Something small and metal. A key. A handcuff key.

"Will you marry me?" he whispered, twisting his fingers and working the key into the lock on his cuffs.

She smiled. "Get your cuffs off," she said. "Then hand me the key and follow my lead, okay?"

He did as she requested, keeping an eye on the twins in the front. They both remained silent, facing forward. When she had freed herself from her own cuffs, she leaned into him again.

"Are you ready?" she asked.

"As I'll ever be," he replied.

She sat completely still, eyes wide and watching a battered minivan pull up on the driver's side of their SUV. The minivan inched ahead of them, just enough so that its dented flank blocked the driver's side door from opening but not the rear door. Dean already knew how fast Xochi was, but it still amazed him to watch her in action. She kicked out the back window, reached through the hole to open the door from the outside and took off down the busy street in the time it took Dean to suck in a single breath.

The guy driving hit the breaks, swearing and trying to open his door. It opened a little less than six inches and then banged into the minivan. The guy on Dean's side was already out and drawing down on Xochi's running back with some kind of preposterous Dirty Harry hand cannon.

"Get down!" Dean yelled, diving out of the SUV and taking off after Xochi. He heard shots and the screams of bystanders as everyone in the street ran for cover.

Dean risked a look back and saw that the driver had climbed across the seat and out the passenger side. He had a snub-nosed pistol in his fist. It looked like a toy next to the cannon wielded by his clearly overcompensating buddy.

Up ahead, Xochi was zigzagging like a rabbit through the frozen traffic, staying low and never providing a clear target.

Dean could see bullets striking sparks off an abandoned cab a few feet ahead of him and before he could register how dangerous that was, the cab went up in a toxic cloud of choking black smoke and shimmering flame.

Dean threw himself down on his belly between two cars just as the cab blew with a strangely flat, eardrum-crushing sound like giant clapping wool-gloved hands. Dean felt like that same giant had just boxed his ears.

When he dared to look up again, Dean saw mad chaos all around. Women grasping crying children, running through the street. Men leaning out of windows to see what was going on. A dozen small retail stands had been knocked over. People selling corn-on-the-cob, bootlegged DVDs and magazines, toys and cheap silver jewelry all had their wares scattered into the street. Dean could see Xochi peeking up between a beater hatchback and a more fortunate taxicab and ran toward her.

When he reached her, she gripped his hand and pulled him toward the debris of the street vendors.

"They won't change their form in front of all these people," Xochi said. "So we have a chance to outrun them. But I have a better idea."

She ran through the broken mess of plastic toys, looking back over her shoulder toward the twins, almost daring them to follow her. Of course, they did. As she ran, she scooped up a black-velvet tray of cheesy silver rings and pendants.

"Put these on," Xochi said as they ran, handing Dean a handful of rings. "Both hands."

He got what she was planning almost right away, so he did as she'd said, cramming as many goofy pot-leaf and skull rings as he could fit onto all his fingers. Moments later, she ducked into a little bakery and Dean followed close behind.

Inside the bakery, two older women were decorating a wedding cake. One was fat and sweet-faced, wider than she was tall with white hair coiffed into a fancy updo and wearing a floral apron. The other was pale and thin with a large, narrow nose, dyed red hair cut mannishly short and pink T-shirt that said "SEXY" in glittery silver letters. When they saw Dean and Xochi, they froze, pastry bags full of pearly white frosting held up like weapons.

Xochi asked them something in Spanish, and the fat one responded, indicating a door in the rear of the store. Xochi ran for the door, which opened into a narrow back alley full of trash and illegible graffiti.

"When the first guy comes through the door," Xochi said, flattening herself out against the wall. "Let him have it."

"Right," Dean said, pressing his back to the opposite side of the door and trying to keep his breathing under control.

He was still scared, but it was the good kind of scared. The action, adrenalin-fueled kind of scared, rather than the trapped, helpless kind of scared he'd been feeling since the arrest. This was what he was good at, kicking monster ass. He had this.

The first *Nagual* came barreling through the bakery door and Dean spun toward him, firing off a straight right and aiming for exposed skin, for the guy's unshaven chin. He connected, a spike of hot pain jolted his wrist, but the guy went down like he'd been shot, skin burning and blistering from the impact of the silver rings. Dean dropped to one knee beside him and followed through with a few more for good measure.

When the second shifter came through the door, Xochi garroted him from behind with a thick silver chain. The silver smoked and burned like it was molten hot, sinking deep into the flesh of the *Nagual's* throat. He fell to his knees, then collapsed on one side in the slimy gutter. Xochi let him go and relieved him of the enormous gun, which turned out to be a Smith & Wesson model 500 .50 caliber Magnum. Dean took the snub-nosed .38 from the shifter he'd KO'd and swiftly patted him down for other weapons. He found a full-sized .45, a nasty-looking telescoping baton, a Leatherman multipurpose tool that would definitely come in handy, and a flint knife kind of like Xochi's, only this one had a hideous, skull-faced woman carved into the handle.

"Leave the *Nagual* knife," Xochi said. She had found a similar one on her shifter and let it drop to the pavement like it was rotten. "It is unclean. An instrument of evil."

Dean looked the flint knife over. Shrugged. Let it drop.

The two ladies from the bakery stuck their heads out the back door, expressions curious. Xochi said something that sounded apologetic. The sweet-faced one in the floral apron leaned over and spat on the prone body of the shifter who'd been garroted.

"*Pinchés federales!*" she said.

Dean had to stifle a laugh.

"Wow," he said. "How does she really feel?"

"People here have no love for the *federales*," Xochi told Dean. "Many are corrupt, tied in with the drug gangs." She leaned in closer to drop her voice and whisper. "It's better if grandmas like these two don't know what these men really are. Safer for them."

Dean got it. He nodded.

"Let's get the hell out of here," he said.

THIRTY-THREE

As they made their way on foot back to the hotel, Dean filled Xochi in on what was going on with Sam. She was furious; she looked ready to slug someone. Anyone.

"Dean," she said, hand on his arm and looking up at him with emotion leaking around the edges of her intense gaze. "We'll find Sam. I swear to you, on my mother's soul. I won't let anything happen to him."

Dean nodded and looked away, thinking of what had happened to Xochi's own little brother. Hoping she was right.

"This is my fault," she said, pressing a clenched fist to her temple. "So stupid of me. We should have stayed together."

"Yeah," Dean said. "But what would have happened to Claudia if she'd been arrested with us? Maybe you can fight off those scumbags with your bare hands, but I doubt she could. Maybe it was wrong to bring her at all."

"Well," Xochi said. "Better she be with us than following her mother on her own. Besides, I didn't say anything because I didn't want to scare her, but the *Nagual* will be tracking her by now. They know she is our link to the Borderwalker and they will want to take her out."

Dean felt like bad luck was shadowing him everywhere he turned and sloshing over onto everyone around him. It seemed like anybody he'd ever set out to protect always ended up worse off than they would have been if they'd never met him.

Xochi stopped on the way to buy a pair of prepaid cell phones from a small electronics shop and gave one to Dean.

"Call your friend Bobby," she said. "I will make some calls and see what I can dig up about who might have taken Sam."

Dean turned on the phone and dialed Bobby.

"You touch a hair on that boy's head, so help me..." Bobby said.

"Bobby," Dean said. "Take it easy, it's me."

"Dean," Bobby said. "Jeez, what the hell happened to you?"

"Got arrested," Dean said. "But I released myself on my own recognizance. Xochi's with me."

"Who?"

"Yeah, well never mind that now," Dean said. "What have you heard from the people who have Sammy?"

"Nothing since that first call."

"Did you wire the money?" Dean asked.

"Not yet," Bobby said. "Not that I've got that kind of money laying around, but they've given me till midnight and I didn't want to do anything until I heard back from you. I tried calling the American Consulate to see if there was any way to spring you, but they've been giving me the runaround."

"Okay, just hang tight, man," Dean said. "Xochi's making inquiries."

"So who is this Xochi person anyway?"

"Long story," Dean replied.

"A female kinda story?"

"What the hell does that have to do with anything?" Dean asked.

"Oh, nothing," Bobby said. "It's just nice to hear that you're getting back into the action."

"Bobby," Dean said. "I'm hanging up now. I have to find my brother."

He ended the call.

Xochi was talking a mile a minute into her phone as they rounded the corner and came upon the hotel where Sam and Claudia were supposed to be holed up. She ended her call and cranked up her pace, nearly running to the double glass doors.

"I'm not finding anything yet," she said. "But I'm not giving up. Let's go in and see if maybe Claudia is still here."

The lobby of the hotel was a strange sort of mash-up of bland, corporate franchise and bizarre, over-the-top local color. There were a few stray, striped polyester couches that looked like they'd been stolen from a Best Western in Scranton back in 1981. When Dean looked closer, he noticed that they were the same approximate color scheme, but didn't exactly match. The carpet was hot pink, which also didn't exactly match. Framed swap-meet paintings cluttered the walls, a strange, incompatible mix of gory bullfighting scenes, cute little boys in oversized sombreros and images of the Virgin Mary. Hovering over the blond fake-wood check-in desk was an enormous, asymmetrical brass and glass chandelier that could have doubled as some kind of medieval torture device. The mousy young girl at the desk looked like she lived in constant fear of being decapitated by that light fixture at any moment.

"Hey there," Dean said. "I'm looking for my brother. He's a big guy, about…"

"Mister Swierczynski?" she asked. "Just checked in this morning with his niece," she looked down at her book. "Jennifer. With that…"

She pointed to her lower lip.

"That's them," Dean said.

"She your daughter, huh?"

Xochi stepped up and took Dean's hand.

"Our daughter," she said. "Yes."

"Room 418," she said.

"Did you see either one of them leave since they checked in?" Dean asked.

She shook her head.

"No," she said. "They didn't come out this way, but there's another door in the back."

"Okay, thanks," Dean said.

"My pleasure," she said. Then she leaned in and said something to Xochi in Spanish.

"What she'd say?" Dean asked as they walked over to the elevator.

"She said she wouldn't let her daughter wear a lip ring."
Dean shook his head.

"Why did you say Claudia was our daughter?" Dean said.
"Nobody's gonna believe that. What, did we have her when
we were in high school?"

"I didn't go to high school," Xochi said. "And of course
people will believe it. Why wouldn't they? My own mother
was only a year older than Claudia when she had Teo."

The elevator came. They got on in silence and rode
to the fourth floor. In spite of everything else that was
on his mind in that moment, Dean was struck again by
the complexity of this strange yoyo connection he felt
with Xochi. They had developed an intense foxhole
camaraderie almost immediately, and there were times
when he felt so close to her, like they had so much in
common. Then there were other times, like now, when
he really felt the gulf of vast cultural differences that lay
between them.

"You have any kids?" Dean asked as the elevator slowly
counted off the floors. He didn't know why it had never
occurred to him to ask before.

"Someday maybe," she said. "There is pressure from my
family, of course, but I'm not ready. Not yet. Not after what
happened to my brother. What about you?"

Dean thought of Ben. Shook his head.

"No," he said.

The elevator opened on the fourth floor. Xochi got out.
She didn't say anything else. Dean didn't know what to say
either, so he just kept quiet.

Room 418 was inexplicably right next to the elevator. Dean knocked.

"Claudia?" he said. "It's Dean, you in there?"

The door opened. Sam was standing there with a bottle of water in one hand.

THIRTY-FOUR

"What the hell happened to you guys?" Sam asked.

Dean let out a yelp of relieved laughter and pulled his brother into a bear hug, not even caring that Sam just let himself be hugged like a patient dog getting loved-up by an over-enthusiastic toddler.

"What happened to us?" Dean asked incredulous. "What the hell happened to you? I thought you'd been kidnapped!"

"Kidnapped?" Sam frowned. "Why would you think that?"

Dean told him about the call from Bobby. Sam patted his pockets, unable to find his cell phone.

"Kid bumped into me by the soda machine," Sam said. "Must have clipped my phone. Man, that's a pretty good scam."

Dean handed Sam the prepaid phone and told him to call Bobby. Xochi headed into the bathroom to change out of her bloody shirt and into a spare tank top. Claudia was sitting on the bed with the TV remote in her hand, scowling at the bolted-down television. Dean could see that she'd been crying again. He felt kind of bad for leaving her alone with Mr. Sensitive. Dean was the first one to admit that he was a lousy grief counselor, but he was Dr. Phil compared to Sam in his current condition.

He walked over to her.

"You okay?" he asked.

She looked up at him, fresh tears spilling down her chubby cheeks. She stood and threw her arms around him, nearly knocking him back a step.

"Hey, take it easy now," he said, shifting uncomfortably and looking over at Xochi. "Come on, kid, it's gonna be okay."

That sounded so lame. He wouldn't even have believed that kind of tripe back when he was Claudia's age.

"Listen," he finally said, extracting himself from her damp clutches and sitting her back down on the bed. "Xochi, Sam and me, we're not social workers. We're hunters. I know you're hurting right now, but there's nothing any of us can do about that. What we can do is work this hunt, the four of us together. We can beat the evil bitch who's responsible for what happened to your mom, but in order to do that, we need your help. We need you on the team."

"He's right," Xochi said. "We need you to be strong now. To be a grown woman. Can you do that?"

Claudia hung her head, looking down at her hands in her lap.

Xochi came over and sat beside Claudia, motioning with her chin for Dean to beat it. He was happy to oblige.

"I'm fine, Bobby," Sam was saying into the phone. "Really, it was just some kind of scam. The guy probably called every single number on that phone, just to see if anyone would fall for it."

Xochi was talking low to Claudia in Spanish. Whatever she was saying seemed to be working. Claudia finally raised her head, swiping at her tears. When she turned to Xochi and saw the shiner, her smudgy raccoon eyes went wide.

"Whoa," Claudia said. "What happened to you?"

"Cops," Xochi said. "We'd better get out of Nogales."

"Cops? Wow."

Claudia was obviously tremendously impressed by the idea of Xochi being some sort of outlaw. She turned back to Dean.

"Are you okay, Dean?" she asked. "Did you get beat up too?"

"Nah," Dean said. "Guess I wasn't their type."

"Right, okay," Sam said to Bobby. "We'll stay in touch, but in the meanwhile, see what you can dig up on an Aztec goddess called the Clawed Butterfly. How do you spell that name again, Xochi?"

"I-t-z-p-a-p-a-l-o-t-l," Xochi replied.

Sam repeated the spelling into the phone. Nodded, listening.

"Yeah, that's her," he said, smirking at Dean. "Smokin' hot, actually." Pause. A laugh. "Tell me about it." Another pause. "Right, later."

"So what do we do now?" Dean asked, ignoring Sam. "We need to get some new wheels, right?"

"There's a good chance that the Rover and the bikes may still be where we left them," Xochi said. "We should at least check it out."

"Then what?" Sam asked.

"If we can score another shotgun," Dean said, "I'd love to pay a visit to your buddy who makes those silver slugs."

"Okay," Xochi said. "So we head for Chihuahua. We can stop along the way to see if Huehuecoyotl will speak to us. It will be best at night, somewhere far from any cities. Claudia, any idea of where Elvia is now?"

"I'm not sure," Claudia said. "I think she doesn't really know where she is either. Only that she is moving south."

"Well, then we better get moving too," Dean said.

Sam gathered up his laptop and files and shouldered the bag, while Claudia went into the bathroom to fix her eyeliner.

"What did you say to her to make her turn off the waterworks?" Dean asked Xochi after Claudia closed the bathroom door.

"I told her that you like tough girls," Xochi said.

"Aw man," Dean said. "Don't encourage her. You're just making it worse."

"It worked, didn't it?"

"It's not even true," Dean said.

"No?" She arched a knowing brow at him, then shrugged. "My mistake."

By some crazy miracle, the Rover was right where they had left it, both dirt bikes unmolested in their trailer. The only thing missing was one of the two helmets. And the keys, of course. Confiscated by the cops when Xochi was arrested.

The kid with the gun seemed to be apologizing profusely for the missing helmet. Xochi gave him more money anyway. He gave them two thumbs-up and scampered off down the street. Dean didn't want to think about what he would be spending that money on.

"What did he say?" Sam asked.

"He said another kid ran off with the helmet," Xochi said, bending down to pick the driver's side lock. "And that he would go find that kid and get it back, but I told him we didn't have time to wait. I told him if he did get it back, he could keep it."

She popped the lock and opened the car door, getting in behind the wheel. Dean jumped in the shotgun seat and Sam and Claudia got in the back. Dean watched Xochi swiftly and efficiently hot wire the Rover and start it up.

"Okay," she said. "*Adios*, Nogales."

They hit the road.

THIRTY-FIVE

Dean had no idea where they were or what made Xochi pick this particular spot to pull over. The desert they rode through was virtually identical to what they'd encountered in Arizona, but it still felt infinitely strange and foreign. Wilder, more dangerous. By they time they'd arrived at what Xochi deemed to be an appropriate location, it was full dark.

"After what happened in Nogales," Xochi said as she killed the engine. "We stay together no matter what, okay?"

"Okay," Sam said. "But we've only got the two bikes."

"No problem," Dean said. "Claudia can ride with you and Xochi with me."

"Why can't I ride with you?" Claudia asked. "Let Xochi ride with Sam."

"I'm sorry, Dean," Xochi said, ignoring Claudia. "I'm afraid it will be you who will be riding behind me. Someone needs to lead the way, following the ley lines."

"You could just tell me which way to go," Dean suggested, knowing full well that that wasn't going to happen.

They got out of the Rover and Sam unlatched the trailer, dropping the ramp and rolling one of the bikes down. Xochi jumped up onto the trailer and tossed the only remaining helmet to Claudia before bringing the other bike down onto the road.

Claudia pouted and put on the helmet, climbing reluctantly onto the dirt bike behind Sam and locking her arms around his waist. Xochi mounted up on the other and looked back over her shoulder at Dean.

"Hop on, tough guy."

When Dean got onto the bitch seat behind Xochi, he knew right away what he was in for. He hadn't had a decent, uninterrupted stretch of privacy since he'd started working this hunt, and he knew damn well that if he spent more than a few seconds pressed up against that ass he was going to be loaded for bear. When she cranked the engine and took off into the desert, Dean grabbed the edge of the seat behind him with white knuckles, struggling to maintain a cushion of respectable space between his crotch and Xochi's ass. But the rugged Sonoran terrain was so challenging that within the first five minutes, Dean had no choice but to hold on to her tiny waist or risk falling off the back like a drunken biker chick.

They were passing through a desolate, moonlit landscape that could have easily passed for the surface of an alien planet. Cryptic rock formations towered over them and arroyos branched across the bone-dry ground like veins and arteries. Tumbleweeds bounded and spun through their slipstream.

Dean wasn't paying attention to any of that. He was too busy trying to think about fat, smelly old bag ladies. Or trying to think about wiping out on the dirt bike and smashing his bare head to bits on the jagged rocks. Or trying to think about pretty much anything other than the way that Xochi's tight, leather-clad ass was bumping and sliding against him. Trying and failing. She kept on raising and lowering her hips over and over, deftly compensating for the dips and shifting her weight with the twists and curves. It didn't help that he had to move and shift his own weight with hers, following her lead and leaning with her into the turns to keep the little dirt bike stable beneath them.

When they came into a narrow box canyon and Xochi braked, then eased the bike to a stop, Dean didn't know whether to be relieved or disappointed.

Sam pulled up beside them, Claudia hopping off and removing the helmet before he'd killed the engine. Dean got down from behind Xochi, using the bulk of the bike to hide what was going on below his belt from Sam and Claudia.

Xochi put down the kickstand and dismounted, pulling a small Maglite from one of her pockets.

"Come on," Xochi said, clicking the flashlight on and focusing it on an indentation in the sand about twelve feet away from the bikes. "This way. See that little clearing?"

Sam turned on his own light and headed for the indicated clearing. Claudia silently followed him. Dean hung back.

Xochi looked over her shoulder at Dean.

"You coming?"

"Sure," he said. "Let me just punch myself in the face a few times first."

Again, that little half-smile, the arched brow. She turned and headed off after Sam. Watching her walk away really wasn't helping.

Dean had no idea how the hell he'd managed to get himself so wound up like this, but he figured he'd let it go just about far enough. The world was full of women with nice asses, and he'd always been able to take them or leave them. Besides, there were plenty of bigger, more important things to worry about right now. Dead serious, end-of-civilization-as-we-know-it kind of things. He needed to start thinking with his big head for a minute and try to put things in perspective. This was nothing serious, just a basic mechanical issue. He'd take care of that as soon as he had a chance, but in the meanwhile he needed to channel Toshiro Mifune or some other equally stone-cold bad ass. Man the hell up and stop acting like a horny teenager.

He followed Xochi into the little clearing.

Claudia was gathering kindling, while Sam ran the EMF meter and Xochi laid out a bunch of herbs and ritual tools on a striped blanket.

"Weird," Sam said. "I'm getting a pretty strong reading, but it fluctuates. Kind of like a tide coming in and out."

He looked up at Dean.

"You okay?"

"Peachy," Dean snapped.

Claudia looked up at Dean with a worried expression and Dean immediately felt like a jerk.

"It's just been a long day," Dean said, softening his tone. "For all of us."

"It's not over yet," Xochi said. "What we are doing right now is very dangerous. Not physically dangerous, but emotionally dangerous. Do you understand? Huehuecoyotl is a trickster. He will lie to you, play with you. He will turn any negative emotion against you and turn us against each other just to entertain himself. We have no secrets that he cannot know. If he tries to exploit your most private thoughts and feelings, you can't let it hurt you."

She turned to Sam, taking one of his hands in both of hers.

"I am trusting you, Sam," Xochi said. "You must be our anchor, holding us steady in the stormy water of our emotions. Huehuecoyotl will not be able to play with you the way he will play with us. Especially Claudia, because she is most vulnerable."

"Man, this is bad," Dean said. The last thing he wanted was to share his innermost thoughts with anyone. Especially not right now. "Are you sure she should even be here?"

"We have no choice," Xochi said. "I need both you and Sam here with me and she cannot be left alone. We must protect her at all times."

"I'm not a baby," Claudia said, placing the sticks she'd gathered in a small pile at the center of the clearing. "You should give me a gun."

"Ever handled a firearm before?" Dean asked.

"Well, no," she said. "But you could teach me."

"We can talk about that later," Xochi said, stacking the sticks for a fire. "For now I need you all to try and clear your minds. Focus."

She lit the kindling with a Zippo and then lit a tight bundle of sage leaves, blowing on the end until it gave off a thick, pungent smoke. She waved her hand to direct the smoke and motioned for Claudia to come forward first. Xochi bathed each one of them in smoke, moving the burning bundle over their bodies. Dean scrunched up his nose, trying not to cough. Trying to clear his mind and not having very much luck.

He felt like a side of cured bacon by the time she was done. He was pretty sure he was never gonna get this hippy stink out of his clothes and hair. Xochi tossed the rest of the sage into the fire and then started crushing a bunch of other herbs and plants in a wooden cup. She added water and then passed the cup around. Sam took a sip and passed it to Dean. Dean frowned into the cup, less than thrilled about the muddy, acrid liquid inside.

"Come on," Sam said. "Drink up, fannybaws."

"What did you just call me?" Dean asked with a baffled frown.

"Hey," Sam said. "Unlike you, I didn't have my head in an airsick bag for the whole flight to Scotland. That cute little blonde stewardess from Dundee taught me all kinds of linguistic curiosities."

"I'll bet," Dean said.

"Please," Xochi said, flashing a warning scowl. "A little respect."

"Sorry," Sam said, swiftly rearranging his features into a more serious expression.

Dean bit the bullet and took a slug of the strange herbal liquid, trying not to wince at the nasty, bitter taste.

"Sorry," he said, picking a twiggy fragment off his lower lip and passing the cup on to Claudia.

Claudia drank deep without flinching and handed the cup back to Xochi, who drained it. Then she took out her snake-handled stone knife.

"Now, we cut ourselves," she touched the tattooed heart on her chest. "Here, over the heart. We must each make a blood sacrifice to Huehuecoyotl."

"Awesome," Claudia said holding out her hand for the knife. "I'll go first."

"I will go first," Xochi said firmly. "Watch me and do exactly what I do. No joking, okay?"

Claudia nodded, watching eagerly as Xochi held the blade to her own chest.

"First, touch the left side of your chest with your fingertips," Xochi said. "Moving them until you feel a strong heartbeat. When you find the strongest spot, make a small cut, moving the knife upwards, like this." She flicked her wrist, making an inch long perfectly vertical cut in the center of her tattooed heart.

"Then, you catch the blood on the blade, like this." She ran the edge of the knife up the length of the cut, letting the blood flow over the pale stone. "And let the blood run into the flames. Okay?"

Xochi held the knife out over the fire, then passed it to Claudia.

Xochi was in her usual tank top. Claudia had on a deep V-neck shirt and Sam a button-down. None of them had any problem exposing the necessary anatomy without removing any clothing. As Dean watched first Claudia and then his brother perform the ceremonial cuts, he really wished he was wearing anything other than a high necked T-shirt. There was just no way around the fact that if he was going to do what Xochi wanted, he would have to remove his shirt. Which wouldn't be any kind of big deal at all if he didn't have a crushed-out teenybopper staring at him like he was the second coming of Elvis.

Sam handed him the knife. He shrugged and pulled his shirt over his head, figuring it would be best to just get this over with. He focused on the flames in front of him as he ran his fingers over his left pec, just below the pentagram tattoo. He could feel Claudia's eyes on him but he ignored her, concentrating on tracing the pulse of his heart beneath his skin. He made the cut.

He gathered his blood on the blade and let it run into the fire, then handed the knife back to Xochi. He couldn't help but notice that Claudia wasn't the only one watching him as he put his shirt back on.

Xochi spoke some strange, melodic words and then fell silent.

"Now what?" Sam asked.

She took out a handful of copal and tossed it into the fire.

"Now we wait," she said.

* * *

Nothing happened for a good twenty minutes. Dean just stood there, feeling hostile, exhausted and really not in the mood for any of this. He wondered how many cumulative hours of his life he'd spent hanging around waiting for something spooky to show up. He could hear coyotes in the distance, moving closer.

When Huehuecoyotl finally appeared, Dean was unnerved and more than a little angry to see the trickster god wearing his face.

It was Dean's image, but it wasn't like looking in a mirror. More like looking at a heavily retouched photo. This version of Dean didn't have the two-day stubble or the sleepless dark circles and budding crow's feet around his eyes. It didn't have the annoying zit Dean could feel coming in just above his right eyebrow, or the scatter of freckles he'd always hoped he'd grow out of but never did. This version was also wearing skin-tight black-velvet lace-up pants that Dean wouldn't be caught dead in. When that other him smiled at Claudia, Dean saw a teasing hint of vampire fangs and felt a sick helpless anger in the pit of his belly.

"*Huehueteque*," Xochi said. "You honor these humble hunters with your presence."

"The honor is mine, *Xuihxochitl*," he replied stepping up to Claudia and touching the cut on her chest. "Tell me, who is this little seer?"

"My name is Claudia," she said determinedly. "I'm not afraid."

"No?" He turned to look at Xochi. "Such strong magic in this one." He took Claudia's chin in his hands, leaning close enough to kiss. "But you've always known you're special, haven't you? That's why the others don't understand you. They are jealous of your power."

"Take your hands off her," Dean said, stepping forward.

"Dean," Xochi said. "Stay calm."

"She's just a kid," Dean said.

"And who are these white men?" Huehuecoyotl asked, never breaking eye contact with Claudia.

"With respect," Xochi said. "They are my friends." She took a step closer, trying to take his attention away from Claudia. "We want your advice, to help your lost granddaughter. To cure her affliction and make her human again so that the *Tzitzimimeh* cannot use her to enter our world."

"That was your idea, wasn't it?" Huehuecoyotl asked Claudia.

"Yeah," she said, even though it had been Sam who had originally suggested it.

"Smart as well as beautiful," he replied, caressing her flushed cheek.

"Look," Dean said. "I'm not just gonna stand here and let an underage girl get hit on by a thousand-year-old pervert dressed up as me."

Huehuecoyotl turned to Dean, green eyes flashing like a cat's in the dark. He backed away from Claudia.

"Righteous Dean Winchester," he said. "Brave protector of innocents. An angry boy wearing his dead father's shoes. Tell me, Dean, how did it go the last time you tried to play Daddy?"

Huehuecoyotl's face flickered, going ugly and animal for

a brief heartbeat. Then he became Lisa.

No make-up, dark hair tousled from sleep. Dressed in nothing but an old flannel shirt that she loved and Dean always threatened to donate to charity while she was in the shower. He never thought he'd see that ugly old shirt again, and seeing it now made him coldly furious. He refused to be manipulated that easily.

"She cries every night," Huehuecoyotl said. His voice was Lisa's voice, rough with tears. "Alone in the bed you once shared. She is broken inside forever because of you. She wishes she'd never met you."

The thing that looked like Lisa stepped closer to him. Close enough that he could smell the vanilla-scented moisturizer she always put on before bed. He clenched his fists.

"And in her darkest heart," Huehuecoyotl said looking up at him with Lisa's big brown eyes, "she wishes Ben had never been born. Because every time she looks at him, she sees you."

"Ben is *not* my son," Dean said. He could feel a small muscle bunching up and pulsing at the hinge of his jaw. "She did a blood test."

"Did she? Interesting how this test was able to eliminate you without a obtaining a sample of your blood. Modern science has made such miraculous advances."

Dean narrowed his eyes, defensive.

"She probably got a sample from that bartender first and it matched, so she didn't need one from me."

"Right," Huehuecoyotl smiled. "That bartender."

Dean didn't say anything. The doubt that had always been there in the back of his mind was off the leash and raging.

"Lisa was afraid to tell you the truth because she didn't want the boy to become a hunter like his father. Especially after you almost killed him."

"Don't listen to him, Dean," Sam said. "Remember what Xochi said. He's just messing with you."

"Don't listen to Lisa," Huehuecoyotl said with a slow smile. "Because, let's be honest. You don't really care about Lisa and Ben anymore anyway, do you? I know what you really want."

His form flickered again and he became Xochi. Hair unbound, topless and fire lit.

Claudia ran, sobbing from the circle.

"Claudia!" Xochi called.

"Go on," Dean said. "Go after her. I got this."

"Are you sure?"

"Go," he said.

Xochi turned on her flashlight and ran after Claudia. Sam looked intently at Dean, silently asking him if he was really sure. He was. He didn't meet his brother's gaze, keeping his focus on the fake Xochi in front of him.

"That your best shot, dogboy?" Dean said, raising his eyebrows, defiant. "Because I'm still standing." He took a step closer to Huehuecoyotl, bringing them nearly nose to nose. "You think I don't know that I hurt Lisa? That I could have killed Ben? There isn't a damn thing you can say to me that I don't already torture myself over, a hundred times a day."

Huehuecoyotl didn't respond.

"And sure," Dean continued, on a roll now. "I'd love to nail Xochi. I don't think that's exactly breaking news to anyone here, except maybe Claudia, so good job making a teenage girl cry. But you know what? Just because I *want* to nail Xochi doesn't mean I will, and that has absolutely nothing to do with how I feel about Lisa and Ben. So, whenever you're done with your cute little puppet show, you let me know and then maybe we can get down to brass tacks and do some business. What do you say?"

Huehuecoyotl shifted again, first to a large black coyote and then to a handsome young Native American man with parallel scars on each cheek and heavy obsidian disks in his stretched earlobes.

"Why should I help you, hunter?" he asked. "And don't say because the world will end. *Your* world will end, not *mine*."

"Because it'll be fun," Dean replied.

THIRTY-SIX

Huehuecoyotl didn't respond, he just looked intently at Dean. His black eyes shone in the firelight. Dean could feel Sam's questioning gaze but he didn't break eye contact with the trickster.

"If Teo and the *Nagual* succeed with their plan to piggyback the Star Demons into our world, it'll be a straight-up massacre," Dean began. "Now maybe that kind of thing is pretty entertaining to someone like you. But you know what's even more entertaining than watching a massacre? Watching a war."

Dean studied that stony, scarified face, searching for clues. Was it working? Was he getting through? It was impossible to tell.

"Think about it," Dean continued. "How would you rather spend your pay-per-view dollars? On a solid, even match-up that you know is gonna go the distance, or a one-sided beat-down that'll probably end in a first-round knockout? Just give us a fighting chance against these things and we'll give that Clawed Butterfly bitch a run for her money. It'll be must see T.V. That's a promise."

"I cannot cure the corrupted Borderwalker," Huehuecoyotl said.

Dean forced his clenched fists to open, letting out a slow breath. Huehuecoyotl looked away into the distance, squinting against the smoke from the small fire.

"But I can help you find someone who can," he said.

Dean knew full well that the trickster might be lying, but he finally felt like he had a foot in the door.

"I'm listening," Dean said.

"I will tell you alone," Huehuecoyotl said. "Tell the empty one to leave us."

"Uh uh," Sam said. "No way."

"It's okay, Sam," Dean said.

"I don't know…"

"Go on," Dean said. "I'm good."

Sam gave Dean a searching look, then nodded and left the circle.

"I'm all yours," Dean said. "Let's hear it."

"I knew a woman once," Huehuecoyotl told him. "The most beautiful woman I've ever seen. *Metzlicihuatl* was her name. A midwife's daughter. From the first time I saw her, I knew I had to have her. But once I took what I wanted, she wouldn't let me go. She became the first Borderwalker. The mother of all the others."

"You mean the Alpha?" Dean asked.

"Yes. The Alpha, as you say." The trickster gave Dean a

knowing look. "She doesn't care that I broke her heart. She loves me to this day."

Dean wasn't about to let himself be needled when he was so close to what they needed.

"So you're saying the Alpha Borderwalker has the power to cure as well as infect?"

"She still has the lump of white copal that I used to steal her heart. She wears it in a deerskin pouch around her neck. If you can convince her to give it you, you can use it to transform the corrupted Borderwalker back into an ordinary human. I cannot help you convince her, but I can help you call her to you."

Huehuecoyotl put out one of his hands and a small ceramic flute took shape, solidifying out of the smoke. It was bright red with a bell-shaped cup at the base, decorated with a trio of bipedal coyotes dancing in a circle. He closed his fingers around the flute and then held it out to Dean.

"Play this flute," he said. "*Metzlicihuatl* will hear it and come to you, thinking you are me. Fair warning, she will be angry when she finds she has been deceived. But you are the kind of man who is easily forgiven by women, aren't you, Dean?"

"Where should I play it?" Dean asked, taking the flute. "Here?"

"Anywhere," Huehuecoyotl replied. "She would cross oceans to be with me."

"Thank you," Dean said.

"Just make it worth my while," the trickster said. "Put on a good show, hunter."

"Will do," Dean said. "We ain't going down without a fight."

"And if you win," Huehuecoyotl said. "Will you keep on standing alone in the rain? Or will you come inside?"

Huehuecoyotl leaned close to whisper in Dean's ear, shifting again as he moved. Shifting back to Xochi.

"Forgive yourself."

The trickster turned and walked away into the desert, Xochi's image fading slowly into smoky transparency before disappearing all together.

Dean found Sam, Claudia and Xochi standing together by the dirt bikes. He showed them the flute and explained everything that had happened.

"Find the Alpha Borderwalker," Sam said. "Genius. Why didn't I think of that?"

"We only have a couple of hours before the sun comes up," Xochi said. "We don't want to be out here when that happens. We should head back to the Rover and then find a place to catch a few hours of sleep. We can visit my friend in Chihuahua during the day and then summon the Alpha tomorrow night. Okay?"

"Yeah," Dean said. "I'm pretty beat."

"We all are," Xochi said.

Xochi carefully buried the fire and gathered up her ritual objects. Claudia was silent and stoic, waiting. Dean thought maybe he ought to talk to her, apologize or something, but he had absolutely no idea how to even start a conversation like that with a fifteen-year-old girl, so he just kept his mouth shut.

Sam got his dirt bike started and Claudia climbed on the back, strapping on her helmet. Sam hit the gas and took off down the trail. Xochi was about to mount up on the other when Dean stepped up next to her.

"I'm sorry about all that," Dean said. "You know, before. Is Claudia okay?"

"She will be," Xochi shrugged. "She's young. Easily hurt but resilient."

She was about to throw one leg over the bike seat, but Dean put a hand on her shoulder, holding her back.

"Can I ask you a favor?"

"What?"

"I remember the way," he said. "Let me drive the bike back to the Rover."

"Why?"

"Honestly?" he said. "Because I don't think I can take another lap dance like the one I got on the way out here. Have a little compassion, will ya? These are my only pants."

She laughed, but she let him drive. They made it back to the Rover without incident.

Sam was the only one who wasn't half asleep at that point so he drove while the rest of them dozed. When Dean woke up the sun was starting to rise and the Rover was parked in the lot of a Ramada in Chihuahua. Xochi and Claudia were still asleep in the back seat.

He got out of the Rover to stretch his aching body and spotted Sam coming out the door, two sets of hotel keys in his hand.

"Come on," he called.

Dean was about to tap on the back window and wake the girls up when Claudia suddenly jolted upright, her movement startling Xochi. Claudia turned to Dean, hand flat against the window and her eyes flashing wide. Then wakeful awareness seemed to filter into her face and she took a deep breath, opening the back door and getting slowly to her feet.

"I saw her," Claudia said. "I saw Elvia."

Xochi got out of the Rover and came around to stand beside Dean.

"Tell us," she said.

"She…" Claudia paused, frowning. "I think she escaped."

Xochi threw a look of surprise in Dean's direction.

"You need to remember everything," she said. "Start at the beginning of your vision. Don't leave out any details, no matter how small."

"Okay," Claudia said. "It's just… well it's kinda mixed up."

"Go on," Dean said.

"Well, first she was in a dark place, like inside a truck or something. She was… tied up. Bound somehow. Then, cops. Army guys, maybe? Guys in uniforms. There was some kind of nasty fight happening. Shooting and…" Claudia shuddered, wrapping her arms around herself. "And in the chaos, Elvia broke loose and ran. But she's… sticky. Like one of those poor birds you see on T.V. with the oil all over their feathers. She's too heavy to leave our world. Does that make sense?"

"Yes," Xochi said. "That's Teo's magic, holding her down. Can you see where they are? What can she see?"

Claudia closed her eyes, remembering.

"It's a not a major city. More like a town," she said. "Real pretty and old-fashioned. Narrow, twisty streets. There's a big church. Tan with a big red dome."

Xochi shook her head.

"That could be anywhere," she said. "Can you be more specific?"

"Elvia is hiding in some kind of catacombs," Claudia said. "With dead bodies all around her. But… this is gonna sound weird."

"Nothing sounds weird," Xochi said.

"The bodies aren't in tombs. They're… It's almost like they're… on display. Like in a museum, standing up in these glass cases."

Xochi's eyes went wide.

"These bodies," Xochi said. "Are they dried out, like skeletons covered in leathery, pale-brown skin?"

"Yeah," Claudia said.

"Guanajuato," Xochi said. "They are in Guanajuato."

"Okay," Sam said. "How long will it take us to get there from here?"

"If we drive straight through and don't sleep?" Xochi asked. "Maybe twelve, fourteen hours."

"Come on, man," Dean said. "None of us are gonna be worth a damn if we don't grab a few hours of real shut-eye. Plus we still need to see your friend who makes the silver ammo and have our little chat with the Alpha Borderwalker."

"He's right," Xochi said. "But we can't spare more than three or four hours at the most."

"No problem," Dean said. "That's all I ever need."

"I've already got us checked in here," Sam said. "May as well take advantage. I don't need to sleep, but I could sure use a shower."

"Me too," Xochi said. "A good hot shower."

Their rooms were on the top floor. Sam had splurged on neighboring suites with an adjoining door. Xochi and Claudia took the one on the left and Sam unlocked the one on the right.

"See you in the morning," Xochi said. "I mean, later today."

"Right," Dean said. "See you."

The suite was decent but utterly forgettable. All that Dean cared about was that it was relatively clean and the bathroom door had a lock.

Sam was setting up his gear on the tiny desk. Dean could hear the shower start up next door. He wondered if it was Xochi.

"You need to get in there?" Dean asked, gesturing at the bathroom door.

Sam shook his head. "I'm good,"

"Because I'm gonna be a while," Dean said.

"Have at it, dude." Sam said without looking up from his laptop. "Do us all a favor."

Dean went into the bathroom and locked the door.

THIRTY-SEVEN

Three hours later, Dean felt infinitely more civilized. Rested, as well as ever, and otherwise stabilized. Showered and shaved and caffeinated. Clean socks and underwear. Ready to get out there and save the damn world. Again.

Xochi's friend ran a tiny jewelry store just off the main plaza. Touristy stuff mostly. Lots of turquoise and silver mixed in with gothic crosses, bats and skulls. It was a mother-daughter operation. The daughter running the public half of the shop while mom did business out of the back.

Mom met them at the back door. She was probably close to fifty and dressed like the aftermath of an explosion in the Stevie Nicks factory. Lots of flowing, gauzy lace and frills that hardly seemed like practical work wear for a serious bullet-smith.

"This is Consuelo Morena Valesquez," Xochi said. "Sam and Dean Winchester and Claudia Porcayo."

"You can call me Chelo," the older woman replied with

a wink. Her English was flawless. "All the hunters do. Especially the handsome ones." She took Sam's arm on one side and Dean's on the other. "Come on in."

The back room of the little shop was a scattered mess of bullet molds in varying sizes, ladles, and bricks of pure silver. In the center of the unfinished cement floor was a large cast-iron pot over what looked like the guts of an electric turkey cooker. There was a heavy leather apron on a hook by the door, as well as several pairs of thick, elbow-length gloves and plastic safety goggles. The far wall was covered with Polaroid photos. Chelo posed and smiling beside a hundred different men and women, all heavily armed. All hunters, obviously. It was amazing to Dean how easy it was to recognize other hunters, even in another country. It wasn't just the guns. It was the eyes. The same eyes he saw every day in the bathroom mirror.

"Xochi tells me you have a problem with the *Nagual*," Chelo said. "I have a shorty I might be able to spare. What do you have to trade?"

Xochi and Dean emptied their pockets of all the weapons they'd stolen from the phony *federales* back in Nogales. Chelo picked up the weighty Magnum.

".50 caliber?" She whistled appreciatively. "I'd love to take this one, but it sounds like you need it more than I do. Lucky for you, I just poured a fresh rack of 50s last night."

She turned to a large cabinet and unlocked it with a key that hung from a chain around her neck. After a moment of searching through inner drawers, she turned and handed Dean a sawed-off Mossberg 500.

"You know what," she said. "Just take it. But in return I want a photo with you two handsome boys."

"You got it," Sam said.

She handed an old-school Polaroid camera to Xochi. Sam and Dean both had to slouch down to keep their heads in frame with the petite bullet-smith. Xochi took the shot and handed the developing photo to Chelo.

"Thanks," Chelo said, waving the photo in the air.

Once the image came in, she smiled and pinned the snapshot up on the wall beside an old photo of Xochi that Dean hadn't noticed until just then. In the picture Xochi looked about Claudia's age. No tattoos. Her hair was shorter, chopped into blunt bangs. She was trying for a stony bad ass stare that wasn't quite there yet. Kind of reminded Dean of himself at that age.

"Okay," Chelo said. "So you need 50s, 45s, and 38s, plus the 12-gauge slugs for the Mossberg. Anything else?"

"Got any silver knives?" Dean asked.

"Of course," she said, like he'd just asked if the Pope was Catholic. "How many you need?"

"Three," Dean said.

"Four," Claudia said.

"No," Dean said.

"It's okay," Xochi said. "She has to learn sometime."

"You'd better teach her how to throw it," Dean said. "Because I'm still not letting anything get close enough to be inside her range. I promised I'd protect her and I meant it."

That was the wrong thing to say. Claudia was looking at him all sparkle-eyed again. Apparently last night's embarrassing revelations had done nothing to dim her crush.

Chelo smirked and headed off into a small storeroom.

"We'd better divvy up the firepower while we're at it," Sam said. "Dean, you take the shotgun."

"Right," Dean hefted the Mossberg, checking it over. "What about you? You want the Magnum?"

"Don't need it," Sam said with a smirk. "I got nothing to prove in that department."

"Yeah," Xochi said. "But you also have the largest hands. Me, I prefer the .45."

"Fair enough," Sam said, picking up the hand cannon. "That leaves Claudia with the snubbie."

Claudia reached for the .38 and Xochi grabbed her wrist.

"Not yet," she said. "I'll hold it for you until I have a chance to teach you how to use it. I don't want you to shoot your foot. Or mine."

When Chelo returned she had a huge, teetering stack of unmarked ammo boxes. Xochi stepped up to help her, taking about half the boxes and laying them out on the workbench.

"Dean?" She tossed him a box.

He opened the lid and saw what looked like a dozen ordinary shotgun rounds. But when he pulled one out and turned it over, instead of the usual star-shaped top, he saw a solid, gleaming silver slug with a flattened top and a deep dimpled center.

"Hollow point?" he said. "Hot damn."

"Like you Americans always say," Chelo said. "Ideal for home defense."

Dean loaded up while Sam and Xochi expelled the standard rounds from their respective firearms and reloaded with silver.

"Here you go, *muñeca*," Chelo said to Claudia, handing her a slim silver stiletto with an image of the Virgin Mary on the handle. She leaned in to stage whisper, "I gave you the best one."

She handed out three other, plainer knives, one to each of them, and then dug up a sturdy leather backpack to carry all the ammo.

"Thanks, Chelo," Xochi said, filling up the pack. "You're the best."

"Don't you forget it," Chelo said. "It was a pleasure doing business with you, as always. And you American boys, remember, I ship international. You can order online, anytime."

She handed Sam a business card with a web address and a lot of gothy-looking clip art. He smiled and slipped it into his wallet.

Xochi shouldered the pack and laid a thick roll of Mexican money on Chelo. Chelo tried to refuse in Spanish, but Xochi insisted. Chelo gave Claudia a big hug and then kissed both Sam and Dean full on the mouth.

"Come back any time," she said.

Xochi sold the two dirt bikes and the trailer to another friend before they left Chihuahua, arguing that they had a lot of miles to cover and they could drive faster without the trailer. Dean had been thinking the same thing.

"So where should we stop to try and summon the Alpha Borderwalker?" Sam asked as he pulled the Rover onto *Carretera Federal 45*.

"Anywhere along the way, I guess," Dean replied. "Just make it somewhere pretty far from any kind of civilization."

"Do you see anything around here that looks like civilization?" Sam asked, gesturing through the dusty windshield at the long flat stretch of nothing they were passing through.

"That's for the best," Dean said. "If she's gonna be anywhere near as pissed off as the coyote guy said she'd be, I don't want any innocent bystanders hanging around. In fact, that might be a good time for you guys to teach Claudia how to shoot."

"We're not letting you face the Alpha alone," Xochi said.

"Trust me on this," Dean said. "I can handle it."

"No way," Claudia said. "That's crazy."

"No," Xochi said. "No, I'll come with you. You need someone to have your back."

"Look," Dean said. "Don't think I don't appreciate the offer, but I'm the most expendable person in this group and you know it. You're our native guide, Claudia's our tracker and Sam, well whatever mystical reason you have for thinking you need him to succeed in this hunt, I'm not gonna argue with you on that. That leaves me."

"He's right," Sam said.

"How can you say that?" Claudia asked.

"Tell 'em, Sammy," he said. "I'm just trying to be practical here."

Xochi swore quietly in Spanish.

"I hate it, but I cannot argue," she said.

"But you were the one who said we all need to stay together from now on," Claudia said to her. "You're just gonna let him walk off and get killed?"

"This ain't my first rodeo, kid," Dean said. "I'm not gonna get killed, I'm gonna get that damn chunk of copal. And when I come back, I want to see you shoot the ace out of the ace of spades. Deal?"

"Fine," Claudia said, turning her face away and staring out the window at the non-scenery. "I don't care anyway."

"Atta girl," Dean said. "Sam, why don't you take that little side road there. Just get us a few miles off the main drag."

They passed a few little shack-like dwellings and a sort of roadside restaurant, then more nothing. The sun was starting to slide down into a smoldering-red sunset.

"Here," Xochi said, pointing to a stubbly rock formation on the right.

Sam pulled the Rover off the road and killed the engine. The four of them got out and Claudia threw her arms around Dean's neck, smashing her face into his chest. He patted her back and then pulled away.

"Hey, what did I tell you?" he said. "I'll be fine."

"Be careful," she said. "Promise me you will. We need you."

"Claudia," Xochi said. "Get the ammo bag and a couple of those plastic bottles out of the back."

"Go on," Dean said.

Claudia looked up at him, then stood up on her tiptoes to press a lightning-quick kiss to his cheek.

"Good luck," she said, blushing like a house on fire and turning back to the Rover.

Xochi came over to Dean and held out her flask. He took it. Took a slug. Tried to give it back, but she shook her head.

"Take it," she said. "And this."

She pulled out her sacred, snake-handled stone knife. Spun it in her grip so that the handle was facing him and held it out.

"It's not obsidian," she said. "But it's better than nothing."

He held her gaze for a moment, then nodded and took it.

"Thanks," he said.

"Just bring it back," she said.

She didn't hug him or kiss him. She just turned without another word and walked back to the Rover. He wrapped his fingers around the sinuously carved handle. It was still warm from her hand. He silently promised her that he would bring it back.

He walked away, into the desert.

THIRTY-EIGHT

Dean walked toward the sunset until he couldn't see the Rover anymore. The sound of Claudia's target practice gradually faded into the distance. He couldn't see any man-made structures anywhere. He couldn't see the road or the car. He was utterly, completely alone. He eventually slowed and then stopped.

Reaching into his pocket, he took out the flute Huehuecoyotl had given him. He held it up, turning it over and over in his hand. It hadn't occurred to him until that second that he had absolutely no idea how to play a flute. He'd never even touched one, not even a toy when he was a kid. The only toy instrument he'd ever had was a drum, and his frequently hung-over father had told him that it had "got lost" only two or three days after Christmas.

The flute had four holes in it, evenly spaced along the top. It was pretty obvious that you were supposed to put your mouth on the skinny end and blow into it, but he had no idea what the holes were for.

He lifted the flute to his lips and blew experimentally into it. The breathy, resonant note that came out was so achingly beautiful that it startled him into momentary silence. It was an inexplicably sexy sound, like a woman's knowing, intimate laughter. The kind of laugh that let you know you were in. That you'd gone from flirting to making love for the first time. That she was yours.

Dean shook his head to clear it and raised the flute to his lips again, ready this time for the seductive effect of the music. He moved his fingertips over the top of the flute and realized that he could make the tone move up or down by covering or uncovering the holes. He was nowhere near an actual song or anything, but he was able to sustain several varying notes that echoed out over the ancient landscape like a beacon.

The air around him began to shimmer and blur. An undulating ribbon of soft white light appeared, bisecting the sunset and forming a deepening rift in the skin of the sky. The Alpha Borderwalker appeared out of the rift, the strange shimmer clinging to her long black hair as she stepped down onto the sand as casually as if she were getting off a train.

Huehuecoyotl had said that she was the most beautiful woman he'd ever seen, and he obviously wasn't lying. She was absolutely breathtaking. Dean had always been partial to women with dark hair and eyes and she was a stunning example of his ideal type. Wide-set, mesmerizing espresso eyes behind heavy black lashes. Impossibly lush mouth.

Regal cheekbones. Flawless without a hint of make-up. But something about her beauty was disturbing. It was too perfect, so unreal that it was almost terrifying. Monstrous. Inhuman.

She was nude, but the soft, brown human skin below her collarbones graduated into sleek, mottled scales like a rattlesnake, making her luscious curves seem almost clothed. Her fingers ended in hooked black claws. An enormous pair of black-and-white condor's wings sprouted from her shoulder blades, flexing and stretching wide, stirring the sand around Dean's boots. This was a magnificent, terrible creature. Nothing like the miserable, tortured abomination they'd battled back in the States. This was what a Borderwalker was supposed to be.

"Who are you?" she asked, her voluptuous lips unmoving, as if her words were being whispered directly into Dean's mind. "You are not my lover."

The flute in his hand turned to smoke, drifting away on the desert wind. He stood his ground, unflinching.

"Huehuecoyotl sent me," Dean said. "He told me that you would help me."

Her heavy eyebrows bunched together into a slight frown. She took a step closer, the rich, amber-like scent of copal dizzying at close range, and reached out a talon-tipped finger to touch his throat, just below the line of his jaw. He could feel Xochi's stone knife pressed against the small of his back, tucked into the waistband of his jeans, but there was no way to get to it in time to stop her from slitting his throat ear to ear if that's what she wanted.

"I do not help human men," she said.

"This help," he said. "It's not for me. It's for a woman. Her name is Elvia Reveultas."

"Elvia," she said, the name barely louder than a breath inside Dean's head.

"You know her?" Dean asked.

"I know what has been done to her," the Alpha said. "I could do worse to you, human. With pleasure."

She caressed his throat with the flat of her palm, the sharp point of her thumbnail sliding up into the soft spot behind her ear. He needed to think fast. To say something. Anything.

"Wow," he said. "This really isn't the kind of welcome I was expecting."

"You know nothing about me," she said, unmoving lips inches from his. "Or my welcome."

"I just meant…" He swallowed against the crush of her hand on his trachea. "After everything that Huehuecoyotl said about you…"

She released some of the pressure on his neck.

"What did he say about me?" she asked.

"Nothing important," Dean said. "It doesn't matter."

"Tell me," she said. "Or I will gut you and leave you for the vultures."

This was way too easy.

"Well it wasn't so much what he said." Dean shrugged. "You know how guys are. We hate coming right out and saying how we feel, but…" He paused. Let her hang for a second. "The way he talks about you, he's obviously still crazy about you."

"You lie," she said. "You lie like he does."

Of course he was lying, but, like he'd told Claudia, this wasn't his first rodeo. Dean was a professional. A black belt, grandmaster, superfly liar. He'd been lying all his life and he knew that the easiest lie to sell is the one that someone really wants to believe.

"Yeah, what do I know?" Dean said. "I must be wrong."

He turned like he was going to walk away. She let him, hands held palm up and open. He took a step, then another. Then, that sibilant whisper inside his head.

"Tell me what he said."

"He told me about the time he spent with you," Dean said, turning back to her. "I think that was the only time when he was ever really happy. He said you made him feel human."

She was listening intently, claws clicking as she nervously opened and closed her hands.

"He still carries this awful guilt over what happened to you," Dean continued. "He only left you because he wanted to protect you and ended up hurting you anyway."

"I don't understand," she said. "Protect me from what?"

"Protect you from his own inner darkness," Dean told her. "He knew he could never be the kind of man you deserve. That loving him would only bring you pain."

She took a half a step back, wings folding inward and dark eyes suddenly wet with very human tears. Dean had to look away from the weeping monster, because he was starting to wonder who was the real monster here. That didn't stop him from moving in for the checkmate.

"He wanted to help Elvia," Dean said. "To make up for

not being able to help you. But he can't. Only you can save her now."

"I know the pain of all my daughters," she said. "Elvia's pain, it is unspeakable."

"Then help me help her," Dean said.

"How?"

Dean frowned. For some reason, in all the time he'd spent scoping her snakeskin cleavage, he never noticed she was not wearing a necklace. Not until that moment.

"Huehuecoyotl said that you still have the lump of white copal that he gave you." Dean touched his sternum. "He told me you kept it in a deerskin pouch around your neck, but…"

Her mouth twisted into a smile and Dean heard a low smoky laugh echo inside his head.

"A necklace?" she said. "That's what he told you?"

She delicately circled her own sternum with a clawtip. The heart beneath her skin began to flicker, pulsing with a hot, ruddy glow.

"That lump of copal is deeply embedded inside my heart," she said. "Just like the man who gave it to me. I cannot give it to you any more than I could give you my own beating heart."

Dean made a solemn promise to kick that shifty coyote in the nards the next time he saw him.

"You know him," Dean said. "Probably better than anyone." Dean tried to remember what Xochi said about Huehuecoyotl. "His lies are more revealing than the truth, right? What do you think he really meant?"

"I have never tried to take away my affliction," she said. "Only share it."

Dean thought back to the cure Bobby had mixed up for him when Dean had been turned into a vampire. One of the main ingredients was the blood of the vamp that turned him. Clearly the Borderwalker that turned Elvia was dead, killed in the transition, but if these Borderwalkers have copal smoke for blood, then maybe all of them share the same smoke flowing through their veins. Smoke from the original piece of copal, currently burning inside the Alpha's heart.

THIRTY-NINE

"Okay, look," Dean said. "Don't take this the wrong way or anything, but can I…? Well…" He thought of the *Monty Python* sketch where they take out that guy's liver while he's still alive. There was really no good way to ask a question like this. "Can I have some of your blood?"

"My blood?"

"I know it's a lot to ask on a first date—" Dean began.

"Give me some of your blood, human," she replied. "Or how about I just take it? All of it."

She took a step closer and he backed up, showing his palms.

"Okay, okay," he said. "What I mean is, I think that's what Huehuecoyotl was talking about when he said I could use the lump of copal he gave you to cure Elvia." He knew he was on a highwire with this. One wrong step and he was screwed. "He didn't really mean I should take the whole thing. He wanted you to give me some of your blood."

"And if I do…"

He waited, afraid to push too hard.

"You understand that my blood is smoke?" She tilted her head. "How do you propose to carry smoke?"

"Right," he said. "Yeah, well…"

Good question. How the hell was he going to carry smoke? More than that, how was he gonna get it out of her body and into whatever he was going to carry it in?

She slid one of her hands around his body and down over his butt cheek. For a second he though she was trying to cop a feel, but she took Xochi's flask out of his back pocket and unscrewed the cap.

"Hey wait…" he tried to say, but she emptied the flask into the sand before he could finish. "What did you do that for? I could have emptied that for you."

"You will have to breathe my blood," she said.

"Wait, what?"

"Breathe my blood," she said. "And then blow it into this flask."

"Are you sure about that?" Dean frowned.

"Do you want my blood or don't you?"

"Yes," he said. "Of course."

"Remember," she said. "I do this for him. Not for you."

Dean considered himself to be pretty open-minded, but what happened next was probably up there in the top ten weirdest things he'd ever done with a naked woman. Well sort of naked. Sort of a woman. Anyway it was pretty damn weird.

She wrapped her fingers around the back of his neck,

claws sliding up through his hair in a way that was kind of sexy and kind of creepy at the same time. With her other hand, she pressed the claw of her index finger to her left breast. Her skin parted between the snake scales and thick, perfumed smoke began to flow from the cut. She pulled his head down to her breast.

"Breathe," she said.

As he put his lips around the edge of the cut, it occurred to him that he really shouldn't actually breathe the smoke into his lungs. He was no Bill Clinton, but he had no way of knowing if any kind of microscopic particles of it might be absorbed into the tissues of his lungs, diluting and weakening the blood that he exhaled. It had to be full strength and they weren't likely to get a refill.

He could feel his cheeks puffing up like Satchmo as he sucked at the smoke, trying very hard not to think about how utterly weird and wrong this was in every possible way. When he'd filled his mouth up as much as he possibly could, he pulled away, eyes watering and motioning for the flask. She handed it to him and he wrapped his lips around the neck, letting the smoke flow out, filling the flask. He screwed the cap on tight.

He coughed, feeling sure that he'd gotten her blood up his nose. That heavy amber scent felt embedded in his sinuses. The tissues inside his mouth felt dry and strange. He was so thirsty that sucking on the sand where the Alpha had poured out Xochi's whisky was starting to seem like a really good idea. He pocketed the flask and tried to think of something clever to say. Nothing came to mind. Talk about awkward.

"Wow, yeah, okay," he said. "So, thanks for that. I'll call you sometime."

She didn't answer. She just stretched out her arms in a crucifixion pose, closed her eyes and fell backward. Before she hit the sand, the sky opened and swallowed her. In an instant, she was gone.

Dean really hoped this was going to work.

When Dean finally made it back to the Rover, it was full dark. Xochi and Claudia were still shooting, using the headlights for illumination. Xochi was standing behind Claudia, shaking the girl's shoulders to try and loosen up her posture. Claudia still looked tense, her whole body flinching with every shot. But she was hitting the plastic bottles more often than she was missing.

When Dean called out to them Claudia turned to him, gun pointed unthinkingly in his direction. Xochi grabbed Claudia's arm and pushed it down so the barrel pointed at the ground, slapping the girl in the back of the head with her free hand.

"Don't ever point a gun at something you don't intend to kill," Xochi said.

"Sorry," Claudia said, scolded puppy eyes all remorseful for a fleeting second, then bounding enthusiastically over to Dean.

To his surprise, she didn't throw her arms around him, although she obviously wanted to.

"Well?" she asked.

"What can I say?" he asked, pulling the flask and

shaking it. "Chicks dig me."

"What is it?" Xochi asked. "Not whisky?"

"Blood," he said. "From the Alpha Borderwalker. Let's get on the road and I'll tell you the whole story."

Dean took the first shift driving, explaining what had happened with the Alpha, but leaving out the details of how he had talked her into helping him.

"So let's say this works," Sam said. "Which we really have no way of testing until it's too late. But say it does, how are we supposed to administer this blood to our Borderwalker? You can't put smoke in a syringe. Or can you?"

"Maybe you need to breath it into her mouth," Xochi said.

"And you think she's just gonna let me make out with her?" Dean asked. "What if she bites my lips off?"

"I thought you said chicks dig you," Xochi said. "I'm sure you can convince her."

"Hey," Claudia said. "This is my mom we're talking about here."

"Sorry," Dean said.

"I'll call Bobby," Sam said. "We'll see if he has any ideas. Meanwhile, we'd better stop for chow and supplies."

A while later they pulled into a strange little roadside stand that was the only thing open for miles. It was mostly outdoors with a tin roof on four poles covering a few cheap tables and a terrifying out-house kind of toilet with an old lady sitting on a lawn chair by the door. She had a moustache like Burt Reynolds. It took Dean a second to realize that she was selling toilet paper. By the individual square.

Xochi and Claudia ordered a big mess of mysterious food, which turned out to be blazingly spicy and amazingly good, even after Dean found out that it was actually goat meat.

After they finished their meal, Dean and Xochi headed over to the cooler for more beer. Claudia was buying something from a candy vendor. When she turned toward Dean, he saw that it was a pack of cigarettes. He watched her open it and stick one in the corner of her mouth.

"Hey," he said. "You can't smoke."

"Why not?" She pulled out a lighter and lit the cigarette. "Because it's bad for me? We're all probably gonna die anyway."

Dean took the cigarette out of her mouth and dropped it to the ground, crushing it under his boot heel.

"Because you're fifteen," Dean said. "And because I say so."

He held out his hand for the pack. She frowned.

"What," Claudia said. "It's okay for you to get all bombed every night, but I can't have one cigarette?"

"That's right," Dean said. "You know why? Because I'm over twenty-one and you aren't. Don't like it, you can write your local congressman."

"We're not even in America," Claudia said.

"I said no," Dean said. "And that's final. Now gimme."

Dean was expecting a big teenage tantrum, but she just bowed her head and handed him the pack. Dean handed the cigarettes back to the vendor, who gave Claudia a ziploc bag full of strange pastel-colored candies instead.

"You are a good daddy," Xochi said to Dean, watching Claudia walk back to their table with her candy.

Xochi paid the beer lady, handed a beer to Dean, then took one for herself and cracked the cap using an opener on a chain locked to the handle of the cooler. Dean thought about his own father. About Ben and what Huehuecoyotl had said. He opened his beer.

"I think that's what her crush on you is really all about," Xochi said, taking a swig from her bottle. "She just wants someone to zip her up inside his jacket."

Dean nodded. He took a swallow of his beer. There wasn't anything he could do about that. He was going to do everything he could to protect that kid, but it would ultimately be up to her to sink or swim.

FORTY

Before they left, Xochi bought a bottle of tequila and some purified water. While Sam gassed up the Rover, Dean bought three weird, bootleg CDs from a blind kid who had his wares spread out on a plastic tablecloth by the side of the road. Dean paid a dollar for all three. Probably outrageously over-priced, but he didn't care.

"We're covered tune-wise for the rest of the drive," Dean said, showing the CDs to Xochi. "Check this out. This is gonna be Sam's new favorite disk right here."

He held up a disk that was hand-labeled "SEX ROCK!!!" No information at all about what was actually on the disk. The other two were labeled "*Lo Mejor de* Led Zeppelin" and "*Los Grandes Exitos de* CLASSIC ROCK."

When they got back on the road, Xochi took the wheel and Dean rode shotgun, playing DJ with his new disks. The Zep CD was just what you'd expect and the "Classic" one was an interesting mix of obvious hits with more obscure tracks, but the "SEX ROCK" disk was the clear winner of the bunch. An astoundingly cheesy grab-bag of dirty hair-metal songs that seemed scientifically engineered to the precise specifications that would most annoy his brother.

Three songs in and Sam and Claudia were ready to stage a bloody mutiny against Dean. He responded to their threats by singing along. When "Hot Cherie" by Hardline came on, it got immediately rewritten by Dean as "Hot Xochi."

"You get me hot, Xochi," he sang, loud and shamelessly off-key. "I want what you've got all over me."

"You want this all over you?" she asked, showing him a gloved fist.

Dean ignored her, singing even louder.

"I'm ready to rock you long and rough!"

Xochi swore in Spanish and hit the skip button on the CD player. Next up was "Smooth Up In Ya" by the Bulletboys.

"Dean," Sam said from the back seat. "I'm about ready to throw that damn CD out the window. I never thought I'd actually say this, but why don't you put Led Zeppelin back on."

"Witnesses!" Dean said, pointing to Xochi and Claudia. "You both heard him say that."

"If I have to hear 'Misty Mountain Hop' one more time," Claudia said. "I'm going to shoot everyone in this car. I can do that now, you know."

"In fact," Sam said. "You know what? Pull over. It's my turn to drive. Claudia, you got shotgun. I'm leaving the tunes up to you."

"Yes!" Claudia said, fist in the air.

"No way," Dean said. "This is not a musical democracy."

"It is now," Sam said.

The fact that Dean was still able to get on Sam's nerves with his musical selection was weirdly reassuring. It was one of the few connections that he still had with this stranger in his brother's skin. It gave him hope that Sam really was still in there.

Xochi pulled over onto the dusty shoulder and got out from behind the wheel, stretching her arms up high above her head. Dean got out too.

"You giving up?" Dean asked Xochi. "Just like that? I thought you were on my side."

"I'm not giving up," she said. She pulled out the bottle of tequila and cracked the cap. "I just know when it's time to let someone else drive."

She took a slug and then handed the bottle to Dean.

"Good point," he said. "I'll drink to that."

Settled into the back seat with Xochi and the bottle, Dean realized that he was probably in for another night of sleeping with her but not really sleeping with her. This was going to require very careful calculation of alcohol consumption on his part. It either had to be less than the amount that would having him thinking it would be a good idea to make a play for her right then and there or else it had to be so much that something like that wasn't even an option and he'd just pass out. Judging by the size of the bottle and the fact that he was sharing it with a thirsty girl like Xochi, he was thinking he'd better go with option A.

Claudia was searching across the radio dial when a lush, dream-like song came on featuring a melancholy male singer crooning in Spanish.

"This is *Caifanes*," Xochi said. "'*Los Dioses Occultos*.' I love this song."

"Cool," Claudia said. "Sounds almost like a Mexican version of The Cure."

This sort of music was way too girly for Dean, but he wasn't really listening anyway. He looked out the window at the black nothingness they were driving through and then down at the bottle. Thought about what they were driving into. About the fact that this was probably the calm before the storm. Their last quiet night. He took his last swallow of tequila and handed it back to Xochi. Watched her drink. She offered the bottle back to him and he shook his head.

"I'm good," he said.

She looked at him with questioning eyes, then shrugged and took another pull.

The hypnotic, drowsy music had a soporific effect on everybody in the car. Everyone but Sam, driving silently and lost in his own unknowable thoughts. Claudia had curled up like a cat in the front seat. Dean felt weary and tired, but still wound-up and unable to completely relax. There was nothing to look at in the dark cocoon of the Rover except Xochi. He watched her wrap her lips around the mouth of the nearly empty bottle, the muscles in her long neck working as she swallowed. She was making short work of that tequila.

"It is funny, no?" she asked.

She was watching him too.

"What's funny?" he asked.

"I will admit to you something about myself," she said. As she drank, her English got rougher, blurry around the edges. "I have never sleep together with a man as many times as I sleep with you." She shook her head, waving the hand that held the bottle. "Only one other man. My husband. *Ex*-husband." She shrugged. "With lovers, I do not sleep. I make love, and then I leave."

"Yeah," Dean said. He looked away, at the dark nothing outside the window. "Me, too."

She downed the very last of the tequila and let the empty bottle drop to the floor behind the driver's seat.

"Sex is not trust," she said. "Sleep is trust. And trust is difficult for me."

He didn't say *me too* again. He didn't need to.

"But I trust you, Dean," she said. "You and Sam. I shouldn't, but I do. You are like my family."

Dean had no idea what to say in response to something like that. She clearly had quite a buzz going and was veering dangerous close to *I frickin love you, man* kind of drunk buddy talk. Under different circumstances it would be way too easy for Dean to steer that kind of talk in an entirely different direction.

"Speaking of sleep," he said instead. "We should probably get some. It's gonna be dawn before you know it."

"Yes," she said. "You are right."

She slid across the seat and laid her head down on his chest. He just sat there for a minute, stunned and unsure what to do with his arms. Eventually, he gave in and put them around her so he wouldn't have to keep holding them up the air. She snuggled against him with a wordless, sleepy noise, her hand sliding across his belly and around his waist. He looked up and saw Sam watching him in the rearview mirror with smug amusement. It was going to be a long night.

FORTY-ONE

Xochi woke up in the back seat of the Rover with her face pressed into Dean's armpit. She looked up at him and saw that he was not sleeping. He was looking down at her with his stubbled mouth twisted into a smirk.

"How's my deodorant holding up?" Dean asked.

"Not so good," she said, sitting up and sliding away from him.

"Admit it," Dean said. "You kinda like my man stink, don't you?"

She could feel her cheeks flush hot. She would rather die than admit it to him, but she did. The raw, natural scent of men's bodies had always played a major yet not entirely conscious part in her decision to have sex with them. It didn't matter how good-looking they were, if she didn't like their scent, it wasn't going to happen. And if she did, well, then they were a lot harder to ignore.

"Where are we?" she asked Sam, pushing a few stray

strands of hair out of her eyes and peering out through the window.

They were no longer in the middle of nowhere. The road was lined with tire shops and garages, bars and warehouses and storefront churches. Still mostly closed. There was the slightest flush of dawn on the edge of the eastern sky.

"Just outside Guanajuato," he replied. "We'll be there before the sun comes up."

"I think we should…" she began.

Claudia cut her off with a sharp gasp, suddenly sitting bolt upright in the passenger seat.

"What is it?"

"They're coming," she whispered.

A *Nagual* woman leapt up onto the hood of the Rover, fist smashing through the driver's side of the windshield and shifting from a human hand to a broad panther paw.

Sam swerved, fighting to keep control of the big, unresponsive Rover on the rough road. The *Nagual* swiped at him with her claws, slashing his shirt. To Xochi's surprise, Claudia reacted quickly and efficiently by drawing the snub-nosed .38 and firing through the hole in the glass. She hit the *Nagual* in the chest and the creature shrieked and rolled off the hood.

There was a brief, almost comical moment where Xochi and Dean both drew their guns and tried simultaneously to push each other protectively back and out of harm's way. It took less than a full second for them to focus in on the danger and start working together to get Claudia out of the front seat. The front passenger side window shattered as Dean reached around the seat and hit the lever that dropped it straight back, while Xochi grabbed Claudia and hauled her backward, into the back seat between them.

Five or six huge crows swooped and dove around the roof of the car while another panther-woman ran beside the smashed passenger window, human from the waist up and holding a thin black reed to her lips.

"Are you hit?" Dean asked.

"I don't think…" Claudia began.

One of the crows dive-bombed the windshield, shattering the already cracked glass and shifting swiftly into a man with long black hair, crouching on the front seat and reaching for Claudia with black clawed hands still hooked and bird-like.

Dean let the *Nagual* have it with the shotgun at point-blank range. The thunderous sound was deafening inside the car and the crow man's entire upper half disintegrated into a spray of glowing cinders and feathers. Xochi could see but not hear Dean let out an exuberant cowboy whoop. She pushed Claudia's head down and took aim at another crow circling the car. The first shot missed but the second hit, sending the bird spiraling and shifting until it hit the ground fully human.

Xochi saw Dean grab Sam's shoulder, mouth making the shape of his brother's name, probably yelling, though she still couldn't hear. She saw that Sam was driving with one hand, the other on the side of his neck. A thin, feathered dart was sticking out from between his fingers. He swerved to avoid an oncoming truck and then slumped over the wheel, laying on the horn as the Rover left the road and slammed into the flimsy wall of a neighboring warehouse.

The back door on the driver's side flew open, throwing Xochi and Claudia out onto the oily concrete floor while the Rover plowed into a large stack of boxes filled with plastic flip-flop sandals.

Xochi rolled into a crouch and tried to stand, but the damaged structure of the building was giving way, heavy beams crashing down all around her. She ducked and weaved through the chaos, trying to make her way to Claudia, when something hit her in the back of the head, making the world go red.

She staggered and fell to her knees, palms on the concrete. She didn't seem to have her gun. Her hearing was starting to come back and she thought she heard Claudia screaming her name but her vision was blurred and eclipsed with spangles. She felt around her on the floor until her fingers found the handle of the .45.

"Dean," she called. "Dean, protect Claudia!"

She shook her head to clear it and struggled to her feet, forcing her eyes to focus. Sam was still slumped behind the wheel. Dean had just shoved the other back door open and was crawling out, shotgun in one hand and ammo bag in the other, squinting against the blood that flowed from a cut just below his hairline.

Claudia was nowhere to be seen.

Xochi ran to the massive hole the Rover had torn in the warehouse wall. She was just in time to see a trio of crows carrying Claudia away, one clutching each shoulder of her shirt, the other the waistband of her jeans. She hung ragdoll loose in their grip. Not struggling, probably not conscious. Maybe not even alive. Xochi didn't dare fire at the *Nagual*, for fear they would drop Claudia to her death. If she wasn't dead already.

Xochi sank to her knees in the street, gun falling from her numb fingers.

FORTY-TWO

When Dean crawled free of the wrecked Rover, he couldn't see Xochi or Claudia anywhere, but all he could think about was Sam. The first thing he did when he got himself up on his feet was to run to the driver's door and pull Sam out from behind the wheel. Sam was limp, a dead weight lolling against Dean's chest as he half dragged, half carried his brother away from the leaking wreck.

"Sammy," Dean said. "Come on, don't do this to me, man. If you're dead again, I swear I'm gonna frickin' kill you."

Dean's legs felt weak as he got Sam out of the collapsing building and laid him out on the side of the road. A small crowd of curious spectators had gathered, advising Dean in Spanish and waving their arms. He ignored them, concentrating on his brother.

He pressed his ear to Sam's lips listening for breath. Nothing. He pulled the dart out of Sam's neck and then felt around for a pulse. It was there, but barely, weak and slow.

"Okay," Dean said. "Okay, stay with me Sammy. You hear me? Stay with me."

This hunt had been a bad idea from the beginning. This wasn't just some entertaining little side bet, this was a nightmare that kept on getting worse with every turn. He should have never agreed to do this, he should have kept on pushing to try and find a way to get Sam's soul back. Because as furious as he may have been when Sam let him get turned by that vamp, as much as it hurt him that this new version of Sam didn't care if Dean lived or died, he just couldn't bring himself to give up on the kid. He'd come close, more than once, but in the end, blood was blood, and Sam was all he had left.

Kneeling there in the dust with his brother's barely breathing body in his arms, Dean realized suddenly that he didn't have a clue what would happen to Sam's soul if his body died. Would it stay trapped in that cage for eternity? There was no way Dean was going to let that happen. They were so deep into this now that the only way out was through.

He thought he heard the word *policia* more than once from the onlookers and turned toward the crowd.

"*No policia!*" he said, waving his arms in a broad negative pantomime. "*Por favor, no policia!*"

That's when Xochi appeared out of the crowd, shouting in Spanish and running to Dean.

"Is he...?" she asked.

"Alive," Dean said. "Barely."

Xochi picked up the discarded dart and sniffed at the tip, then bent down and sniffed at Sam's slack, open lips.

"I think this is a sleep drug," Xochi said. "This dart was probably meant for Claudia."

"How can you be sure?" Dean asked.

"Because if it was traditional *Nagual* poison," she said, "he would be having convulsions and there would be an acidic yellow foam around his mouth."

"Where is Claudia?"

Xochi shook her head, expression grim.

"They've got her."

Dean clenched his fist.

"Dead?"

"I hope not," she said.

A burly young man with long, curly hair and a Cannibal Corpse T-shirt pulled up in a battered, primer black El Camino, honking and hollering for people to get out of his way. He leaned out the driver's window and called out to Dean, motioning at the open truck bed.

"Come on," Xochi said, grabbing Sam's ankles. "Let's get him into the back."

Dean grabbed Sam under the arms and the two of them lifted him into the bed of the El Camino. Dean climbed in back with Sam and Xochi got up front. The driver pulled out into traffic before Xochi could close the passenger door. There was no tailgate, so Dean had to hang on to Sam with one arm and wrap a hank of knotted rope around the other to anchor himself to the body of the truck so the two of them didn't slide out the back every time the driver hit the gas.

The El Camino took them down into the twisted, cobbled streets of Guanajuato. There didn't seem to be any logic at all to the haphazard intersections, winding alleys, and damp, dripping tunnels. If there were any traffic lights or signs, they were more like casual suggestions that everyone ignored. Getting from one place to the other in this town seemed to be more like improvisational theater than actual driving. It was really a beautiful little town, full of gorgeous buildings, churches and theaters, but Dean was watching Sam, willing him to wake up.

The driver pulled up in front a little row of shops, none of which looked open. Xochi got out and came around back to give Dean a hand with Sam. Once they got him down out of the truck bed, Xochi called out to the driver and waved. The driver stuck an arm out the window in salute and then drove away.

"Who was that?" Dean asked, adjusting his grip on Sam.

"I don't know," Xochi said. "He said his name was Alejandro."

"Why did he help us?" Dean asked, watching the El Camino drive away.

"He liked my ass."

Dean laughed, adjusting Sam's weight again.

"I won't argue with that," he said. "Where are we taking Sam?"

"Here," she said, gesturing with her chin to an unmarked door.

She knocked on the door and it was answered by a person

who looked to be in their early sixties. Dean couldn't tell if they were a man or a woman. The features were rough and heavy, mannish and free of make-up, but the fluffy white hair was long, elaborately coiffed and curled. The clothes were plain, loose-fitting, and black, except for a bright purple, sparkly scarf with a beaded fringe. Jeweled rings on every thick finger but nails trimmed short and unpainted. Purple cowboy boots.

Xochi introduced herself and Dean. The person said their name was Lulo and exchanged a few Spanish words with Xochi, before motioning for them to enter. Lulo's voice did nothing to clear up Dean's confusion. It was low in pitch but distinctly feminine in tone.

They were led into a small cluttered room that looked like it had been decorated by the Native American Liberace in 1971. There was a full-sized mannequin suspended from the ceiling as if flying, dressed in an outfit that might have been selected by a drag-queen playing Pocahontas in a Las Vegas show. There were tons of kitschy tomahawks and feather headdresses and other "Indian" knickknacks, all embellished with various glittery, homemade touches. One whole corner was taken up with an elaborate altar covered in candles, incense, coins and small, greenish oranges. Above the altar was a painting of a shirtless guy with a coyote head and a red flute. Dean assumed it was an image of Huehuecoyotl. Lulo motioned for Dean to bring Sam over to a pink-velvet couch covered in thick, clear-plastic slipcovers.

Lulo looked Sam over, touching his wrists and forehead, smelling his breath and pushing his hair back from his face.

Dean wasn't thrilled about the idea of this weird stranger messing with his brother, but he trusted Xochi. He didn't want to and certainly hadn't planned to, but he did. He had to. He looked over at her and she gave him a slight, reassuring nod.

Lulo said something to Xochi in Spanish and left the room.

"Okay," Dean said. "First of all, is that Lulo person a guy or a woman?"

"Lulo is a two-spirit shaman," Xochi answered, as if that explained everything.

"I don't get it." Dean frowned. "I mean, everybody's gotta be one or the other, right?"

"Lulo doesn't."

Dean had no idea what to make of that.

"Well," Dean said, shrugging. "If I'm not gonna date her… him… whatever, then I guess it doesn't matter to me. All that matters right now is whether or not this person can help Sam."

"Sam will be okay without help," Xochi said. "Lulo confirmed that he is only sleeping. But we can't do anything if we have to carry him around like this. We need him awake and able to help us, so Lulo has agreed to mix up a tonic to reverse the effect of the drug."

"And what about Claudia? We gotta find her."

"My guess is that the *Nagual* have drugged her like they drugged Sam. They will want to keep her hidden until she wakes. Once that happens, they will question her."

"Question her," Dean echoed. He knew exactly what that meant.

"They will make her tell them where Elvia is. Then they will kill her."

"Any idea where they might have taken her?" Dean asked.

Xochi shook her head. "But you know who will know where she is?"

"Who? Lulo?"

"Elvia."

Lulo returned with a small pink cordial glass filled with dark liquid, motioning to Dean to lift Sam's head. Dean put his arm around his brother and cupped the back of his head. Lulo held the glass to Sam's lips. Some of the murky tonic dribbled down Sam's chin, but the rest went down his throat. Sam's reaction was immediate and violent, as if he'd received an adrenalin shot to the heart.

He sat bolt upright, gasping, eyes flashing wide and white around the edges like a frightened horse. He knocked the glass out of Lulo's hand and might have actually taken a swing at the shaman if Dean hadn't been right there to grab his brother's arm.

"Hey, whoa," Dean said. "Take it easy, Sammy."

"What the hell happened?" Sam asked. He looked around the room. "Where's Claudia?"

Dean filled him in while Lulo gathered up the broken pink glass off the sparkly linoleum.

"All right then," Sam said. "We'd better go find Elvia."

"I don't know," Dean said. "You really think she's gonna listen to us after we tried to kill her?"

"If you've got a better idea, I'd love to hear it," Sam said.

"If you convinced the Alpha to help us," Xochi said, "you can convince Elvia."

"How did this hunt become all about me sweet-talking chick monsters?" Dean asked.

"It's only because you are so good at it," Xochi said.

"Yeah, but the Alpha was…" Dean struggled for the right way to say this. "Well not exactly normal, but normal for what she is. Elvia, not so much. She's obviously been driven dangerously insane by everything she went through. I don't think she can be reasoned with."

"Come on, Dean," Sam said. "You've had plenty of crazy broads in your life. Remember Niki Drummond?"

"You mean the facehugger?" Dean shuddered. "How could I forget? I thought I was gonna have to chew my own leg off to get away from her."

"You can do this, Dean," Xochi said.

"But I don't think Elvia even understands English," Dean said.

"I will translate," Xochi said. "We are wasting valuable time with this argument. Whatever we are going to do, we need to do it now. Right away."

"She's right," Sam said, getting to his feet. He pulled out that huge Magnum and checked it over. "Did you get the ammo?"

Dean nodded, hefted the bag.

"Okay then," Sam said. "Are we doing this or are we doing this?"

Lulo came over to Sam and took his hand, saying something Dean didn't understand.

"Lulo wants to bless you," Xochi said.

"Bless me?" Sam frowned.

"Lulo says that you also have two spirits," Xochi said, translating as Lulo spoke. "Not male and female, but good and evil, intertwined like connected twins who can never be separated. All your life, gods, demons, and men have been trying to push you one way or the other. But Lulo wants you to know that you will always have these two spirits inside you. That you must learn to accept and embrace that duality and find your own balance between the two. To be your own man, on your own terms. Lulo wants to bless your... your vessel while it is empty, so that when your twin spirits are freed from their imprisonment, the wounded halves will... integrate together more harmoniously."

Dean looked at Sam and could see that his brother wasn't buying any of this mumbo-jumbo. Twin spirits or not, Dean wondered if Sam was still just as dead set against getting his soul back as he was the last time they'd talked about it. They'd been way too busy to get into it again and Dean certainly wasn't gonna be the one to bring it up, but he wondered. And although Dean wasn't really sure if he was buying this mumbo-jumbo either, he did find it interesting that Lulo had said *when* Sam's soul is freed, not *if*.

"Fine," Sam said. "Whatever. Just make it quick."

Lulo put a hand in the center of Sam's chest, eyes closed and humming softly. Sam shot a glance toward Dean but said nothing. After about a minute, Lulo stepped back and nodded, big smile revealing two missing teeth, one on top and one on the bottom. Lulo then handed Sam a black-and-white-striped candle in a glass tube and said something in Spanish.

"Rub this candle on your hair, your face and your body," Xochi said.

Sam looked skeptical but did as requested. Lulo took the candle, lit it and added it to the others cluttering up the glittery altar.

"Can we go now?" Sam asked.

"Yes," Xochi said. "We can go now."

FORTY-THREE

El Museo De Las Momias was still closed when they got there.
Which was a good thing. The last thing Dean wanted to deal
with was crowds of sunburned tourists if Elvia decided to
go on another rampage.

It was an old colonial building, tan and brown with rows
of columns and archways along the front. The place was
locked up tight as a drum, all heavy bars and steel gates.
No windows and only one other side door—some kind of
emergency exit around the corner from the main entrance.
The alarm was a pushover, but the lock was a bitch, a
Medeco 80 series MVP cam lock. Not totally pick-proof, but
a real pain in the ass. Dean sent Sam to watch out for guards
while he disabled the alarm, got out his picks, and went to
work on the lock.

Dean had always thought of locks like women, and he
liked a challenge. He shut out everything else around him
and zeroed his focus down to the smallest micro-movements

of his fingertips. Didn't think about Claudia, or Sam, or the Star Demons. He just concentrated on the feel of the picks against the tumbler. He almost had it. Almost had it—

Then the door opened from the inside, startling Dean and making him step back and drop the picks, hand going reflexively to the shotgun grip. Xochi stuck her head out of the doorway, looked around, and waved Sam and Dean inside.

Sam smiled and held out his hand for Dean to go first. Dean gathered up his picks and ducked into the dark, stuffy interior of the silent museum.

"How the hell did you get in?" Dean asked Xochi.

Xochi gestured toward a young, chubby guard lurking in a distant doorway looking pink faced and smitten.

"You're not the only one who knows how to sweet talk the opposite sex," she said.

She blew the guard a kiss and winked. He looked down, turning even redder. Dean grinned.

"Okay," Sam said. "So how are we going to find Elvia?"

"I think I have an idea of where she might be," Xochi said.

She clicked on her mini-Maglite and led them down a long dark hallway and into an exhibition hall lined with glass cases. Dean followed with his own flashlight and Sam took the rear. Playing his light over the glass cases, Dean knew what he would be seeing, but knowing and seeing are two different things.

The cases were filled with corpses. Dozens and dozens of desiccated dead bodies. Delicate, papery, and dry, with yawning mouths and empty eye sockets. Many still had hair. Some had ragged clothes. Most were naked. Some were laid out flat, others propped up with wire as if standing on their withered, curled up feet.

"What's with these all corpses anyway?" Sam asked.

"They are natural mummies," Xochi said. "Dried up because of certain minerals in the soil. Around the late 1800s, a burial tax was created and if families could not pay for their loved ones, the bodies would be dug up and kicked out of the graveyard. But nobody wanted to just throw the bodies away with the garbage, so they piled them up in storage. This practice was outlawed in the fifties, but soon tourists started coming to see the collection of mummies. That's why they opened this museum."

"Wow," Dean said, shining his light on the box-kite ribcage and shriveled breasts of a mummy with long wispy hair bound into a braid. "Fun for the whole family."

Truth was, Dean knew that while Lisa would probably be less than thrilled, Ben would love something like this. Dean needed to push thoughts like that right out of his mind and stay focused.

"So where do you think Elvia is hiding?" Sam asked.

"Well," Xochi said. "If I was a confused, crazy mama who lost her baby daughter, I think I would want to be with the *angelitos*."

"The what?" Dean asked.

"Little angels?" Sam said, with a questioning tone.

"Yes," Xochi said, pointing at a doorway down at the far end of another long hallway. "The little angels."

Dean raised his light to a sign reading "*LOS ANGELITOS*"and under that in English "The world's smallest mummy!"

The *angelitos* were dead babies. Everything from larger toddlers to the "world's smallest," an unborn fetus that had been inexplicably been removed from its dead mother and displayed separately. Many were dressed up in fancy outfits and laid out on lacy pillows. Some had little plaques explaining who they were and others were unlabeled, mysterious and unknowable.

Xochi froze and put her hand on Dean's chest, holding him back and pressing a finger to her lips. That's when Dean heard it too. A soft, keening sound, like a hurt and lonely dog. One of the cases at the far end of the room was open.

FORTY-FOUR

They'd been forced to leave the obsidian weapons back in Nogales, Arizona, and even though Dean knew he was supposed to be trying to talk to her, not kill her, he still hated going into a situation like this without a suitable weapon in hand.

"Dean," Sam said, gesturing to the open case.

The old-fashioned wooden cases were raised up off the tiled floor on six-inch-high legs, leaving a gap beneath. A long gray hand was reaching slowly out from the shadows underneath the cases. Dean could feel that same weird static charge he felt at Claudia's house racing across the surface of his skin.

"Elvia?" he said.

He crouched down slowly, tilting his head to peer underneath the cases. The Borderwalker was crammed into the narrow space, clutching a mummified baby in a dusty christening dress. Her form was human but abnormally thin and covered in patchy gray hair. Her black-hole eyes bored into Dean, black lips dripping venom and twitching into a snarl. She was breathing too fast, almost panting.

"Elvia, we're not going to hurt you," Dean said, looking back over his shoulder at Xochi.

Xochi repeated his words in Spanish.

She growled, low and harsh, nails clawing at the tile.

"Your daughter's in danger," Dean said. "She needs our help."

Again, Xochi translated.

"Where is she?" Dean asked. "Where is Claudia?"

Xochi got down on one knee beside him and repeated his words.

Silence.

"We should cure her now," Sam said. "Cure her, or kill her."

"What?" Dean said. He kept his eyes on Elvia.

"Now, while we have the chance," Sam said. "We may not get another shot."

"If we cure her now," Xochi said. "She will be an ordinary human again. Her bond with Claudia will be severed. Same if we kill her. Without that psychic connection, we won't find Claudia. Once the *Nagual* know the connection has been severed, there will be no reason for them to keep Claudia alive."

"Look, I'm sorry about that, but…"

"No, Sam," Dean said. "No way. I already see where you're going with this, and you're overruled."

"Overruled?" Sam took a step closer to Dean. "We can't put the life of one girl before the millions of lives that will be lost if the Clawed Butterfly makes it into our world. Including our own. That's just crazy. Suicidal."

Elvia retreated further under the cases, shivering.

"You're scaring her," Xochi said.

"Back off, Sam," Dean said. "Just let me talk to her, will ya? I'll try to get her to accept the cure after I find out where Claudia is. But it's Claudia first. I said I was gonna do everything in my power to protect that kid, and that's exactly what I'm gonna do. You just watch the door and make sure I don't get c-blocked by Teo and those crow-guys."

Dean moved closer to the case, easing himself down onto his belly. Xochi was right beside him.

"Elvia, listen to me," Dean said. "I know you're scared, but your daughter is scared too. You can feel it can't you? How scared she is?"

He waited for Xochi to translate, studying Elvia's shifting face and hollow eyes. She was staring intently at Dean, frozen and tense as a cornered animal.

"She needs her mother," Dean said. "She needs our help just like you do. Tell us where she is and we're gonna get the both of you out of here, okay? I'm not gonna let Teo hurt you anymore."

Those bony gray fingers slid back out and gripped Dean's hand. It was hard not to flinch from her feverish touch, but he managed.

"Where is she?" he asked again.

Her answer came as a brutal blast of raw agony inside Dean's head, accompanied by a powerful sense memory of shoving baby Claudia into a clump of dry brush and a rush of something that wasn't really words, more like a primitive torrent of emotion.

"...*leftherleftherleftherlefther*..."

Dean touched his nose, fingers coming away wet with blood. Elvia's anguished shriek was echoing inside his head like the worst migraine of all time.

"You had to leave her to protect her," Dean said, struggling to keep his thoughts straight. "But now you have a chance to find her again. Find her and save her, Elvia. Tell me where she is."

Elvia let go of Dean's hand and came crawling out from under the cases. No one else moved. Sam's hand was on the grip of the Magnum, eyes narrow, watching.

"Easy now," Dean said.

Elvia dropped the mummified baby, shifting as she crawled. More coyote-like now but hunched and mangy, scabrous skin alive with insects. She was moving away from Dean, toward the doorway of the exhibit hall.

"Where are you going?" Dean asked.

Xochi translated. Elvia ignored them.

"Elvia?" Dean said, getting slowly to his feet. "Elvia, where is your daughter? Where is she?" Xochi's rapid Spanish followed his words.

He could see the muscles in her scrawny haunches bunching up, ready to run. He was afraid he was losing her.

"Elvia, wait, listen to me—" he began. But he was cut off by her answer, echoing inside his skull like the whine of a damaged buzz saw.

"...*here*..."

He caught a flickering image of Claudia, flanked by *Nagual* and standing in front of a row of female mummies.

Elvia leapt, tearing down the hallway.

Dean swore and took off after her, calling back over his shoulder.

"She's here. Claudia's here, in the museum."

Dean followed Elvia down the hall and into a larger room with three doors, the one they came in through, one to the left, and one to the right. Xochi and Sam were close on his heels.

The chubby young guard who'd let Xochi in to the museum was dead, face down in a pool of blood.

There was a soft, rustling sound like the whisper of turning pages or the swish of a woman's skirt. The sound was building and growing in volume. Then a massive, ear-shattering crash as every single glass case in the building shattered simultaneously. Dean grabbed Xochi and hit the tile, covering her with his body, his arms thrown across his face to protect against the spray of jagged glass.

"Sam!" Dean called, raising his head and spotting Sam in the left-hand doorway. "You okay?"

"Fine," Sam said, pulling a shard of glass from his right shoulder. "But we got a problem."

That was an understatement.

The mummies were climbing out of their cases.

FORTY-FIVE

"Awesome," Dean said, shaking broken glass out of his hair and pulling out the sawed-off shotgun. "This is just what we need."

The mummies were surprisingly fast, their movements jerky and puppet-like. Dean let one have it with the shottie, blasting its desiccated head into dust. It kept coming, reaching for him with shaky, skeletal arms. Dozens more were pouring in through all three doorways, separating him from Sam and pushing his brother backwards out the left-hand door.

"You gotta be kidding," Dean said, kicking and swinging, knocking the brittle mummies back—but they just kept coming. "Come on. What the hell is going on here, Xochi?"

"No," Xochi cried, getting up on her knees. "No! Elvia!"

She held her hand out toward the Borderwalker, but the mummies were all over Xochi. They didn't seem to be biting or even really attacking, just crowding her and pushing her back, away from Elvia. Xochi was using her telekinetic spell to smash through the crowd of mummies but they were an unstoppable tide.

Dean risked a look toward Elvia and saw her struggling, enveloped in glowing blue strands just like the ones Teo had used to bind her at Claudia's house.

Xochi screamed something in Spanish. The only word Dean recognized was her sister's name: Teo.

A pair of *Nagual*, one male and one female came in through the right-hand door, animal forms shifting to human as they reached out to grab the bound Borderwalker. Dean took a shot at the man, but several bumbling mummies got in the way, taking the force of the slug and pushing the barrel up toward the ceiling. The *Nagual* and Elvia were gone before Dean could reload.

Xochi had torn a two-foot long piece of wood from one of the shattered cases and was busting mummy heads left and right. Dean followed her lead, breaking off a heavy chunk of wood for himself. It seemed like blunt-force trauma was the way to go with these things. They didn't stop coming until they were smashed to pieces.

"What's with these mummies?" Dean asked. "Why can't we kill them?"

"They are not real," Xochi replied.

"They seem pretty real to me," Dean said, swinging the chunk of wood and caving in a leathery ribcage.

"I mean they are not autonomous," Xochi explained, taking the twiggy legs out from under a half-dressed female mummy. "They have been animated by Teo to slow us down and block us."

"Damn, that bitch is good," Dean said.

Dean heard the distinctive baritone bark of Sam's Magnum, twice, then three times, in the chamber to their left.

"Come on," Dean said, heading for the left-hand door. Xochi followed him.

"Here," Xochi said, putting her shoulder against one of the larger cases right by the door. "Help me."

Dean put his weight against the case.

"One, two…" Xochi counted.

Together they shoved the case over, blocking the mummies from the large room from entering the hallway. There were still plenty of stragglers in the hallway, but it looked like Sam had really cut a swath through the ones on this side of the door. The floor was littered with dry bones and rags and flaps of parchment skin.

Dean dodged the remaining mummies and ducked through another doorway. There, in a long narrow gallery, was Sam, facing off against a single *Nagual* woman. Several of her fellow shifters lay dead around her. She had her arm around a pale and wide-eyed Claudia, stone knife pressed against her throat, using the girl's body as a shield.

Dean raised both his hands, letting the wood drop to the floor.

"Okay," Dean said. "Take it easy. Don't hurt her."

Sam was totally calm and still, expression neutral. The *Nagual* hissed something Dean couldn't understand. Sam raised the Magnum, exhaled slowly and shot the *Nagual* between the eyes.

The *Nagual* went down in shower of sparks. Claudia ran

to Dean, while Sam stepped up to the fallen shifter and gave her a precautionary double tap in what remained of her head.

"You okay, kid?" Dean asked, lifting Claudia's chin and eyeing the trickle of blood where the *Nagual* knife had bit into her skin.

"I knew you'd save me," she said, squeezing Dean's waist so tight he could barely breathe.

"Yeah, well how about a little sugar for Sam?" Dean asked. "He's the one who saved you, not me."

Sam was reloading the Magnum, not paying any attention to either one of them. Claudia let go of Dean and went over to hug Sam.

"Thanks, Sam," she said.

Sam looked over the top of her head at Dean, eyebrows knitting.

"Say 'you're welcome,' Dexter," Dean said.

"You're welcome," Sam said. "Now let's get the hell out of here and figure out how to get Elvia back."

"I heard Xochi's sister saying they needed to get to Mexico City," Claudia said. "But she didn't say exactly where."

"Then we'd better get on the road."

Xochi boosted the only vehicle in the museum parking lot, a bondo-ed pick-up truck covered in religious stickers. Claudia rode up front while Sam and Dean climbed into the bed. The ride was slow and bumpy, constantly thwarted by crazy traffic, and for a good hour, Sam and Dean didn't speak.

"Why did you save Claudia?" Dean finally asked.

Sam didn't answer for a minute, just squinted against the sun.

"Why not?" Sam said. "We still need her, don't we?"

"Yeah, but you didn't know that at the time," Dean said. "For all you knew, Elvia could have been dead at that point."

"I saw that I had a shot. I took it." Sam shrugged. "Couldn't really think of any reason not to."

Dean knew it was impossible, just wishful thinking really, but he found himself wanting to believe that maybe there was some tiny scrap of conscience left in Sam after all. Some little echo inside his head that kept him from taking the easy shot, through Claudia's chest and into the shifter behind her.

A few minutes later, the truck coughed, spluttered and died. Xochi was able to coast over onto the shoulder to get them out of traffic.

Dean and Sam got out of the back while Xochi leaned out the driver's side window.

"This truck has no third gear," she said.

"Lovely," Dean said. "Pop the hood."

He raised the hood, releasing a ton of toxic smoke as he propped it open and peered inside.

"Who knew that you could make a whole engine out of duct tape?" Dean said, waving a hand in front of his face to clear the smoke. He shook his head and closed the hood like it was a coffin lid. "This thing isn't going anywhere."

Xochi got out and fished around in her pockets.

"Let me call Alejandro," she said, unfolding a crumpled bar napkin.

"Who?" Dean asked.

"The guy with the El Camino," Xochi said, pulling out her phone and dialing the number off the napkin.

"He gave you his phone number?" Dean asked.

"Of course," she replied.

She switched to Spanish and turned away from Dean, voice taking on a flirtatious tone.

Dean looked down at his hands. The backs of his hands and forearms were scratched up from the broken glass. Nothing serious.

Xochi ended the call.

"Alejandro is at work right now," she said. "But he's sending his cousin Oscar. He can give us a ride to Santiago de Querétaro. We can get another car there, or, if we find no other choice, we can take the bus into El D.F."

"The bus?" Claudia made a sour face. "I'm not taking the bus. Aren't Mexican busses, like, full of chickens and babies with TB and ten smelly guys mashed up against you?"

"You've been watching too many American movies," Xochi said. "The bus is just a bus. Just normal people, going to work or to visit relatives. No chickens allowed."

"Yeah," Sam said. "But we don't have time to wait for a bus. We're bleeding time here. Every lost minute is an extra mile Teo has on us. At this rate, there's no way we are gonna make it in time to stop her. We still don't have any idea exactly where she's going. Now I've never been to Mexico City, but I understand it's pretty big. "

"You're right," Xochi said. She paused a moment in thought. "Claudia, have you ever tried consciously to link minds with your mother?"

Claudia shook her head.

"It just kinda happens," she said.

"I will teach you," Xochi said. "Once we get on the road. This may be our only chance."

They waited for over an hour in the dusty swelter before a guy pulled up in a ridiculously tricked-out white mid-eighties Monte Carlo SS. He looked about twelve years old, but with way too much hard living around the eyes. Dressed in a shiny, sharkskin suit and a screamingly loud fuchsia-silk dress shirt. He was so short, Dean was surprised he was able to drive without sitting on a phone book. This guy had to be Oscar.

Xochi greeting him in Spanish and made introductions. Dean just nodded and smiled. Xochi sat up front while Dean and Sam had to cram themselves into the back seat with Claudia between them.

As they crept through the snarled and snail-like traffic, the prepaid phone Xochi had given Dean back in Nogales rang in Sam's pocket.

Sam took out the phone, glanced at the screen. He took the call.

"Bobby?" he said. "What have you got?"

Sam listened in silence for several minutes.

"Right," Sam said. "Okay."

He ended the call.

"What did he say?" Dean asked.

Sam kept his voice low, even though it seemed pretty clear that Alejandro's cousin didn't speak English.

"Not much on the possibility of curing Elvia using the Alpha's blood," Sam said. "He says he can't find any info whatsoever on the Borderwalkers, only the most vague allegorical references to the Coyote's Kiss in some old recordings of Native American oral history. We're on our own there. But he had some interesting things to say about the Star Demons."

"Great, let's hear it," Dean said.

"Those soul-chewing teeth," Sam said. "They're a weakness as well as a strength. Probably the Star Demon's only weakness."

"How?" Dean asked. "I don't get it."

"The teeth are made of obsidian. Obsidian is a type of naturally occurring volcanic glass, razor sharp but also brittle and easy to shatter. A couple of good cracks in the mouth with a blunt weapon would essentially defang the demon. The only problem would be getting cut by the flying shards."

"Not to mention getting close enough to score a hit like that," Dean said.

"Right now," Sam said. "That's pretty much all we've got."

The ride to Santiago de Querétaro was agonizingly slow. Xochi tried to make polite conversation with Oscar, but she could feel every passing second cranking the tension inside her higher and higher.

Once they finally got into town, Oscar dropped them off in front of the bus station. Unfortunately, massive lines snaking out the main door made it clear that the bus wasn't going to be an option.

Dean managed to boost a halfway-decent Caddy El Dorado that didn't look like it would fall apart on them, but getting the car out of the city was a whole other challenge. Xochi could tell that dealing with improvisational Mexican driving was making Dean homicidal. He was leaning out the open window, shouting hilariously creative American profanities and shaking his fist at the motorbikes and taxicabs, but there was nothing she could do about that now. She needed to be in the back seat with Claudia.

"Now I want you to listen very carefully to me," Xochi told the girl. "What I am teaching you is not easy. Normally you would need to learn how to link with someone who is right next to you before you would be able to link with people who are far away, but we have no time. You must learn to run before walking, but your natural ability and your bond with your mother are both so strong that I believe you can do it."

"I hope you're right," Claudia said.

"First you must clear your mind," Xochi said. "I know this is hard with so much happening, but it is a critical step. Imagine that you are a glass pitcher and all your thoughts and worries are pouring out of you like water, until you are empty."

Claudia took Xochi's hand and closed her eyes.

"Slow your breathing," Xochi said. "Shut out all the noise around us."

Claudia did as she was told.

"Now," Xochi said. "Say these words after me."

Xochi slowly spoke the ancient words of the mind-linking spell, carefully and clearly enunciating the complicated string of syllables. Claudia stumbled on some of the pronunciation, and Xochi had to struggle to keep her own mind calm and breath even.

"Start again," Xochi said.

She spoke the spell again, even more slowly this time. Claudia followed along, but before she could finish she sucked in a sharp gasp, clutching Xochi's hand tight.

"I see her," Claudia said.

"What do you see?" Xochi asked.

"A huge swap meet," Claudia said. "With all these different color tarps. Hundreds of stalls selling all kinds of weird, cheap stuff. I see the *Nagual* taking Elvia into an empty storefront. A green building."

"Show me," Xochi said, pressing her hand to Claudia's forehead.

A stream of images flooded Xochi's mind. She recognized the place at once.

"Tepito," Xochi said. "El Barrio Bravo. This is a rough neighborhood in the Cuauhtémoc section of Mexico City."

Claudia's eyes opened, looking into Xochi's with a kind of stunned wonder.

"I did it," she said.

"Yes," Xochi said. "You did."

"Tell me about the area," Sam said. "How rough are we talking here?"

"We will have dangers there," Xochi said. "Human and inhuman. But I know the area well. It is full of good people as well as bad. Many of my closest friends are Tepiteños."

"Okay then," Dean said to Xochi. "Now that we got that cleared up, I think it's time for you to drive, before I add a dozen counts of intentional vehicular homicide to my rap sheet."

FORTY-SIX

They made Mexico City by sundown. The area of Tepito was easy to find. The flapping, colorful blue-and-yellow tarps were just like Claudia had described them. Tall wire racks of merchandise. Knock-off perfumes. Fake designer watches and purses. Pirated DVDs. Piles of second-hand clothing and small appliances. Paper flowers and cheap nylon panties. Dean had never seen anything quite like it.

Xochi parked the stolen El Dorado on a side street. They all got out of the car, gathering and checking their weapons, but Xochi seemed distracted, staring up into the night sky. She turned to Dean with real fear in her eyes.

"Dean," she said. "The *Tianquiztli* cluster, can you see it?"

"The what?"

"That's a constellation." Sam said. "The Pleiades, right?"

"You call it 'the seven sisters,'" Xochi said. "We call it 'the marketplace.'"

"I don't see it," Sam said. "Maybe it's just too smoggy.

Or the bright city lights are hiding it."

"Can't you feel that breeze?" Xochi said. "The night is clear. All the other neighboring stars are clear. This is a terrible omen."

"What kind of omen?" Dean asked. "What does it mean?"

"It means the end of the world," she said. "It means demons will devour the earth. It means the *Tzitzimimeh* are coming."

"Are coming?" Sam asked. "Or are here already?"

"Don't you see?" Xochi said. "It's all connected. This place, Tepito, it is the ancient second marketplace. In the time of my Aztec ancestors, this place was a ghetto market for disreputable, lower-class merchants who were not allowed in the main marketplace. Stolen goods have been sold here for hundreds of years. It is now and has always been a place of much illegal activity, and it is the perfect place for Teo and *Itzapapalotl* to conduct their illicit business. Now the celestial marketplace is gone from the sky. It has already begun. The Star Demons are on their way, if they are not here already."

"What's that music?" Claudia asked.

"Sounds like *mariachis*," Xochi said.

They turned the corner and found the street choked with people. There was some kind of parade or street fair in progress. Every tenth person seemed to be holding a large doll, each one wearing a different frilly, elaborate outfit. It took Dean a second to realize that all the dolls had skull faces.

"What is this?" Sam asked.

"No," Xochi said, her voice full of dread. "No, this is terrible. We need to get these poor people out of here!"

"It's a *Santa Muerte* festival, isn't it?" Claudia asked.

"Yes," Xochi said. "And all these people will be meeting the Skinny Lady much sooner than they expect if they stay here tonight."

"Saint Death?" Sam asked. "They worship Death?"

"They think they are Catholics," Xochi explained. "But really they are worshiping the Aztec death goddess *Mictecacihuatl*. Death is neither good or evil. She comes for all of us. We are all equal to her."

"My Tia, Izzy, has an altar to *Santa Muerte* in her backyard," Claudia said. "She put it up after her son got shot. My mom always said she was nuts." Claudia looked down at her hands. "I mean, my adopted mom…"

"Come on," Dean said. "We need to find Elvia."

There was a group of Aztec dancers in full traditional dress gathering up their drums and equipment at the edge of the crowd. A man in a huge, elaborate skull and feather headdress spotted Xochi and raised a hand.

"Javi!" she called to him.

He came running over to where they stood and swept Xochi up in his arms, lifting her off her booted feet and laughing. He was broad-chested and ripped within an inch of his life, wearing nothing but an elaborately embroidered loin cloth. She spoke to him in Spanish, kissing him on the mouth and getting his black-and-white skull make-up on her lips. He set her down, cupping her the curve of her ass with one hand and speaking close to her ear in a low, intimate tone.

"This is my friend Javi," Xochi said. "Dean, Sam, and Claudia."

Dean nodded in silent greeting, biting back on an involuntary and ridiculously powerful surge of competitive, testosterone-fueled dislike for the buff dancer.

Xochi spoke to Javi in rapid-fire Spanish, pointing down the street. Javi nodded and took off in that direction.

"Wow," Claudia said. "Is that your boyfriend?"

"Sometimes," Xochi replied.

"If that was my boyfriend," Claudia said, staring after Javi, "it would definitely be *all* the time. We'd never leave the house."

Dean looked over at Sam, who was suppressing a smirk.

"Looks like you're not the center of the female universe after all, dude," Sam said.

"Come on," Dean said. "I'd look good in a loincloth too, wouldn't I?"

"I don't ever want to know the answer to that question," Sam replied.

Xochi came over to Dean.

"I told Javi to spread the word that one of the gangs is planning a drive-by," she said. "If we're lucky, that will get some of these people out of the street. Meanwhile, we need to start searching these storefronts to see if we can find the empty green one from Claudia's vision. This is where Elvia will be opening the gate."

There was a low rumble under their feet, like the subway or a passing truck. Xochi gripped Dean's arm.

"They're here," Xochi said. "Can't you feel it?"

"I don't feel anything," Sam said.

But Dean did. It was horrible, a pulsating, unnatural resonance that felt like a more subtle version of the work that Xochi's grandmother had done on his wounded soul. The healing scar on his hand was throbbing like a second heart.

"Look!" Claudia said, pointing to a small skirmish going on about a half a block away. It resembled a chaotic bar fight, except more than half of the participants had large, gaping wounds on their arms and faces. Mortal wounds that didn't seem to be slowing them down or affecting them in any way. The fight was swiftly spreading through the gathered celebrants. People were screaming and frantically trying to get away, but it was too crowded and there was nowhere for them to go.

Then, the plate-glass front of one of the shops exploded outwards and Dean got his first look at a Star Demon.

The creature was so big that it had to crouch down to fit through the shattered plate-glass storefront. The first thing Dean saw was long, black machete-clawed fingers clinging to the edges of the broken window. Then a massive head the size of a La-Z-Boy. Corpse-white skin, tiny matte-black eyes, and a wide, under-slung jaw like a lantern fish. Its crooked, obsidian teeth were slick with blood. In place of hair was a crown of gory, bone-white horns and glossy black quills. As it crawled free of the pale-green storefront, Dean could see its emaciated torso was distinctly female. A necklace of severed human hands and impossibly beating hearts swung between the grayish flaps of its crone-like breasts. Blood-shot human eyes studded the long white arms and legs, blinking and rolling as it stood to its full height of nine feet or more.

"Run!" Xochi said.

The four of them tore down the street with a riot on their heels. The soulless zombie victims were spreading through the crowd as swiftly as the mounting panic, and both ends of the street were blocked by competing taco trucks set up to serve the festival crowd.

"In here," Sam said, pushing open the door to a small shoe store and waving them inside.

As soon they were through the door, Sam and Dean worked together to pull down the security gate while Xochi shoved Claudia behind a rack of high-heeled boots and drew her .45. Seconds later, the glass shattered and a dozen bloody, reaching arms were shoved through the spaces in the gate, rattling it on its hinges.

"Headshots?" Dean asked, raising the shotgun.

"Yes," Xochi said, demonstrating by putting a bullet into the forehead of a screeching, middle-aged woman with a bad perm, wearing a sparkly red tube-top.

The moment the zombie fell, three more took her place.

"Come on," Sam said, gesturing to an open door that revealed a flight of stairs on the other side.

Xochi sent Claudia up the steps first and Sam followed close behind.

"Go," Dean said, letting an old guy in a Raiders cap have it with the shotgun.

The security gate was starting to give, peeling loose from its moorings in one corner. The zombies would be in the shop in under a minute.

Dean shot a skinny young man trying to push through the gap and then ran backwards toward the stairs, reloading as he went.

He got to the door just as the zombies busted through the gate. He slammed the door, shoved a large metal garbage can up under the doorknob, then followed Xochi up the stairs.

The second floor was just a bunch of empty offices so they continued up to the roof. The roof access door was reinforced steel, locked with a key lock. Another damn Medeco.

"Dean?" Sam asked.

"On it," Dean said, stepping up to the door and pulling out his lock picks.

His hands were shaking with adrenaline. He took in a long deep breath and struggled to focus, shutting out everything but the feel of the tumbler.

"Dean," Xochi said urgently. "They're in the stairwell."

"Come on, baby," Dean whispered between clenched teeth. "Come on, come on, come on."

Sam and Xochi were firing down the stairs, but Dean ignored it. Focusing.

The lock gave, and popped open.

Dean let out his breath in a shaky laugh and pushed the door open.

"Claudia!" he yelled, pushing the girl through the door and out onto the roof.

Sam followed Claudia and then Xochi. Dean was about to go through the door himself when he felt clutching hands grab the back of his shirt.

FORTY-SEVEN

Dean twisted his body around to face Xochi's friend Javi. His chin was slick with gore, skull make-up smeared and ruined. He'd lost the feathered headdress at some point and there were giant teeth-marks in his shaved scalp. He screamed, blood-webbed teeth snapping inches from Dean's face. Dean fought to shove Javi back far enough to raise the sawed-off for a headshot but the dancer was incredibly strong. Several more zombies were barreling up the stairs behind Javi. Dean had only seconds before they would be on him.

Then, the crack of a gunshot inches from Dean's ear and Javi's forehead burst open with an explosion of brains and bone. Dean kicked the dancer back down the stairs and Xochi was at his side, pulling him through the door and slamming it in the faces of the oncoming zombies.

Xochi and Dean both pressed their backs against the door, expecting to need all of their weight to hold it shut.

Amazingly, the lock Dean had picked re-engaged itself as soon as the door closed and after a few moments, the two of them cautiously stepped away.

Dean looked over at Xochi. Her face was stone, eyes cold and emotionless as she efficiently reloaded the .45.

"Thanks," Dean said.

Xochi nodded without meeting his gaze. He knew better than to say anything else, knowing that this was exactly the way he would react if he were in her shoes. Now was not the time for emotion. That would come later. If there was a later.

Sam and Claudia were both standing at the edge of the roof, looking across an alley at the neighboring building. Dean joined them, looking down at the balls-out chaos ruling the street below.

A second *Tzitzimitl* had crawled out of the empty green shop to join the first, cutting a swath through the terrified crowd. Zombies were everywhere, ganging up on the few remaining living people and dragging them down.

"Where the hell are the police?" Dean asked.

"Police do not come to this part of the *Barrio Bravo*," Xochi replied. "We need to find a way across to the green store where Elvia has opened the gate."

"It's too far to jump," Sam said. "But look…"

Dean looked at the roof of the building on the other side of the alley. There was a large wooden extension ladder lying near the fire door.

"If we could get that ladder," Sam said. "We could climb across and from there the buildings are all connected. We could get down into the green shop from above and get to Elvia."

"And how do you propose to do that?" Dean asked. "If we could reach that ladder, we wouldn't need it."

Sam didn't answer. He didn't have to.

"Oh, hell, no," Dean said. "Don't even think about it."

"The zombies, they're chasing souls, right?" Sam said. "So are the Star Demons. I don't have mine, so wouldn't they leave me alone?"

"We have no way of knowing that for sure," Dean said. "What if you're wrong?"

"What if I'm not?" Sam asked. "I can sneak past them and get into that other building, then lay the ladder across the gap for you guys."

"Dean," Xochi said. "This is why I needed Sam for this hunt to be successful. It wasn't clear until this moment, but I think this... this is his destiny."

Could that be true? Could it be that Sam was sent back from Hell without his soul for a reason? Could this be the reason, to stop yet another apocalypse? A double-blind deep cover mission into a foreign land where Castiel and all of Heaven's minions were not allowed to interfere? Maybe so and maybe not, but either way, Dean just wasn't seeing any other option.

"Dammit, Sammy," Dean said. "I hate this plan."

Sam headed over to a rickety fire escape hanging off the side of their building.

"I got this," Sam said.

Claudia ran to Sam and hugged him. He looked up at

Dean and then put his arms briefly around the girl's shaking shoulders, face still neutral and expressionless.

"Good luck, Sam," Claudia said.

"I don't need luck," Sam replied.

He started climbing down the fire escape, toward the street.

Dean watched his brother descend toward the madness of the street with his fists clenched and his heart in his throat. This *had* to work. It just had to.

When Sam reached the second floor, the fire escape simply ended, the ladder meant to reach the ground level either missing or stolen. He had no choice but to jump down to the sidewalk, right into the thick of the zombies. Which meant there would be nowhere to run if the zombies did go after him.

Sam looked up at Dean, acknowledging him with the slightest nod—then jumped.

He landed hard, knocking over a pair of punk kids with brightly colored mohawks. A heartbeat passed, then another. No reaction from the zombies. They just looked right through Sam.

"Hot damn," Dean said. "He made it."

"Dean," Xochi said softly.

"What?"

"Can I have my hand back?"

Dean looked down and saw that he had one of Xochi's gloved hands in a vice grip. He let her go and she opened and closed her fingers like they were sore.

"Sorry," Dean said.

"Where is he going?" Claudia asked.

Dean looked back down at the street and saw Sam weaving through the crowd of zombies, walking right past the door to the neighboring building. He was headed straight for the pair of *Tzitzimimeh*.

"Is he crazy?" Xochi asked, as Sam picked up a broken-off, four-foot length of rusty rebar.

There was about a ten-foot clear area around the long, skinny legs of the demons, littered with skull-faced *Santa Muerte* dolls and mutilated corpses. Sam slowly approached the edge of the clearing. The two demons were turned in opposite directions, one chewing through the rag-doll body of a teenaged girl and the other tipping its massive, oversized head like it was listening to something only it could hear.

Sam took a cautious, sliding step closer, raising the rebar like a samurai sword. Neither demon seemed to notice him.

"They can't see him," Xochi said, astounded disbelief in her husky voice. "He is invisible to them."

Sam lunged at the listening demon, swinging the rebar and shattering nearly half the obsidian teeth in its massive jaw.

The demon screamed and swiped at Sam with its knife-like claws, but Sam danced back and to the left, while the creature lunged right. It was fighting blind, swiping at nothing while Sam snuck up from behind for a second shot.

"He's going for the teeth," Dean said. "Just like Bobby said."

"Without those teeth, it can still attack," Xochi said. "But it can make no more zombies. It can eat no more souls."

Sam struck again, knocking out the flailing demon's remaining teeth then leaping back, out of the way. His arms and face were laced with bleeding cuts, but the cuts were only flesh wounds. He had no soul to eat.

The other demon attacked the now toothless one, the two of them crashing together into the side of a toy store. One of them kicked out at a parked minivan, sending it flying and crashing into the window of the empty green storefront they'd crawled out of.

Sam let the attacking demon have it in the back of the knees, buckling its lanky legs. It spun toward him, jaw snapping inches from Sam's face as he faded back and then swung for the fences, obsidian teeth fragments flying everywhere.

The first demon lunged at the second, retaliating with wild, vicious swipes of its bloody claws. The two went down together, scattering cars and vendor's tables.

Sam ran, dodging through hoards of milling, confused zombies and heading for the open door of the building opposite the one where Dean, Xochi and Claudia were trapped. He ducked inside, pulling the door closed behind him.

They waited. Just under five minutes later, Sam appeared on the neighboring roof, ladder in hand.

"What did I tell you?" Sam called. "Piece of cake."

"I never thought I'd say this," Dean said. "But after that stunt, I think you might almost be as bad ass as me."

"Almost," Sam said, laying the ladder across the gap. "Now get your bad ass over here will ya?"

"Claudia first," Xochi said. "Sam, Dean: hold the ends of the ladder.

Claudia looked down at the zombies below. They had spotted the activity on the roof and were scrabbling at the walls, trying to climb over each other and reaching upward.

"Don't look down," Dean said.

Claudia started across, inching slowly along. She was a little less than halfway when she slipped and nearly fell, clinging desperately to the rungs, legs swinging.

"Come on!" Sam called. "Keep coming."

"I can't!" Claudia wailed, clinging tighter. Frozen with terror.

Xochi swore.

"Hold on," she said. "I'm coming."

Xochi made her way across the ladder, which started to bend beneath their combined weight.

"I'm slipping!" Claudia cried.

"You're not slipping," Xochi said. "You're fine. Give me your hand."

"I can't!"

"Yes you can. Give me your hand."

Claudia looked down at the reaching zombies, then squeezed her eyes shut.

"Don't look down," Dean said again.

Claudia reached a shaking hand toward Xochi and Xochi heaved her back to safety. Together, they made it across the rest of the ladder. Sam was there on the other roof to help Claudia down on the other side. Xochi joined them and then turned back and motioned to Dean.

Dean looked around for something to secure the ladder when he crossed. He weighed it down with a discarded clay plant pot and then began to cross. As he made his way across the splintery ladder, he could feel that the joints where the extensions met had been weakened by Claudia's struggle. He was almost to the other side when the stressed joints gave way. Dean felt himself slipping, falling.

Sam caught the back of Dean's shirt with one hand and his arm with the other, hoisting him awkwardly upward while the pieces of the ladder crashed down on the howling zombies. Dean could feel his shirt ripping. He didn't look down, just locked his grip on Sam's wrist.

Sam was as calm and stoic as always. No sweat. But even though he hadn't seemed particularly worried that Dean might fall and end up zombie chum, he'd still grabbed Dean. He didn't let Dean fall. Dean looked up into his brother's cold eyes. Looking for something that he knew wasn't there. Or was it?

Sam pulled him up.

"What are you?" Dean said to Sam as he climbed up onto the roof. "Captain Frickin' America all of a sudden?"

"Yeah, whatever," Sam said. "We have work to do."

"You know," Dean said, fighting to catch his breath. "For a guy with no soul who doesn't give a damn about anyone, you're turning out to be quite the hero."

"Just trying to be practical," Sam said.

FORTY-EIGHT

Xochi stayed close to Claudia, trying not to think about Javi. He had been a good lover, even though he always wanted more emotionally than she was willing or able to give. She knew that the adrenalin pumping through her body was numbing that particular pain, though she knew that the second she slowed down, it would come back to knee her in the gut. But she couldn't worry about that now. She had to stay focused on Claudia.

"Here," Xochi said, tucking a single marigold behind Claudia's ear. "You take the last one."

"Thanks," Claudia said.

Sam had played out his role as if he'd been born to do it, now it would be up to the girl to complete the puzzle and fulfill her own destiny. Whatever shape that destiny may take.

But was Xochi ready? Ready to face Teo? All this time, with everything that had happened, she was still deeply conflicted. She felt such poisonous anger toward her sister, but blood was blood. Teo was still the person who'd raised Xochi, who went without food so that Xochi and Atlix would have enough, who'd taught Xochi to read, to shoot, to hunt. Xochi had idolized her big sister for years, struggling to copy her hairstyles and her swagger and the way she held a gun. Then, after their brother's death, Xochi spent the subsequent years distancing herself from Teo, trying to do everything she could to prove that she and her sister were nothing alike. But there was just no escaping the truth, that Xochi wouldn't be the hunter she was today without the conflicted gravitational flux of her relationship with Teo. Was she really prepared to do whatever it took to stop Teo? Including killing her?

Crossing the connected roofs was no problem. Getting down through the building and into the empty shop was more of a challenge. It was crawling with zombies and *Nagual* but Sam and Dean were ahead of her, clearing the way for Claudia like a supernatural SWAT team.

As they came down the last flight of stairs, a violent tremor shook the building, sending them all staggering into one another and clutching at the handrails. One of the pursuing *Nagual* came tumbling down the stairs between them and Sam took her out the second she hit the bottom.

When they got to the first floor, they found that it was one big empty storefront. A painting project was half completed, with tarps, cans and brushes stacked against one wall. The crushed minivan was protruding sideways through the broken glass front. At the other end of the shop, where there should have been a back wall and maybe an emergency exit, was an open, pulsating gate, spiraling down into dizzy, sickening nothing. And front and center, Teo. *Itztlitlantl* in her hand.

"You're too late," Teo said in English. Then she switched to their ancient native language. "*Elvia is bringing Itzpapalotl through the gate right now. The rest of her sisters are following close behind her. I can't stop it now and neither can you. It's over.*"

"No," Xochi said. "*This is insane. Think about what you're doing, Teo.*"

"*I have thought about it,*" she said. "*This isn't the end of the world, little sister. It's the beginning of a new era.*"

Elvia crawled out of the gate, smoking from a dozen slashes, her stuttering form bleeding out into the air around her. Close behind her was a mammoth shape, coalescing out of the nothingness, all gleaming black teeth and howling hunger.

Claudia made a move toward her mother and Teo lunged at the girl with the obsidian knife. Sam and Dean both drew down on Teo, but Xochi was quicker, drawing her own stone knife, countering and knocking her sister back. They rolled together across the floor and away from Claudia.

"Don't you touch her," Xochi said in English, putting all her telekinetic power into her knife hand.

"*Why fight me, Xochi?*" Teo asked, countering with her own telekinetic power and forcing Xochi's hand back. "*This is our moment. The birth of an era of rampant monsters. An era in which skilled hunters like you and me will live like queens. The world will be a paradise of wild game and desperate humans willing to pay anything for our services. Even your little boyfriends will have more wealth and action than they will know what to do with."*

Claudia threw her arms around her mother. Elvia shifted again, pale and human now in her black hooded sweatshirt.

Dean watched Xochi and her sister fighting out of the corner of one eye, then took the flask from his back pocket.

"Elvia," Dean said. "We can help you, but you need to drink this. I mean… breathe it. Dammit, just tell her, Claudia. We have to shut this gate right now."

Claudia translated while Dean crouched down beside her and held out the flask to her mother. Elvia looked up at Dean for a minute, then reached out her hand.

Suddenly the whole building was rocking and rolling as a volley of tremors came out of the shimmering gate. Dean stumbled, battling to keep his balance on a floor that felt more like the deck of a ship in a thunderstorm. The flask slipped from his hand, spinning away toward the yawning gate.

Dean dove after it, but when it hit the cement floor, the cap popped off, and the Alpha's fragrant blood wafted out and dissipated into the air.

Dean slammed his fist against the floor.

"Our mother would be ashamed if she could see you now," Xochi said to Teo. *"What you've become."*

"Don't talk to me about shame," Teo retorted. *"You know nothing about our mother."*

Shuddering shockwaves came rolling out of the gate like a dozen simultaneous earthquakes. Cracks appeared in the walls and floor, spiderwebbing outward from the gate as the form inside became more solid, an enormous toothy head and long reaching arms now visible.

"*I know she died a warrior's death,*" Xochi said. "*She died performing her sacred duty.*"

"*I only let you believe she died an honorable death because you were so young and heartbroken,*" Teo responded. "*And because I didn't want you to share the shame that I still live with to this day. The shame that made it impossible for me to keep on buying into the family's pretentious posturing about 'balance' and 'sacred duty.'*"

"*What are you talking about?*" Xochi asked. Though she wasn't sure she wanted to hear the answer.

"*Our mother died on a routine job, cleaning out a fledgling vampire nest,*" Teo said. "*She died because she was drunk, and had been for years, drinking to kill the pain of a job that had ceased to have any meaning for her. She got drunk and she got sloppy and she got killed by a hungry newborn. Pathetic.*"

The telekinetic power in Xochi's hand faltered and Teo pushed her advantage.

"*After that,*" Teo said, "*the job ceased to have any kind of deep spiritual meaning for me either. I saw it for the hollow lie it really was and realized that the only thing that mattered in this life is the pleasure you can squeeze out of every day.*"

"*And killing me will bring you pleasure?*" Xochi demanded. "*Your own flesh and blood? Is that how depraved you have become?*"

"*Your death will bring me no pleasure, little sister,*" Teo said. "*Only the pleasure of victory.*"

* * *

"Claudia," Sam said, raising the Magnum and drawing a bead on Elvia. "Step back."

"No," Claudia cried, pushing Elvia's knotted hair back from her tear-stained face. "No, there has to be another way."

"Look at her," Sam said. "She's dying anyway—can't you see? We have to close the gate. We have no choice."

"I'm sorry, Claudia," Dean said. "But there is no other way."

"There is," Claudia said. "Remember, Dean, you told me there's always a choice." She turned to Elvia, whispering in Spanish, then English. "Change me."

"What?" Dean took a step closer to Claudia. "No way, I'm not gonna let you do that. Come on, you don't have to be all tough just to impress me."

Claudia looked up at Dean, anger in her eyes.

"This isn't about you," she said. "This is our only hope. Even if you kill her now, it's too late to close the gate. Look, the Clawed Butterfly is already coming through. But if I become a Borderwalker, then together Elvia and I can carry the Star Demons back through the gate. She doesn't have the strength to do it alone."

"She can't change you," Sam said flatly. "Borderwalkers can only share the Coyote's Kiss with dying women."

There was a beat of silence. *Iztpapalotl* was fully formed now and starting to crawl out through the gate, huge gray-and-black moth wings unfurling and brushing the ceiling.

Then Claudia had the silver knife in her hand. The one

with the Blessed Virgin on the handle, given to her by the silversmith in Chihuahua.

"No!" Dean yelled. "NO!"

Claudia plunged the knife into her own chest.

FORTY-NINE

"Change me," Claudia said, bleeding and collapsing against her mother. "Change me, or we all die."

Dean ran to Claudia's side, but Elvia took her daughter's hand, tears spilling down her pale cheeks as she reached out to touch Claudia's face. The two of them levitated up off the cracked floor, flickering, shifting, and twisting as Elvia's power flowed into her daughter. Claudia's face became a coyote's face, then human again, her heart visible and glowing through the skin of her chest.

The two of them flowed like drifting, intertwining smoke moving toward the gate and the almost fully emerged Star Demon. Claudia grabbed one of the demon's bony shoulders and Elvia the other and together they pulled *Itzpapalotl* back down into the void.

The Clawed Butterfly screamed as she spiraled down and away, the sound violent and deafening inside the storefront. The gate was reversing, a black hole now pulling everything toward it. Sam and Dean hung on to the exposed struts to stop themselves from being sucked into the nothingness. But Xochi and Teo were loose and were rolling across the floor, forced toward the gate.

Xochi managed to grab hold of a flapping tarp with one hand. Teo was digging her fingers into one of the cracks in the floor, fighting to hold on and losing. She had dropped *Itztlitlantl* and the knife lay just within Xochi's reach, but was swiftly sliding away toward the gate.

Xochi realized she had a choice: she could grab the knife or grab her sister's hand. Even now, it was no choice at all.

"Teo!" she cried. "*Take my hand!*"

Her sister looked up at her, eyes stony and guarded as ever. She lunged for the sliding knife instead, gripping it and slashing at Xochi. Xochi flinched away and Teo went tumbling down into the void, *Itztlitlantl* clutched to her chest.

The tarp Xochi was holding on to started to tear.

"Xochi!" Dean yelled, diving for her and managing to catch one of her kicking boots just as the tarp tore loose, flapping away like a bat into the yawning gate.

He held fast to her ankle, hooking his other arm around a nearby support beam.

"I've got you," he shouted. "I've got you!"

The minivan that had been lodged in the store window came loose and flew down the gaping throat of the gate. Right behind it, first one, then the other, de-fanged Star Demon, screeching and flailing as they fell. A dozen zombies came swarming in after them through the now open storefront.

Dean could let go of Xochi to draw his gun or hang on to her and wait for them both to be eaten alive.

But, as the demons were swallowed up by the void, each one vomited up a coiling stream of bluish-white light. The light shattered into fragments, engulfing each of the oncoming zombies and stopping them in their tracks. They fell to their knees one after another, covering their faces with their hands.

For a moment, Claudia was visible in the mouth of the gateway, condor wings spread wide, eyes bright and heart burning. She raised her hand to Dean, then fell away, the void folding in around her as the gate closed, leaving nothing but a plain concrete wall.

Xochi struggled to her knees, leaning heavily against Dean. He held her for a long minute, unable to do anything else. It was a grim victory, resonant with painful losses. They were both shell-shocked, beaten and bruised to hell and back. But they were glad to be alive.

Sam offered Dean a hand, pulling him to his feet. Dean in turn helped Xochi.

"We did it," Sam said.

"Claudia did it," Xochi corrected him.

"I'm sorry about your sister," Dean said.

"I know," Xochi replied flatly. "She made her choice. Like we all do."

All around them, the former zombies were getting to

their wobbly feet. They seemed disoriented and confused, but otherwise back to normal.

Xochi grabbed an older man in a Hawaiian shirt and spoke to him in Spanish. He replied, a puzzled look on his face.

"They remember nothing," she said. "When the demons were pulled back through the gate, they spit out all the souls they had eaten. The souls went back into their owners but it seems the owners have no memory of the events that happened while they were soulless."

Dean looked at Sam. Didn't say anything. Xochi put one arm around Dean's waist and the other around Sam's.

"Come on," she said. "Let me take you boys home."

FIFTY

On the street outside Chato's body shop in Nogales, Arizona, Dean stood by the driver's-side door of the running Impala. He had a lurid, bilingual newspaper in his hand, headline reading "DRUG RIOT IN MEXICO CITY SLUM!" It didn't surprise him at all that no one believed what had really happened. They never did.

He tossed the paper in the back seat, watching Sam hand Xochi her gun-belt from the open trunk. She buckled it securely around her hips, fastening the straps around her thighs and checking both pistols. Sam closed the trunk and turned away, looking down the road, but she took his face between her hands and turned him back to her. She stretched up on tip-toe, looking intently into Sam's eyes and speaking softly to him. Dean couldn't hear what she was saying. "Gimme Shelter" by the Rolling Stones was blasting from the Impala's speakers.

Then Xochi turned to Dean and came to him slow,

sliding her arms around him like she had done that first night. This time he didn't push her away.

"Dean—" she began.

"Stay," he said, hushing her by pressing the pad of his thumb against her parted lips, fingers tracing the strong curve of her jaw. "Just for tonight."

She closed her eyes and leaned into him. Mick Jagger was wailing for shelter. Dean felt like he'd forgotten the meaning of the word until that moment. Not home. Not happily ever after. Just one night out of the rain. Just *shelter*. He could feel a thousand knots coming unbound inside him. He cupped his hand around the back of Xochi's neck and kissed her.

It was not a sweet, romantic kiss. It was rough, aching, and full of hunger. A survivor's kiss. And she kissed him back, just as hard and just as hungry. Everything else went away.

Until she broke the kiss and stepped back, pulling free from his embrace. There was desire in her dark eyes, but also a melancholy kind of understanding. Even though the night was warm, his body felt chilled where she was no longer pressed against him. He had to curl his hands into fists to stop them from reaching for her.

"Go to your brother," she said. "He needs you. He can't tell you this, but he does. It seems to me, he has fulfilled his destiny, and now you must help him get his soul back. Stop at nothing. Whatever it takes."

"But…"

"Goodbye, Dean," she said.

Dean watched her walk away, down the dusty road, for as long as he could. Watching the swing of her long braids, moving in rhythm with her pistol-packing hips. Wanting her to turn around. Willing her to turn around. She didn't.

He turned back to Sam.

His kid brother was standing by the rear bumper, big hands stuffed in his pockets and shoulders hunched, lost in thought. After everything they'd been through, Sam still seemed so impossibly young, still the same pensive kid he'd always been, so full of unrecognized potential. Dean felt like he was a hundred years old and then some. He walked over to Sam, mock-punched him on the shoulder.

"Come on, Sammy," he said. "Let's get the hell out of here. We got work to do."

Dean got behind the wheel of the Impala. Sam took the shotgun seat. As Dean pulled away from the curb and headed north, the Rolling Stones song ended and another song started up.

"Carry On, Wayward Son," by Kansas.

That's just what Dean did.

THE END

ACKNOWLEDGMENTS

Thanks to H. Pascal for introducing me to El D.F., to my old comadre Libertad, to Gerardo Horacio Porcayo for letting me borrow his name, and to Macarena Muñoz Ramos for turning me on to Caifanes.

ABOUT THE AUTHOR

Christa Faust is the author of ten novels including the Edgar and Anthony Award nominated *Money Shot*, the Scribe Award winning novelization of *Snakes on a Plane*, and her latest, *Choke Hold*, forthcoming from Hard Case Crime. She lives in Los Angeles.

SUPERNATURAL™

THE OFFICIAL SUPERNATURAL MAGAZINE

features exclusive interviews with Jared and Jensen, guest stars, and the behind-the-scenes crew of the show, the latest news, and classic episode spotlights! Plus, pull-out posters in every issue!

TO SUBSCRIBE NOW CALL

U.S. 1 877 363 1310
U.K. 0844 844 0387

For more information visit:
www.titanmagazines.com/supernatural